Dinner with Trixie

The South Settles an Old Score with the North

Janis A. Pryor

DINNER WITH TRIXIE

Copyright 2019 – Janis A. Pryor

Printed in the United States of America

ISBN – 978-1-949802-00-9

Published by Black Pawn Press

FIRST EDITION

...This is dedicated to one of my oldest friends,

Elizabeth Strong Ussery,

who struggles to understand the complexity of

this madness called racism,

and to one of my sisters from another mother,

Robette Dias,

who lives with and fights systemic racism

for the good of us all...

Chapter One:
Dinner

"Where did he find this woman?" Jeanette whispered to her husband, Carl Davidson. "Why can't he do what he's told?"

Whispering back, Carl said, "Tom is your brother. So much for business this evening." Carl sipped his glass of chilled, crisp, Chardonnay wine while trying not to stare at the woman. She was, by all accounts, a real piece of work in her navy blue suede over the knee high heeled boots, and her Armani suit. Her bright, black eyes and wavy blonde hair were a visual contradiction in the same way the Archangel Michael is often portrayed, a heavenly being with a sword.

Her blonde hair, thick as honey, came from the womb and not from some beautician's bottle, Carl thought as he discretely eyed her. There was also something about the look in her eyes. They were sparkly, devious, passionate and dangerous. When you looked into them, it was like peering into a bottomless pit. This woman had a powerful kind of authenticity that you could almost taste. It made Carl uneasy.

Jeanette Capwell-Davidson gave a painful smile and asked her, "Why don't you tell us about yourself? How did you meet my brother?"

The woman's eyes lit up, and she eagerly responded. "Tom and I met at a car wash in Boston this morning." Her eyes, that rarely missed anything, noted that Jeanette's right hand was trembling slightly.

"Really? Well, imagine that," said Jeanette as she sipped her martini and wondered what the hell had happened. She had ordered the servants to use their best china, polish the silverware, iron the monogrammed linen napkins and clean everything! This was supposed to be a business dinner with the head of Grant Family Companies, the Capwell ticket to solvency and safety. Instead, Tom brought home a bimbo in a designer suit!

Tom Capwell was getting nervous. He really wanted his sister and Carl to like Trixie, and he wanted Trixie to like them. But she made sure he didn't have time to tell Carl and Jeanette about her, and so much was riding on this meeting. Tom wondered if prayer would help right now while his eyes darted from face to face. Trixie's eyes were like laser beams with all the heat and intensity of a roaring fire. Jeanette's mouth was struggling to hide a sneer and Carl's forehead was home to a disapproving frown as he watched Trixie. But that uneasy feeling was creeping into his gut. What was his body trying to tell him that his brain couldn't detect? Carl realized he had stopped breathing! He took a deep breath, let it out, and smiled at Trixie.

Trixie didn't really talk. She bubbled over with nothing short of enthusiasm and charm usually associated with white Southern women. Tom had learned about that deceiving charm in between the vowels and consonants of Trixie's stunning Southern accent earlier that day. The memories caused small beads of sweat to form on his forehead.

"Well, it's a good thing we met at the car wash because I was just about to place a personal ad in the paper," she said while looking at an array of flatware next to her plate. Frowning at the place settings, Trixie couldn't figure out why there were two spoons, two forks and two glasses. "Y'all have a lot of flatware here for a simple, little dinner."

Jeanette cleared her throat while Carl, with raised eyebrows, stared at Tom. Taking another sip of her martini, Jeanette looked at Trixie and asked, "What in the world would you put in a personal ad?" Jeanette rolled her shoulders as if she was trying to shake off the idea of Trixie placing a personal ad that was in any way connected to her brother. Jeanette wanted to gag thinking about a relationship between her brother and this woman. Rather than gag, Jeanette kept drinking her martini.

The maid walked in with a platter of Cornish hens and placed it on the circular mahogany dining table, within reaching distance of Carl.

"Oh my God," Trixie exclaimed! "Whatever happened to those tiny chickens? I've never seen a chicken that small. Did you get them on sale someplace?"

Jeanette glared at Trixie, and then Carl, trying to suppress the gagging sensation that was working its way up her throat. She wasn't sure she could get through an entire meal with this woman.

Tom touched Trixie's arm and said, "They're supposed to be small. Those are Cornish hens."

Trixie gave Tom a vacant stare and said, "Oh… Well, I knew that. I did. I was just playin' with y'all." She winked her eye at him.

"Trixie, the personal ad? What would you ever write?" Jeanette asked and tried not to grimace. She was doing her best to uphold the family tradition of extending minimal courtesy to those beneath them. Although Trixie wasn't scraping the bottom of the barrel, Jeanette was convinced Trixie was damned close!

Bubbling up again, Trixie said, "I think I have a rough draft in my handbag. Let me go get it."

"No, no," Carl said and he rang a little bell next to his plate. Out of nowhere, the butler appeared. Carl asked him to find Trixie's bag and bring it back.

Trixie's eyes followed the butler out of the dining room and into the hall.

Meanwhile they all sat in horrible silence. Trixie looked around and thought to herself that this place is a museum! Fresh air was needed along with some bright colors. The rooms Trixie had seen when she arrived were painted universal beige, not white, not ecru or cream, but non-controversial beige. It was a color that added nothing to any setting as far as Trixie was concerned. There were too many dark brown pieces of furniture, all of them looking older than dirt. This was the kind of furniture that provided comfort to stodgy, pretentious people who had no taste or they didn't want to call any attention to themselves or their bank accounts. That's how old money operated, stealth like, and absolute with the grace and swiftness of a steel hand in a velvet glove. The average person would have no idea that all of this very unattractive, antique furniture cost a fortune.

Trixie looked at Jeanette and Carl's faces and realized they didn't like her, and probably didn't like each other either. What a shame, Trixie thought to herself. What a terrible shame. This was going to be a very long evening, or not. A smile slowly surfaced on Trixie's face as she noticed that Jeanette also had a small facial tic underneath her right eye matching that slight tremor in her right hand. Bring it on, Trixie thought. Bring it on! Damned fools.

Tom was lost in the morning memory of meeting Trixie at a car wash that was a block or so from the hotel where she was staying. He noticed a limo pulling up. The chauffeur opened the door for her and Tom turned to see who this was. The first thing he saw was her long leg hugged by an over the knee high heeled suede boot. The second leg followed. His eyes widened as she got out and walked over to him. With those boots, she had to be close to six feet, and Tom didn't know what to do as she approached him. She took her sunglasses off, extended her right hand and said, "Thomas Capwell? I'm Charlotte Alison Grant also known as Charles Grant, CEO of Grant Family Companies. How are you this morning?"

Tom's mouth parted slightly but he pulled himself together and managed to say, "I'm fine... What a coincidence."

She smiled and told him, "We knew you were here. I've had you and your family under surveillance for quite a while. Let's go back to the hotel and talk."

"Well, sure…but I need to wait for my car…" he said and looked towards the cars being pulled through the swishy, watery device that washed them.

Trixie walked over to her limo, opened the front door on the passenger side, said something to someone that Tom could neither see nor hear. A massive, unsmiling man with copper skin, black eyes, and a long black braid stepped out of the car wearing only a dark suit. He and Trixie walked back to Tom.

"Tom, this is my cousin, Wallace. His brother and he handle security for the family. Our cousin, John, whom you'll meet later, handles security for Grant Family Companies. Wallace will take care of your car and drive it back to the hotel."

Robotic, Tom walked over to the limo and got in the back seat. Trixie slid in next to him. Tom heard the car doors lock and jumped. Trixie smiled and said, "Don't worry, Tom. You'll be fine. There's so much we have to go over."

Tom was staring at the Cornish hens, wondering how much of a disaster this dinner was going to be. Trixie made a "strict suggestion" that he was to give her a "lot of room" to play with Carl and Jeanette tonight. The problem from Tom's perspective was Trixie was the only one having fun!

Without making a sound, the butler appeared at Trixie's side with her handbag. She thanked him and asked, "Where're you from?"

The butler looked at Jeanette and then Carl. He didn't know what to do. Trixie saw the dilemma written on his face and said, "Don't be shy. I won't hurt ya' and neither will they! Where're you from?" she asked again knowing he was afraid to speak.

"I'm from the Philippines."

"Well, I declare! What's your name?"

"Joseph," he said barely breathing.

"Joseph? Just Joseph?"

"No. Joseph Alejandro, Jr."

"Well, Mr. Alejandro, thank-you so much. You don't need to wait on me hand and foot. I'm sure you have your hands full with the Capwells."

Joseph vanished with the same silence that delivered him to Trixie who was still smiling. She caught Jeanette staring at her handbag. It was one of those very high-end, uber expensive, designer bags. The leather was so soft you could easily imagine it melting in your hand. Trixie knew Jeanette had a precise idea what the price tag was for that handbag. It cost more than what some people earn in a year. A clenched jaw paralyzed Jeanette's mouth, and Trixie continued to smile with the same stillness referred to in the twenty-third Psalm; "He leadeth me beside still waters…"

Barely able to look at Trixie, Jeanette said, "We don't engage the servants in conversation, Trixie. It confuses them about their place. Boundaries are important."

Trixie gave Jeanette a hard look and said, "Is that right? Well, I'll be damned," Trixie muttered. "Anyway," she said and pulled out a piece of paper. "Here it is. This is what I wrote. Get ready. 'Crazy yet kinda cute woman who lives the bucket life is seeking the experience of driving a John Deere tractor with an experienced driver on a farm and actually tending the soil. Not just a quickie!'"

"That's enough. We get the idea," Carl said. He turned to look at Tom, leaned closer to him, and quietly asked, "Does she know who you are? Who we are?" and he poured himself another glass of wine.

Tom looked at his brother-in-law and whispered, "Do you know who she is? Her last name is Grant." Winter was approaching outside and the dining room was "cool" as many old houses in New England normally are during winter, but Tom was sweating. His entire face was shining like a lit candle. He didn't dare drink anything other than water. He needed to keep a clear head.

Carl gave Tom a confused, perplexed look that slowly transformed into panic. All signs of life boycotted his face leaving it blank and ashen. Now he understood his uneasy feeling. Something was very wrong and there was nothing Carl could do about it.

Jeanette looked at the men and hissed, "Please! Stop." Turning to Trixie, Jeanette forced herself to smile and say, "I am so sorry. Men can be so rude. Let me explain." Jeanette was still eyeing Trixie's clothes. Something was not adding up, or more accurately, every item of clothing Trixie had on added up to an astronomical amount of money. Her clothes had the kind of elegance and simplicity that only money could buy. And the jewelry; she wore one of those rose diamond Cartier trinity rings on her wedding finger. Trixie's style was impossible to find on the floor of a retail store. Her style was customized. There were too many inconsistencies about this Trixie woman. Jeanette's head was hurting from trying to reconcile the contradictions.

Trixie's bubbly smile had become perversely serene. "By all means, explain it to me, Jeanette."

"Well, the truth is, Tom was supposed to have a very important meeting earlier today with a potential buyer for one of our companies. You may not know this but our family owns several companies across the country, and in some Southeast Asian countries, including China. There's a small company that's been in the family for at least two hundred years that we want to sell, Capwell Fabrics. Tom was going to meet with a potential buyer earlier today to try and butter them up before we got down to hard business tomorrow, and then, if all went well this morning, bring them here for dinner so we could get to know each other a bit. The irony is our families have been doing business for generations going way back, before the Civil War. But recent generations have never actually met face to face. We were looking forward to Tom bringing home the CEO of Grant Family Companies. Instead, he brought you, Trixie. No offense, but we were expecting a different kind of meal tonight with a very different kind of person."

Tom cleared his throat before speaking. "Jeanette..."

Trixie placed her hand on Tom's and cut him off. "Well, tell me about this buyer. Who is it?" Trixie asked. "They sound interesting."

Jeanette sighed and said, "Well, it's very well known, an established conglomerate that operates out of Atlanta. It's also a family owned establishment, led by Charles A. Grant, who's the fourth or fifth generation of Grants. Apparently, he keeps a low profile. We couldn't find anybody who would talk about him, or even describe him! People seem to be very protective of this man. He's a bit of a mystery. Supposedly, Charles is very bright, increased profits. You can see why we wanted to meet the leader of this generation of Grants. No offense, Trixie, but we are a little concerned that this is a southern company. Given the history of the south, it makes us uncomfortable, but business is business." Jeanette looked at Trixie and met Trixie's hard, calm gaze.

"Jeanette, stop talking," Tom said as he took his handkerchief and dabbed his forehead.

She glared at her brother and said, "What do you mean, 'stop talking'? Thomas!"

"Jeanette, Carl," Tom said and looked at Trixie, "This is Charles A. Grant."

Trixie, or Charles, calmly smiled, and sipped some wine. A chill set in as the Capwells froze. The room became as still as an iceberg. It seemed like everyone had stopped breathing, except for Trixie. She fought hard not to burst out laughing.

"My God," Carl said. "This is so embarrassing." Carl's intestines continued to twist. His stomach dropped like a stone to the bottom of a pool. "Please accept our apologies." He wanted to throw his hands up in the air and leave, but he didn't.

Jeanette sat there; stiff, only able to bite her lower lip for a moment. "Well," Jeanette said. "I guess we need to be filled in." She looked directly at Tom and tried to suppress her desire to spit nails, in rapid succession, at her baby brother. If only she could!

"Trixie and I met coincidentally this morning at the car wash a few blocks from her hotel before our meeting. It was just luck, or something…"

Leaning forward and putting her elbows on the table, Trixie said, "I pulled up to the car wash and lo and behold, there he was! The Lord works in mysterious ways. His wonders to behold," Trixie said. She leaned back with the same assurance and strength as a long legged cheetah after cornering its prey. She was getting ready to use the truth the same way a cheetah uses its legs. With speed and strength, she was getting ready to pounce.

Carl and Jeanette stared at Trixie with disbelief. Carl let out a sigh that defied description. It was somewhere between panic and regret. Looking at his glass of wine, he thought, "This isn't going work out well, if at all. My God."

"But your name…what is that? Charles," said Jeanette. "I don't understand."

"My full name is Charlotte Alison Grant. I often use Charles A. Grant for business. It's legal and very useful when you're doing business with some country where women are still relegated to the kitchen and the bedroom. Trust me, I have some very good lawyers, and my brother runs our legal department. My father called me Trixie ever since I was a little girl. People I like, people who are close to me, call me Trixie. I like your brother, Jeanette, but right now I don't like you or your husband very much. I'm sure you can understand that." Now there was only a hint of Trixie's southern accent as she spoke to them. "Jeanette, as you said, business is business, and I know not only do you want to sell Capwell Fabrics, you have to sell it. You need an infusion of cash, quickly, or your whole empire will collapse. Yes? And it's the only company you can sell that won't attract a lot of attention from the Feds much less those busy bodies on Wall Street. Selling Capwell Fabrics will generate just enough cash to cover up your mistakes. Do I have that right because y'all have had some difficulties, criminal difficulties? Something about embezzlement, large amounts of cash just missing, personnel problems, discrimination suits coming up. Jeanette, it's no wonder you're on medication."

Jeanette's eyes stretched wide with shock. She wondered how this woman knew she was on any medication.

Carl looked at Trixie and said, "Yes. But we've cleared most of that up. It was just a misunderstanding."

"You cleared it up because you have connections. Not because you didn't break the law," Trixie said. "That's not the only criminal difficulty you've had, Jeanette. That temper of yours needs to be reined in. I'm hoping that's what the medication is for, yes?" For a moment, time and space were suspended. They all looked at each other trying to do quick assessments of the entire situation. Jeanette and Carl were barely breathing and Tom wanted to cry. The Capwells knew everything was wrong. Trixie continued to watch them suffer with an abnormal patience.

Swallowing the rest of her martini, Jeanette took a deep breath, and said, "I don't know what you're talking about."

"Your children know, don't they?" Trixie asked. "Not to mention the maid you paid off to be quiet."

Jeanette wrapped her hands around the flatware and glared at Trixie. Carl shook his head and stared into his plate of untouched food.

"So, tomorrow morning," Trixie said. "We'll meet at my hotel, 10 AM, and see what we can work out. This may take a full day or two because I have a lot of questions that I need y'all to answer. Jeanette, your Daddy gave you his empire and now you have controlling interest. Carl, you've been a hands on CEO for over ten years with Tom as COO for almost five years. Somehow, y'all have managed to run Capwell Enterprises damned near into the ground."

There was more silence as Trixie looked at each one of them. You could almost hear time passing. Faint kitchen noises where the butler and cook were working floated through the air.

Carl cleared his throat and said, "We've had some difficult years."

"I know. Carl, every business has difficult patches. It's just the nature of the beast. Y'all are way past difficult. Tom and I had a long conversation today. We're all going to have a longer conversation tomorrow. I surely want to hear about that branch of Jeanette's family that came over on the Mayflower. This generation of Capwells and Grants have never exchanged credentials, have we? And I know how important pedigree is to the Capwells. Our families have been doing business for so long. We have history and I just love history. So, I think I should leave now. I'm sure y'all want to talk."

Trixie stood and everyone jumped up. No one had eaten much. The Cornish hens, the wild rice, the green beans were abandoned. The salad? Full of fluffy lettuces, cherry tomatoes, marinated artichokes resting in a large crystal bowl untouched, never tossed, abandoned.

They followed her to the front door and Jeanette asked, "I wasn't paying attention to how you got here. Did Tom drive you? Do we need to call a car service?"

"Oh darlin', no," said Trixie. "My limo is waiting right outside."

Jeanette's face fell. "Oh."

"Tom, you be sure to tell them all about the car wash." Trixie winked her eye at Tom again and smiled.

"I will," he said and helped Trixie put on her navy shearling coat.

She turned and saw some photographs on a narrow table near the coat closet. Picking up one with two young people, Trixie studied the photo for a few seconds before turning to Jeanette. "These're your children?" Trixie asked.

"Yes."

"Harrison and Jennifer I assume," Trixie said and placed the photo back on the credenza.

Carl asked, "How did you know that?"

"Oh, I make it my business to know as much as I can about the people I do business with," Trixie said. "And that personal ad? I was just playin' with y'all. I actually found that in some little local paper from up north where we were skiing before we came down here to meet with you fine folks."

"Whose we?" Jeanette asked as she held her right hand to hide the tremor.

Trixie, violating Jeanette's personal space, took a step closer to her and said. "My family. I always have some family with me. Family is everything, at least it is to us." Trixie could feel Jeanette's warm, erratic breath spread over her face. Jeanette wanted to throw up. She took a step back from Trixie and bumped into Carl. He barely felt Jeanette but did step away from her. Tom didn't know if he should laugh or cry. For a second he considered shooting himself! His father's gun collection was still in the house but guns terrified Tom.

Trixie buttoned up her coat, and looked past Jeanette at Carl. "You know, you're a perversely honorable man," Trixie said. She studied each one of them before continuing. "Be prepared to stay for most of the day. We have a lot of ground to cover. Anyway, this has been so interesting. I'll see y'all tomorrow." She started to walk out and then stopped. "Oh, one more thing. I hope y'all can explain tomorrow why there are so few people of any color working in management positions for Capwell. It just pops out at you when anyone looks at your website or reads through your reports, especially the minutes to your board meetings. Your website is lily white. Jeanette we know about your problem with black folks. But my God, where are the Asians, the Latinos? Maybe you're hiding them somewhere. C'mere Jeanette. Let me show you something." Trixie took Jeanette's hand and walked her over to a wall tapestry that was hanging in the dining room. "Look at this beautiful wall tapestry." Trixie lifted several dangling threads and revealed two small holes in the lower right hand corner. She poked the tips of her fingers through the holes. Jeanette was still trying to adjust to having Trixie touch her!

"You should take care of that before the whole thing becomes undone. One ravel can do that. But two or three? Total destruction of a beautiful piece of work. Once that happens, you can't ever put it back together the same way. Gotta pay attention, Jeanette." She let go of Jeanette's hand and finally walked out as Jeanette followed. Trixie shut the front door like she owned the place, leaving Jeanette watching her from a side window near the door.

Chapter Two:
Explanations

The minute the limo pulled away with Trixie, Jeanette whipped around from the window and looked for her brother. Tom was nowhere to be found.

"Thomas! Where did you go?" Jeanette screamed Tom's name again. Carl threw one hand up in the air, clutched his glass of wine with the other, and walked into his study. The butler looked out from the dining room to the foyer, and saw the look on Jeanette's face. He ran back into the kitchen where the maid was muttering her concerns and fears. If only she could afford to quit this job she would without a second thought.

Tom was standing at the top of the staircase. "What is it, Jeanette?"

"Come down here and talk to me, right now!" She stomped her foot thinking that would make Tom move faster. Her face was reddened and the look in her eyes came from some other dimension. It was hard to tell if Jeanette's eyes were focusing on anything visible.

Loosening his tie, Tom slowly walked down the stairs while glaring at his sister. "Okay, I'm here," he said and leaned against the banister. He needed something to hold him up.

"Why didn't you warn us? You could've called or texted or whatever it is they do today. You spent the day with her. What is wrong with you?"

"I had one chance to call you, Jeanette, and when I did do you remember what you said?" Tom straightened up and faced Jeanette, but he didn't let go of the banister.

Jeanette stood there. Her mouth was slightly open as she tried to remember the events of the day. "I don't know what you're talking about."

"Oh, well, let me repeat what you said to me, and I quote, Tom, don't bother me now. I'm getting fitted for a suit." He made a clicking noise with the inside of his cheek and tongue, and then sat down on the stairs. It was a noise he learned to make as a child and it drove Jeanette nuts! That's why he did it. That's why he still does it.

She clenched her jaw. "You could've called back," Jeanette said, determined to ignore that clicking noise her brother was making. It made her think her head was going to explode.

"No, no I couldn't Jeanette. I didn't have a chance. I was in the presence of a hawk! When I called you it was from the bathroom. That was the only time I was alone. When Trixie left the room, somebody else was always there watching me. Let me give you some advice."

"What? What kind of advice?" Jeanette put her hands on her hips and glared at Tom.

"Get ready, big sister. Get ready. This woman is no joke."

"What did you tell her? I need to know exactly what transpired."

"I didn't have to tell her much because she's got files on all of us, every last one of us, including your children. She's been watching us ever since the payments stopped. How do you think she knew about Jennifer and Harrison?"

"What are you talking about? Watching, how?" Now Jeanette reached for the banister. Maybe, he thought, she was having a dizzy spell. That often happened when she got upset. "Tom, answer me!"

"As in surveillance. Photographs. Private Detectives! That's what I mean, Jeanette. We have no secrets from her. I'm telling you, she's found every skeleton."

Jeanette just stood there for a moment, still trying to steady herself, before speaking. "Why would she do that?"

"She just told you why. She wants to know whom she's doing business with! I hope you haven't been doing anything that would look bad," Tom said with a smirk on his face. "I don't put anything past this woman. She's no dummy. Trixie is the one in charge of Grant Family Companies. She's a friggin' force of nature and damned smart." Tom became still, took a second or two, and continued. "For as long as I can remember there's been this family rumor about the Grants and the Capwells, Civil War and slavery. I thought it was just talk or an exaggeration, but after today... She's on to us Jeanette. She wants this over, all of it. That's why the payments stopped. She figured it out. She doesn't need to buy Capwell Fabrics. She's already made more money than she'll ever be able to count or spend. She's going to finish us off."

"Oh, I can't believe that, Tom," Jeanette said. "She's a bubble head! And a southern bubble-head at that. It's just a lot of razzle-dazzle! Don't you believe her. We're still in control of this." Jeanette, holding onto the banister, was having trouble focusing, and the hallway had started to spin.

Tom stood up and walked back up the stairs, waving his hand in the air as if to say, it's over.

Jeanette took a deep breath and tried to ground herself. If only the hall would stop spinning. If she focused on one object, maybe Carl's desk that could be seen from the hallway, the dizziness would slow down. Exhaling, she carefully put one foot in front of the other, walked into Carl's study, and confronted him.

"How did this happen? Didn't anybody do any background work? Wasn't there a photo of Trixie on the website?" She waited a second or two and heard nothing but silence from Carl. "Carl! Answer me!" Her voice hit the air the same way finger nails screech across a blackboard.

"First, my darling wife, you need to lighten up on the southern animosity. That's what's gotten us in this mess to begin with, okay?" Carl shifted in his chair, leaned forward and said, "There were no photos of Miss Trixie, or Charles, on the company website. It's a very sophisticated, elegant website. No photos of the Grant family. Lots of photos of happy employees! People of all colors and stripes damned grateful to work for Grant Family Companies. Lots of information about the money they make." Carl looked at his wife and said, "Sit down. Look it up yourself."

Ignoring him, Jeanette asked, "Why didn't you have my assistant call me or send me some kind of briefing paper?"

"Your assistant?" Carl grinned and took another sip of his wine. "You mean that poor young woman you drove crazy?"

"Her name is Courtney," Jeanette said while debating whether she should sit down or not. If she sat, Jeanette was afraid she wouldn't be able to get up.

"She resigned two weeks ago," Carl said and put his hand across his mouth. Laughter was just dancing in this throat, desperate to become audible.

"What? Why?" Jeanette grabbed her right hand still trying to hide the tremor and maintain her balance.

"Said she got a better offer, and said it was no longer in her best interest to work for us." Carl gave his wife a sarcastic smile.

Jeanette stared at him for a second. "That doesn't make any sense. People can't just walk away from a job! She's not rich! She comes from a working class family. Went to Bunker Hill Community College. Those people are hopeless. Who's she going to work for?"

Carl finished his wine and took his time saying, "Grant Family Companies. When she told me, I got the distinct impression she's just the first rat deserting a sinking ship." Carl leaned back in his chair and pushed away just enough so he could put his feet on the desk.

Jeanette's face was hot with rage, her facial tick growing more pronounced. She glared at her husband, turned and walked out while saying, "This is on you Carl."

He put his feet down, leaped up, and screamed, "Oh no it isn't! This mess started long before any of us were born. I've been busy the past twenty years or so trying to save our children from you with one hand, and this damned Capwell empire with the other."

Jeanette walked back into the study and said. "Don't start, Carl. That's behind us. Everyone's fine."

"Fine? My God, Jeanette." Carl unlocked the bottom drawer on the left side of his desk, reached in and pulled out a plastic bag. There was a child's hairbrush covered with blood stains. He held the bag up for Jeanette to see. "You remember this?"

Jeanette was silent and looked away.

Carl still holding the bag with the bloodied brush said, "This is the real crime. I don't give a damn about anything else. I don't care about this company. I don't care about you, and I sure as hell don't care about this damned Capwell legacy. I care about our children. Thank God the maid was here when you went fucking crazy and called me! It wasn't the first little episode you had either, was it?" His dark eyes bore holes through Jeanette. Every feature that made him handsome and even sexy to some women, now held the power and mystery of a galactic storm.

Jeanette was breathing heavily and still a bit dizzy, but she was determined to stand her ground. All she had to do was lean against something that wasn't moving. She held onto a chair in front of Carl's desk.

"You never understood how difficult children can be," Jeanette mumbled. "I was here, alone with them. They would cry and scream sometimes. They refused to obey me." Her knees were growing weak. Now her head was pounding and she wanted to collapse into somebody's arms. But there was no one.

"Alone? There were servants here to take care of your every need."

Looking at the brush, Jeanette asked, "Why do you keep those things, Carl? Why?"

Carl ignored her and put the plastic bag back in the bottom desk drawer and locked it. He walked over to Jeanette, and stared into her eyes for three or four seconds before saying anything. Carl was a tall, attractive, dark haired man with a predictable five o'clock shadow who looked ten years younger than his age of fifty-five. "I'm just waiting for our son to finish grad school so I can stop living this lie, this complicated, sick, painful lie. I think Trixie is going to solve a lot of my problems. So tomorrow morning, we're going to walk out of here, meet with her and hope to God she puts us all out of our misery. She knows about this brush and all that it represents."

Jeanette didn't know what to say, so she turned and walked out trying not to stumble or fall while remembering the fleeting joy that enveloped her when Jennifer was born. Jennifer was a seven pound bundle of beauty. Her skin was so soft and she was such a good baby in the hospital. Once they got home everything changed.

"What went wrong?" Jeanette mumbled. Nothing went wrong with Jennifer. She was a perfectly normal baby. "Why couldn't I handle it all?" Jeanette asked herself. She walked in her bedroom and flopped down on the bed hoping the dizziness would subside. "I didn't know what the hell I was doing. I just didn't," she mumbled. "And I almost killed her."

All those memories of Jennifer crying assaulted Jeanette with as much force as she had assaulted her daughter. Staring up at the ceiling and into a space no one else would ever see, Jeanette said, "Oh God! What was wrong with me?" She slowly sat up, bent over, and put her head in her hands as the memories of the first "episode" slapped her. Jeanette threw Jennifer in her crib with great force causing Jennifer to cry louder. It was the nanny who saved Jennifer from Jeanette's abuse during Jennifer's infancy. But there was nobody to save Jeanette. Nobody to help her learn how to be a mother, so she failed. The failure was poisonous and found a home in Jeanette's cluttered mind where there was so much dysfunction. Her children were sacrificed and paid with her physical and emotional abuse. But Jeanette didn't see it that way. She believed that since her children were smart, they should be able to get over it, pretend it never happened, and go on. That wasn't how it worked. So everybody kept paying.

Jeanette lifted her head and looked straight ahead softly muttering, "Maybe my children defeated me, set me up with their infancy, thinking they could control me, but Miss Trixie certainly won't. The Capwells are going to come out victorious, and send those red-necks right back to where they came from."

Chapter Three:
Tomorrow

It was early December and cold. Snow was in the air creating its characteristic heavy stillness. Jeanette, Carl, and Tom were driving down the Massachusetts Turnpike into Boston from the wealthy and discrete suburb of Weston where they all lived in the family "home." It's a mansion, an estate complete with an iron wrought gate, a long driveway and servants. It embarrassed Tom living that way with so much poverty in the world. The growing disparity in wealth was becoming vulgar and shameful in the United States. He never thought he'd be living a life that embarrassed him, but here he was, working in the family business, Capwell Enterprises, carrying on the Capwell tradition, which was riddled with shame, crime, rumors and arrogance. He felt like a hamster running and running on one of those wheels. Just around and around and around unless he found a way to jump off and figure a way out of the Capwell cage.

Tom stared out the window and said to himself, "I wish I were dead. Anything's better than this. What kind of fool am I to even be here? Cowardice has many faces, and one of those faces is mine." He ran his fingers through his strawberry blonde hair. Even though Tom was a grown man, well built, six feet with a great smile, women looked at him and instantly described him as "a cute kid." He didn't wear stress well. It made him look like he was on the verge of tears. Tom had been looking that way for weeks.

He found himself longing for Rachel, the woman he was going to marry. They were studying on architectural fellowships for two years in Rome. It was a simple story of immediate attraction that grew into deep love and respect. They talked about having kids and leaving Massachusetts. He was going to convert to Judaism for her over the objections of his father and Jeanette. Two months after they were engaged, Tom noticed a small lump in her left breast along with a rash spreading across both breasts. Rachel had a virulent form of breast cancer. A year later she was dead. She died in his arms, mid-afternoon in their apartment in Milan. Most of her extended family died in the holocaust. Her father had died of a heart attack while she was in college, and she was estranged from her mother. She was an only child. Tom was her family.

He gave up after Rachel died, returned home to Weston and barely went out of the house for almost a year. He surrendered to grief and spent much of his time painting and drawing. He let go of his passion for residential architecture, and eventually found himself caught up in the Capwell madness as Chief Operating Officer, something he never wanted any part of. He had little to no qualifications for this position, other than being a Capwell. There was a lot of "o.j.t." on the job training. Tom learned to live with a bad taste in his mouth.

Carl sat behind the wheel of the car, lost in his own thoughts of rage and desperation while driving. He married into this ridiculous family thinking he had it made. His family fortune could be sustained and increased by marrying into another wealthy family. Jeanette wasn't a bad looking woman, and for a short while they were infatuated with each other. Carl's dark haired good looks and Jeanette's genuine affection and sizable fortune generated lust that produced two children, Jennifer and Harrison. Carl thought all was well, but something happened to Jeanette. Carl didn't notice until it was too late. He kept his daughter's hair brush in his desk drawer as a reminder so he wouldn't forget that first time he caught Jeanette beating Jennifer while Harrison watched, crying and shaking in the living room corner. Doris, the maid at that time, called him at work.

In a hushed voice she said, "Mr. Davidson, you must come home. Mrs. Davidson is having... an episode, a very bad one with the children."

Apparently, Jeanette had been having these episodes on a regular basis. It was hard to tell what would trigger her abuse. Like a summer storm, Jeanette seemed to explode. The servants would hear her yelling and screaming. That was Doris' cue to find the children and come up with an excuse to get them away from Jeanette. Sometimes she would hustle Jennifer and Harrison into the kitchen on the pretense of making cookies. Anything, because Jeanette Capwell Davidson had blood in her eyes.

Usually when Carl got home, the children were asleep and all seemed well. And then one afternoon Doris felt morally compelled to call. This time she was frightened for the children's lives. Usually Doris was able to intervene, get the children away from Jeanette, and calm her down, but not this time.

Carl drove home from downtown Boston, ignoring every red light and the speed limit on the Mass Pike. He found Jeanette beating Jennifer with her hair brush. Jennifer's face was bloody. She was curled up in the corner of the living room with her five year old brother crying when Carl got home. Panting, Jeanette sat on the couch, holding the bloodied brush and watching her children. Looking at Jeanette you would've thought she had just finished consuming a meal from a fresh kill. Carl took one look and knew he had to get his daughter to the hospital. He walked past Jeanette and picked up his seven year old daughter and told his son everything would be okay.

"Doris," Carl yelled!

Doris rushed into the living room. "Yes, Mr. Davidson, what can I do?"

"Get me a blanket. I need to wrap Jennifer up. Call her pediatrician and tell him we're coming to Mass General." Jennifer had stopped crying and was unnaturally quiet. Carl held his daughter as close to him as possible. "Doris, get me Harrison's jacket too." Carl motioned for his son to stand by him. Harrison ran over and grabbed his father's leg. The three of them left for the hospital, leaving Jeanette in the living room staring into space.

But that was long over. Jennifer was a grown woman now, and Harrison, in a few months, would have his Ph.D. Jeanette's ugly secret slipped away into denial and suppression. But Carl remembered everything, the legal problems they had, the deal they cut with the court, and Jeanette's mandated therapy. Now Carl had a secret that rescued his sanity, soul, and heart from all that Jeanette created. Eight years ago he found a way out of this upscale hell with Jeanette. It was just a matter of time before he would be able to escape permanently. He had a feeling Trixie was going to provide a way for him to exit early.

Carl woke up one morning almost ten years ago, and realized he could no longer stomach Jeanette. She came to the same realization about Carl when she discovered he had a mistress he'd been seeing for at least a year, maybe two. Jeanette didn't know who or where the woman was, and didn't really care. A divorce seemed impossible because from the beginning their marriage was a business arrangement, an economic alliance (well defined in an explicit pre-nuptial agreement) needed to maintain the lifestyle they'd been born into. They loved money not each other. She felt nothing could change that and Carl was stuck. She knew he would never leave her and appearances could be maintained.

Jeanette sat next to her husband in the passenger seat pretending to read the Boston Globe. "You know," Jeanette said to no one in particular, "The Globe just hasn't been the same since the Taylors sold it to the Times and then to that baseball man. No substance anymore. It's like reading the New York Times 'lite.' So very sad."

"You say that every morning, Jeanette." Carl looked at her for a moment and then stared straight ahead at the road. A plop fell on the windshield. Bird poop.

"How would you know, Carl? Lots of mornings you aren't here. Hell, lots of days, lots of weeks you're not here. The New York offices seem more appealing to you. So how would you know what I say every morning?"

She saw Tom out of the corner of her eye in the back seat. He had closed his eyes for a second, shook his head and said, "Great. This is just great. You guys need to knock it off. Am I the only one who thinks we're about to meet our Waterloo?!"

Carl ignored Tom, turned the radio on and heard, "...love that dirty water! Yeah, Yeah, Boston is my home." Carl smiled. He loved that song and loved dancing to it decades ago. He tapped his fingers against the steering wheel to the beat of the music. Music had always been his emotional safety net. Driving, he smiled, remembering the saying that music could soothe the soul of a savage beast. What a blessing he thought.

Jeanette never turned the pages of the Globe. She was trying to figure out how they let things get so out of hand with the business. What happened to the money? Capwell Fabrics was their oldest company, one of the originals established by her father's ancestors. The family just picked up the business from London, crossed the Atlantic on the Mayflower, eventually set up shop in Boston, and the rest was history. They were tailors and seamstresses, and then they went into manufacturing textiles. The first company was opened in what is now Lowell, Massachusetts. The profits from that company allowed them to expand, buy other companies, and take them over. Eventually they opened up one of the precursors to department stores not only in Massachusetts but up and down the east coast. All of this evolved from a tailor, Joseph Capwell, and his wife, Ruth, who was a seamstress.

This is what America is about for some people, the opportunity to work hard and succeed regardless. Now their descendants, Tom and Jeanette, were being forced to sell the company that started it all. Jeanette clenched her jaw and tried not to cry. To add insult to injury, she was now going to negotiate with a woman whose nickname was Trixie. It was humiliating. Jeanette felt set-up, especially after that fiasco of a dinner last night. She was staring past the windshield into nothingness, and couldn't shake the feeling that Tom knew more than he was telling her. She certainly couldn't depend on Carl. It was Carl who got them into this mess to begin with by not paying attention, and thinking no one noticed the magic math he used to cover up his greed, also known as embezzlement in the legal community. But the Capwell traditions of extortion and blackmail began more than a hundred years ago back in the eighteen hundreds. Carl had nothing to do with that.

"Jeanette, we're here," said Tom.

"Oh!" She snapped out of it and realized they had arrived at one of those hotels that now populated the waterfront. This was what Jeanette called, "The New Boston." She didn't like it. The city was becoming unrecognizable to her. Unlike thirty or forty years ago, international students and people of color had become much more visible in Boston. Black, red, yellow, brown, people she knew nothing about nor understood. She had not the slightest bit of curiosity about them either. Her father told her "those people" were dangerous and uneducated, desperately poor due to their laziness and inability to learn the value of a dollar. To this day, "those people" made Jeanette uncomfortable at best. All her life had been spent in this destructive bubble of wealth, ignorance and extreme privilege where everybody looked alike and everybody thought the same things. She felt safe in that bubble. But now, she felt impinged upon, violated and horrified by the growing numbers of "those people." Jeanette was barely breathing as she watched people walking by. All these new people in the city destroyed her sense of security.

They were different, too different. They spoke different languages and ate food she didn't understand or recognize. Their music was loud and threatening, drums, guitars, bells with rhythms that made no sense to her. And then there was Rap music that made her feel insulted and denigrated with its coarse language and thumping, suggestive beat. A headache was preferable. There was the hair issue with those black women. What was that, Jeanette wondered? Why was it the way it was? What happened? The truth was, Jeanette was afraid of black hair generally, but especially black women's hair. It could do things that her hair couldn't. The volume of black women's hair, its thickness, its versatility, the riot of curls and kink that they could cut within an inch of the skull or could somehow make straight sent the fear of God through Jeanette. How could all this difference exist in the same world she occupied? And then there was their skin color; why were they all different colors?

And black women's skin never seemed to age the way hers was aging. Jeanette hated that. She found it confusing and deceitful giving them an unfair advantage! At least most of the Jews were white. Even though a few had frizzy hair they called "Jewfros" when picked and lifted to style, that white skin gave Jeanette some comfort but not enough to accept them or invite them to dinner. She could only go so far.

Jeanette heard someone say that Boston was now majority minority. That was incomprehensible to her. She didn't know where "they" came from. It sickened her as she scanned the entrance of the hotel. She saw far too many of "them" walking around and asked herself, what right do they have to this country? This is my country, my city, she thought. It was all she could do to make peace with the fact that the Mayor was Irish. She never mentioned this to Carl because he was Irish. But at least Carl's family was rich. That took care of all those differences for Jeanette because money is magic. That's what she was taught and that's what she believed.

Carl got out of the car and gave the keys to the valet, while Tom and Jeanette walked into the hotel.

"Tom, where are we meeting her?" Jeanette asked while they stopped and waited for Carl to catch up.

"She has a suite. She has a few of her people here also."

"A few of her people? What are we talking about?"

"She's got her financial guy and her research person. Remember what she said about family? That's all I know. Oh, one more thing. She has her own security detail."

"What?" Jeanette just stared at her brother. "Why?"

"I don't know. I'm just telling you," Tom said as Carl joined them.

"Are they all staying in the suite?" Carl asked with a sneer. "Are we about to experience Deliverance in designer clothing?"

"Knock it off," Tom said and shook his head with incredulity.

"Okay," Carl said. "I'm sorry. This is your girl. I can't believe we're in this situation, having to do business with a Dixiecrat! Stupid southerners," he said under his breath. "I wonder what her politics are like."

Jeanette turned and said, "We wouldn't be here if it wasn't for you. So you can shut-up. Like you know or care what their politics are."

"This didn't start with me, and you know it. This started with your family. Let's get clear on that and stay clear. I'm just an accessory to this madness."

"Oh yeah, just an innocent bystander," smirked Jeanette.

They got on the elevator and rode up in silence. The elevator stopped so gently they barely noticed it wasn't moving. Tom stepped out first and walked down the hall followed by his sister and brother-in-law. At the end of the hall was that huge man built like a brick wall with smooth, tan skin. This was the man Tom met at the car wash. His straight black hair with one thick, silk like braid snaked its way down to his waist as he stood in front of the suite door. Tom remembered from yesterday that his name was Wallace.

As they approached the door, Wallace's black-eyed stare stopped them.

Tom told Wallace who they were. Without saying a word, Wallace opened the door with his meaty looking hand that reminded Tom of thick filet mignon steaks. They walked into the living room of the suite. There was a magnificent view of Boston Harbor. Jeanette walked over to the window and wondered if she should've taken her medication to help her get through this meeting. But the pills made her feel loopy and she hated that. She stared out at the harbor while Tom took care of their coats. Carl dropped his body into the couch. He was already tired. As he looked around he noticed a coloring book and a large box of crayons on a credenza with a small, fluffy, pink, stuffed bunny rabbit. It made Carl smile. His daughter had a stuffed bunny. "Must be those long floppy ears," Carl thought and smiled.

"Well, good morning everybody," Trixie said. Carl jumped up as they all turned and looked as she entered the room. Trixie had a walk that was smooth, strong, firm and fearless. The impact was daunting highlighted by a subtle waft of very expensive perfume.

Carl couldn't get over her presence, her charisma, that made him think, "Whoa!" It was the kind of energy he associated with heads of state or royalty. She was too real to come from Hollywood but she had that kind of charm that morphed on witchery, mystery and power that you couldn't express but feel.

"Good morning," Tom said. Jeanette and Carl nodded. Trixie was dressed by some of the best designers in the states and

Europe. This morning she wreaked elegance, tailored yet feminine. She was uniquely beautiful and alluring in a non-traditional way. Her black eyes were sparkling, intimidating. Her thick blonde hair glowed this morning. People often mistook her for a model. She had long legs and although she was thin, she was shapely, strong and healthy looking. Trixie's appearance was one part of her personal arsenal. Pointing to the sitting area, she said, "Why don't y'all sit down. Can I get you some coffee, tea? Maybe some hot chocolate? I already ordered all that from room service. It's on its way."

"Tea will be fine," Jeanette said and suddenly noticed another huge man (Frank) standing in a corner. She had a feeling he had a gun. Jeanette walked over to Trixie and asked, "Who are these men?"

"Security," Trixie said. "Business like this requires security," she said and quickly raised and lowered her eyebrows.

"I see," Jeanette said and sat back down, her body now stiff with fear. Who knew what these strange, colored men were capable of, Jeanette thought.

"Listen," Trixie began as they all found seats, "I thought we'd spend the morning talking about y'all's little company that I'm interested in. Just some background, some history, and then we could have lunch and talk hard facts and figures this afternoon. If all goes well, we might have ourselves a fair deal by dinner and close things tomorrow."

"Well," Jeanette said, "I guess we should get to it." She crossed her legs and straightened her back trying to prepare herself for this conversation.

"Great," Trixie said! "But first I want y'all to know about us also, so you understand our motivation and connection that's tied us together for what? Two hundred plus years. This is going to be so enlightening. I can just feel it. Enlightening for all of us. I have found out so much about y'all and according to Tom, y'all still aren't quite sure who I am…"

"No, no – we're clear. I explained," Tom said.

Carl reached in his suit jacket pocket and pulled out a pack of cigarettes.

"Oh my God," Trixie said. "Bless your little heart, you don't still smoke those nasty ol' things, do you? They'll kill ya' for sure. And anyway, I don't smoke, and this is a no smoking suite so don't even light it, darlin'."

"I'm sorry. It's a nervous habit," Carl muttered as he put the cigarettes back in his jacket pocket.

"Well darlin', it is a bad habit."

"Where would you like to start?" Tom asked and sat down next to Trixie.

"You know where I'd like to start," Trixie said to Tom.

"What do you mean by that?" Jeanette asked. "What's going on?"

Trixie looked at Frank and motioned for him to come over. She asked, "Can you get Louis and Madeline to come on in here?"

He nodded and walked out of the room, vanishing down the hallway suite without making a sound.

"Louis and Madeline? Who are they?" Carl asked, hoping he sounded calm.

"Louis is my CFO and Madeline is my special research assistant," Trixie said. "Louis and Madeline are also my cousins. Like I said, first y'all need to know us." They all sat silently waiting for Louis and Madeline.

Tom could hear a clock ticking but he didn't see it. He swallowed and wished the tea and coffee would come. Fixing his eyes on the view of the Boston Harbor he wondered how much this suite was costing the Grants. There were enough fresh flowers to start a florist! Tom wanted to meet in the conference room at the Capwell office building so they would have a psychological advantage over the Grants. He suggested meeting there to Trixie yesterday. She told him calmly but firmly she wasn't doing that. Trixie smiled at him and said, "Nice try, Tom." So much for that. Nothing about this felt right to Tom.

Frank, who resembled Wallace, right down to the long braid hanging down his back, walked into the living room. Trixie turned and smiled at him. Louis then entered exuding a presence that sent another chill through Jeanette. She had never seen a man who looked like that. She was so alarmed she said to Trixie, "This is your CFO? This is your cousin?"

"Oh, he is," Trixie said. "He's family. We're all family. My guards, my staff, all of us."

Jeanette whispered to Carl, "Isn't that man black?"

Louis heard her and said, "Yes, I am as far as you're concerned."

"I'm sorry. You're such a striking, unusual looking man," Jeanette said. "I've never seen a black man with freckles. I mean…I didn't know black people could have freckles." She was desperately trying to clean up her comments. Everyone in the room was now looking at her with expressions of incredulity. Tom started absent-mindedly pulling at his shirt collar and Carl bent forward and covered his face with his hands almost peeking at Jeanette through his fingers. He quickly sat back up, eyes frozen with disbelief at her statement.

"A-huh, I know what you mean," Louis said. He sat on the other side of Trixie and placed a folder on the coffee table. "I've been known to 'pass' in some circles, especially in the north. Northerners just don't have the same kind of visual vocabulary that many southerners and black people have."

"What a clever way of putting it," Jeanette said not knowing what it meant to "pass." Jeanette wanted to vanish. Carl looked her full in the face for a second and turned away.

"It's a little different where I grew up," Louis said. He was an elegant man and he moved with confidence and assuredness. Jeanette, Tom and Carl could see the resemblance between Louis and Trixie. It was something about the shape of their faces. Recognizing that, Jeanette's face reddened with outrage.

"And where was that?" asked Carl.

"Scotland, the Highlands to be specific."

Jeanette was confused. "How did you get there?!"

Louis took his time, smiled, and said, "By plane."

Jeanette stared at him. She wanted to slit his throat! How dare he speak that way to her. Louis' impudent tone was more than she could take and silence fell fast. A fog of fear and rage circled her like vultures.

Madeline walked in, pearls around the neck, perfect hairdo, an Anna Wintour bob cut, conservative suit, and proper but expensive shoes. She too had a thick folder and was also unusual looking, pale tan complexion, a few freckles like Louis, dark hair, but blue eyes. It unglued Jeanette and intrigued Carl. He couldn't take his eyes off of her. Jeanette could not hide her contempt towards this woman. Madeline's blue eyes somehow violated Jeanette's notion of normalcy. She saw Madeline as a freak of nature. What else was "wrong" with her, Jeanette wondered?

"Good morning, Miss Grant," she said.

"Good morning to you, Madeline. No need to be so formal. Pull up a chair and let's get going. By the way," Trixie said, and looked at Jeanette and Carl, "Madeline also spent time growing up in the Highlands. Smart as a whip."

Jeanette blurted out, "She's beige! How did you get two beige cousins?!" She started to laugh and stopped. Everyone in the room was staring at her. Jeanette cleared her throat and hoped that her face was less red than it felt.

"Beige?" asked Trixie. "Is that what you said? Beige? You want to know why I have two beige cousins? Really? You've got to be kidding given what has brought us to this point. Well, darlin', if you don't know, you're going to find out."

"Is that a threat? C'mon, you gotta admit this is a little unusual," Carl said. "I know this is the 21st century, but..." and his voice trailed off realizing Frank was unusually still and focused on him.

Trixie muttered, "This is going to be rich." She looked at Jeanette and said, "You haven't told him the whole story have you?"

Trixie then stared at Carl, and Tom stared at his shoes. He knew it was too early to start drinking. He and Carl had been doing a lot of that lately, drinking at inappropriate hours, commiserating, and trying to find a way out of the Capwell mess.

Room service arrived with coffee, tea, hot chocolate, orange juice, scones and biscuits. Trixie loved biscuits especially with butter and molasses. Louis saw the scones and was disappointed. He wondered where he could get some authentic Irish scones. After all, this was Boston. These triangular things that were heavy and crumbly wouldn't do. He picked up a biscuit and along with everyone else waited for Trixie to begin.

She sighed and looked at each one of them before beginning. Smiling she said, "I bet y'all are wondering why I would be interested in this little company of yours to begin with. God knows we don't need it."

"Well, what are we doing here?" Carl asked. "Maybe we should find another buyer," he said and sipped some coffee.

"There won't be any other offers, Carl," Trixie said. "I've taken care of that."

Carl heard himself think, "Sweet mother of God, what have we done? All those rumors can't be true."

"I noticed something, or rather Louis noticed something. Tell 'em Louis," Trixie said.

"When Trixie's grandfather died a few years ago, I took over his position as CFO. I immediately went through the finances. Everything was fine except for these automatic, quarterly payments of $250,000 that went to some mysterious company. Nobody seemed to know anything about it."

"Granddad personally signed those checks," said Trixie.

"It didn't make any sense, so I stopped the payments. I expected to hear from somebody, but nothing. Very odd," Louis said.

"That's when Louis called me," Madeline said, "to do some research, not about the money, but to whom or what the money was going to. It was going to Capwell Fabrics, your parent company that's for sale. It took forever to figure it out."

Tom held his head in his hands, then looked at Jeanette, "I told you this would happen. You couldn't hide this forever." Tom stood and walked over to the window and stared at Boston harbor while listening to his sister.

"Well," Jeanette began, "what do you want me to say? I'm not sure I understand."

"Why don't you tell me what you think is going on," Trixie said. "I'd love to hear your explanation, Jeanette. Wouldn't you, Louis?"

"Yes, I would," he said as he leaned back and crossed his long legs. "I really want to hear this. I can't believe you didn't know or make the connection," Louis said while looking at Jeanette.

Jeanette, Carl and Tom said nothing as Tom walked back and sat down. Louis, Madeline and Trixie waited. After a full minute passed, Madeline pulled out what looked like a thick report or transcription of some sort. She took a deep breath and said, "Well, just so you know, the story began during slavery when cotton ruled the economy enabled by slave labor of course. The Grant family was one of the most prosperous families in Georgia."

"What is this? A history lesson?" Carl asked, hoping no one could hear his heart pounding.

Trixie looked at him and said, "You'd do well to shut up, Carl. Go ahead, Madeline."

"The Grant plantation was huge and the family owned well over four, five hundred slaves at one point. Cotton was picked and shipped to textile factories that were thriving up north, especially in New England," Madeline said, and she looked directly at Jeanette. "As you know, Mrs. Davidson, one of those factories or mills, belonged to your family, Capwell Fabrics. It's the company you need to sell now."

"To tell you the truth, my memory is fuzzy on all that history. I don't see what it has to do with this transaction," Jeanette said as she flung her hair back.

Trixie's eyes were motionless as she watched Jeanette. "You cannot be serious."

"There's no need to dig up the past that's gone and forgotten," Jeanette said.

"Oh the past is not dead," Louis said. "Far from it. You made that clear when I walked in here." Louis leaned forward and placed his elbows on his thighs. There was a perverse, patient smile on his face. It was hard to know exactly what he was waiting for at that moment.

Trixie looked at Madeline and said, "Let's continue telling Jeanette about that so-called history that's gone and forgotten, that over the years, hell, over the past two hundred years has cost us the equivalent of millions of dollars if not more!"

Madeline opened another folder and handed four stapled pages to everyone. She avoided eye contact with Jeanette, Carl and Tom. The pages illustrated the lineage of the past two hundred and thirty-three years of the Grant family.

Carl took his papers and asked, "What's this?"

"Genealogical charts," Madeline said

Tom looked at his sister, and again shook his head back and forth. He wanted to run out of the room.

Trixie touched his arm and said, "I'm so sorry we have to do this, Tom. I feel badly about it, but not that badly."

Chapter Four:
The Set-up

The genealogical charts were complicated, but Madeline's explanation made it all clear. The boxes, the dotted and straight lines, all led back to the Grant family patriarch Alistair William Grant.

Madeline cleared her throat and drank some of her tea before beginning. "Our family was founded by an extraordinary man named Alistair William Grant. His story reveals the Grant-Capwell connection."

Jeanette's eyes grew wide and she tried not to hyperventilate while clutching the genealogical charts. She saw hands reaching out from the charts to strangle her. It was only for a moment, but it seemed real to Jeanette.

"Extraordinary," muttered Carl. "Another story about a slave owner from the south." As soon as the words rushed from his mouth, Carl wanted to kick himself.

Trixie leaned forward and said to Carl, "What is it about 'shut-up' that you don't understand? Given what we know about you my advice is start praying."

The color drained from Carl's face. Jeanette scowled at him for a moment and felt her facial tic jump several times.

"Should I continue?" Madeline asked.

"Absolutely," Trixie said.

"Excuse me, but how do you know all this? We're talking hundreds of years ago. How could you know?" Jeanette asked.

"We know," said Madeline, "because Alistair kept diaries. All the Grant men did and still do. Anyway, Alistair's diaries were in Gaelic."

"Then how could you possibly read them?" Jeanette asked.

"I studied Gaelic. I can read, write and speak it as well."

Jeanette's face dropped with shock. Carl tried to hide a smile with his hand, and Tom closed his eyes and covered his face with both hands for a few seconds. Carl felt his "pretense of ignorance" about what was going to be told slowly evaporate. He became a vision of stoicism and prepared himself for whatever was coming including some form of contemporary slaughter that was too horrible to imagine. The Grants and their ancestors have thrown the Capwells into an arena to be killed by some horrible animal of vengeance. Muttering to himself, Carl said, "We deserve whatever's coming." His attention returned to Madeline, resigned to the unknown.

"So, what I'm about to share with you are the relevant entries from his diary," Madeline said. "A great deal will be clarified. This is long, so I would make myself comfortable."

Trixie gave the Capwells a look that terrified them.

Chapter Five:
Alistair's Story

September 4, 1782

"I landed in what used to be New Amsterdam. But the Dutch have been long gone and now it's called New York. Anything's possible here. I'm going to find some work, earn more money, and then leave for the South. They say there's land there. The climate's warm, the soil rich, and the prospect of buying some land and a few slaves is promising. I'm going to hold on to the money I made fighting in Liverpool after I left Scotland. I know this much, I am never going to be poor again. Watching my mother and baby sister die because there wasn't enough food to eat is a sin of some sort."

April 18, 1783

"I've got a good feeling about this. Ten acres I acquired. Right now, I've got five slaves. We're going to work this land. I'm going to work right alongside of them. Some of the other landowners made a point of telling me how wrong that was; how I need an Overseer to handle the slaves. The minister rode out here to tell me I'm soft on my slaves. Everybody thinks it's because I'm young and don't know any better. It has nothing to do with my age. This business of slavery sickens me but there's no way I can become a rich man without them. There's a very dark place in hell waiting for all of us who've enslaved these black people. But I'm ready to face God's judgment when the time comes. We don't deserve His mercy. How do you ask for God's forgiveness?"

Madeline stopped to drink some tea and looked at the Capwells. They were frozen in their seats barely breathing. With the grace of a ballerina, Madeline cracked her neck from one side to the other before she continued.

"Based on descriptions and comments I found in some historical documents and a full length portrait we still have, Alistair was a big man, lean but muscular with a strong physical and emotional presence. His black eyes could make a woman swoon or die from fright. Alistair's blue black hair never grayed. We could tell by some of the encounters he wrote about that his physicality seemed to generate a kind of forbidden, sexual heat that women back then found embarrassing but tempting, and men found threatening. In one local paper I found they described his stride as smooth, strong, firm and fearless! The way he walked was a celebration of his determination. People just naturally stepped aside when he walked by. He was intimidating," Madeline said and grinned. She caught herself and regained her serious demeanor before continuing to read. That grin revealed some laugh lines that betrayed her youthful appearance. It was hard to tell how old Madeline was but right now that didn't matter to anyone except Jeanette.

July 2, 1784

The love of my life arrived today, Marie Bridget McCloud. This is the longest time we've ever been apart. We grew up together in the same village. I wrote her last year and told her I'd send for her when the house was finished. I hand-picked seven slaves to work in the house, cooking, cleaning, doing the laundry, sewing. I've been prosperous. Acquired more land and more slaves. There's a young girl I bought a year ago. She can't be more than fourteen or fifteen. The slave trader called her Kate. He was Kate's father. He branded her with his insignia, the letter D centered in a circle with the rest of his name right in the middle. He put the branding on her upper arm. The name was Douglas. I hated doing business with him. One of the many necessary evils of slavery.

Alistair went on to write that the ship's Captain wanted his needs met one night and raped an African woman who gave birth to Kate. It was the Captain who was responsible for her thick, straight black hair and hazel eyes. Her looks made her more desirable to slave owners, and increased her value." Madeline suddenly stopped. There was sadness in her eyes she couldn't hide as she carefully regarded the Capwells wondering what was going through their minds.

Madeline took a deep breath and continued reading from Alistair's diary.

"I've never seen anyone as beautiful as Kate is. The skin that condemns them all because of its color, on her, is radiant. Her hair is thick and straight like black honey. She's smart too. She'll do well in the house."

Trixie shot a look at Carl, Tom and Jeanette, and said, "Kate is very important. Kate is why we're all here."

Jeanette's stomach tightened. Her eyes flitted from Trixie to Louis and then Madeline.

Trixie looked at Madeline and said, "Go on, Maddie."

"It's been rumored that several slaves from the Johnson plantation ran off and are living with the Cherokees. The sin of greed is going to come back and destroy this country one day. Stolen land and slave labor create a weak foundation to build anything on, much less a country. God help us if the red man and the black man united.

Marie and I are getting married, Sunday, right here in the garden surrounded by flowers. There's a lot of talk about it in town but I don't care. Marie waited for me. I'm not going to make her wait any longer."

Madeline sighed and told them that eventually Alistair owned five hundred acres and seemingly enough slaves to populate a small town. He had a Midas touch. The quality of his cotton was unmatched. He had contracts with several mills up north. Yet much to the consternation of his peers, Alistair remained "soft" on his slaves.

June 9, 1788

Ian came over here today and told me there was a meeting last night of all the property owners about how I treat my slaves.

Everyone's concerned because I continue to give them decent shelter, food, and medical care. I told Ian a healthy slave is a productive slave. Ian understood, but he wanted me to know I'm walking a fine line. Something's going to happen, soon. I can feel it. They see me as a threat. I'm going to have to do something especially with the baby coming. Marie's due in a couple of weeks.

Madeline said, "Alistair paid the local doctor, Paul Dunn, well for his services, and to keep his mouth shut about the care Alistair's slaves received from him. When Dunn threatened to tell the authorities that Alistair was breaking some unspoken, but highly enforced law about giving care to his slaves, Dunn demanded additional compensation for his silence. Alistair refused. He wasn't going to work people to death and then throw them away like garbage. Nor would he be blackmailed by anybody."

Alistair wrote that Dunn said, "I don't understand you, Alistair. They're less than human, easily replaceable."

Madeline paused for a moment and then continued. "They ended up getting into a loud, ugly fight with the doctor spitting in Alistair's face. It's noted in Alistair's diary that several slaves witnessed the argument."

Continuing Madeline said, "The doctor left the plantation that day and vanished. According to Alistair's diaries we know that shortly after the doctor left Alistair followed him."

"Alistair's accounting started with the following. 'I ordered Seth to get my horse, a beautiful, black stallion I had bought and named Druid. I mounted him and rode off after Dunn. I caught up with him, stopped the horse that was pulling his carriage and said, get down.

He told me he didn't have time to stop. I got off Druid and pulled the Doctor to the ground. He stumbled and fell but I pulled him back up on his feet. I told him that I didn't like him and didn't like what he said. He's a twisted kind of Christian. I let him know that whatever he was going to do or say would never happen.

Dunn got nervous and thought we were alone. He started to make a plea and said, "Alistair, I have a family. I have children. We don't have nearly what you have. Please."

I looked down at Dunn and said, "You should've thought about that when you tried to blackmail me."

"No, no, no… you misunderstood Alistair. I would never do that. I was simply trying to warn you. People talk. I have to protect myself, my family."

I put my hand around the Doctor's neck and started to squeeze until he stopped breathing. I knew we were being watched. The doctor's body went limp, and I let him drop to the ground. I dragged him off to a wooded area. I looked up and saw two Cherokees and a black man who was dressed like them. Three of my slaves were standing a few yards behind them."

Madeline smoothed her hair and told everyone, "No one knew exactly how Alistair disposed of the body nor what happened to the Doctor's horse and carriage. There's nothing about it in his diary. Who, what, and how remained a secret that they all took to the grave."

"When I returned later that day, Seth took Druid and asked if everything was in order. I looked at Seth and told him that everything was fine. A week later I rode off to meet with a Cherokee woman I'd heard about. She's going to come and care for the slaves when they get sick. The impact of the Doctor's death on the larger community was as I expected. Everybody was frightened, and whispers began among my slaves that I killed the doctor to protect them. The other plantation owners believed that one of my slaves had killed the doctor. People live in constant fear of them. What if they rose up? Rumors about slave uprisings are common. What if they rebelled and killed us all? There were so many ways to do that especially with the house slaves preparing food and in such close proximity to their owners." Madeline stopped for a second and looked directly at Jeanette. She shifted her weight and avoided eye contact with Madeline by staring at her shoes.

Madeline went on to read, "Some of the slaves have strange ways, and like the Cherokees, know things about plants and roots. The Indians seem to be everywhere and nowhere, silent, invisible, seen only when they want to be seen. It would make anyone nervous."

"I mean after all," Madeline said, "This massive land was theirs. They were the rightful owners. There were stories of slaves escaping into the woods, living with various tribes, and intermarrying all over. That's how black Indians came to be, that and living amongst them for generations."

"Whoa," exclaimed Carl! "What are you talking about, black Indians? I've never heard of that, nor seen a black Indian." The strain to understand was balanced by the wide eyed look of a curious child on Carl's face.

Louis turned towards Carl and said, "There's a lot you don't know Carl. You're in the presence of three black Indians and one of them has a gun. Don't interrupt my sister again."

Carl's eyes darted over to Frank. Could Frank be one of those? Carl quickly reassessed Frank's looks, especially his long, black hair. Frank's face? Was that why his cheekbones are so pronounced, his demeanor so...stolid, Carl asked himself? And who is this third copper skinned man in the expensive suit seated in the corner? My God, Carl thought, what else don't I know? Who are these people? I mean who are they really?

Madeline read, "I went to a town meeting where I was confronted by my neighbors again and what passed for the law. I told them my slaves didn't have enough sense or cunning to murder anybody. They were barely human anyway. They couldn't think. They couldn't reason. They were children at best. Their only value was brute strength. It made me sick to have to say that, but after days of talking everyone seemed to accept that my slaves had nothing to do with the disappearance of the doctor. But everyone was still terrified. I heard later that many became harsher with their own slaves to let them know who ruled just in case they had some fantasy of rebellion."

Jeanette was growing weary of listening to Madeline talk about how slaves on nearby plantations would pray to be bought by Alistair William Grant; how they considered him a savior of some sort, the South's very own Oscar Schindler. Jeanette was beginning to squirm in her seat. Grant's slaves would be fed and well taken care of until they died and blah, blah, blah. On the Grant plantation there was a good possibility that their families could stay together and not be sold off to some other plantation or individual. Jeanette snickered quietly and thought, "He didn't give them their freedom. He wasn't that much of a savior!"

July 1, 1785

Today was the most joyful and heart breaking day of my life. Marie gave birth to our daughter, Elisabeth, early this morning. The baby's healthy and beautiful. We think her thick blonde hair is from Bridget's father's family, Viking blood. Elisabeth has these bright black eyes that make me think about our Celtic heritage. I look at her and think of the stories my mother told us about the old ways, Druids, fairies, magic. But by sunset, heart break was upon us. Marie was dead. The midwife couldn't stop the bleeding. I went out to the garden, dropped to my knees, cried, screamed. I could see Marie standing in front of me, telling me to get up, take care of our daughter, that I had to lay the groundwork for an extraordinary family that would thrive for hundreds of years. She told me I'd love again and have more children. That I can't imagine. Then she was gone but I can feel her spirit. I know she'll always watch over our baby girl. Marie Bridget McLoud will always be the great love of my life. She was uniquely beautiful with black hair, gentle eyes, high cheekbones, skin softer than a cool breeze on a hot day. She had the hands of royalty, graceful, long fingers. Elisabeth will be my salvation. Everything I do will be for her now."

Madeline told everyone that after Elisabeth's birth he kept writing how the buying and selling of black people and the increasing slaughter of red people were making him sicker and angrier. The cruelty repulsed him. He wrote, "I watched Abraham Carrington beat a female slave until she was too weak to cry out and she was with child. What price will we all pay for being part of this? An eternity in hell awaits. You can't serve God and money. But the truth is I love money more than I fear hell. And that's what the Bible says, the love of money is the root of all evil."

"Alistair desperately wanted more children, if for no other reason than to keep Elizabeth company but it would be five years before he remarried," Madeline said.

Trixie looked at the Capwells and said, "Y'all listen very carefully now. Keep going Madeline."

"During those five years, he fathered two more children, a boy he named Sinclair, after a friend of his up north, and a girl he named Bridget, after his late wife. He referred to his baby daughter as little Bridget, and called her his Goddess of Magic sent from heaven. But the mother of Bridget and Sinclair was Kate, the slave, who now served as housekeeper," Madeline said. "Kate had become a tall, striking, young woman, lean, with soft, butterscotch colored skin. From Alistair's descriptions of Kate, she could've easily become an haute couture model today."

Jeanette stiffened and didn't want to hear anymore. Tom had emotionally checked out shortly after Madeline began, and Carl was looking more troubled and more uncomfortable as she continued telling the story of Alistair William Grant. Carl loosened his tie and poured himself a glass of water. What would they say if they knew his secret? Questions and thoughts tumbled around his brain, like wet clothes in a dryer, as he tried to reconcile the contradictions of his life. Staring off into space for a few seconds, he shook his head slightly. The irony he was living made him sweat and nauseous. Something had to change.

Trixie got up and sat next to Madeline whose eyes were filled with tears. Taking her hand in hers, Trixie softly asked, "You okay? I can take it from here if you want." Madeline nodded her head and gave all the diaries and papers to Trixie.

Carl and Jeanette looked bewildered for different reasons. Jeanette didn't understand why Madeline became so emotional. Carl was beginning to empathize with Madeline. Something clicked in Carl's brain as his thoughts turned inward. Tom looked equally miserable because he knew why Madeline had to stop. He was beginning to connect the dots. All those rumors he heard growing up were about to be proven true. The weight of carrying this around for roughly two centuries was beginning to rest on Tom's shoulders. He realized that he was in no position to shoulder that weight nor the regret that the Capwells should be feeling. He wasn't that strong. What happens when you're not strong enough? Who do you go to for help? His late brother, Daniel, could shoulder anything and think nothing of it. He would have no regrets. Daniel's only concern would be what benefitted him.

Trixie looked at Alistair's diary and like a runaway locomotive started to read. "Kate will be more presentable than these other African women with the strange, thick hair that can be braided and twisted into odd configurations. I heard in town that their heads were often shaved before they were sold because slave traders knew those strange hairdos carried messages. Their hair styles were often a key to what tribe they belonged to, so, the slave traders took no chances and eliminated every possible way for slaves to unite or communicate with each other." The speed with which Trixie read left Carl, Tom and Jeanette almost breathless. Wide eyed, it had a suffocating effect on them. There was no going back.

"It didn't take Kate long to assume the appearance of a grown woman. It was obvious by looking at Sinclair and Bridget who their father was. He kept them at the house, raised them with Elizabeth as family. The slaves knew and said nothing. The whites knew and snickered. It was an open secret," Trixie said. "An open secret," she repeated, and spit the words directly at the Capwells.

"Alistair eventually remarried and when he did, he explained to his new wife, Ella, that Kate, Bridget and Sinclair, were not to be bothered or displaced. They stayed in the house in two rooms in the attic, not in the slave quarters. And if Elizabeth needed to be disciplined, he would do it. Alistair was a big step up for Ella, so she kept her mouth shut about the irregularities. There was too much to gain, too much money, too much status, and all that land," Trixie said.

He wrote, "Ella tried to argue with me about Kate. I told Ella she would have to adjust to the fact that all of my children were learning to read, write, and do their numbers. Sinclair, Bridget and Elizabeth would learn a foreign language, and understand how the upper classes lived, behaved and worshipped. Ella told me she had heard about my reputation for defying tradition and the law when it suited me. I asked Ella who would tell? Ella was shocked with the implication, but I'm now the wealthiest and most powerful man in the county with fifty of the five hundred acres I own devoted exclusively to farming. We can sustain ourselves. God's blessed me with success. The cotton has already made me a rich man ten times over. We ship most of it, up north, to Massachusetts where it's spun into cloth by the Capwell company. I'm growing a new strain of cotton on ten acres to see how it turns out. I'm hoping it'll be the quality dressmakers in France and England would want. Trixie looked up at them and said, "Y'all understand? You following this?"

Carl took a deep breath and said, "Yes, go on." Shoulders slumping, he sank into the couch withdrawn and somber.

"We know from his diaries, that Alistair remained physically strong all his life. Everyone knew he could still beat a man senseless within minutes. But he could hold his baby daughter with all the care and gentleness one held fine crystal or a flower."

Trixie reached for her glass of water and drank some before going on. Nobody else dared move.

"Shortly after they married, Ella went to inspect the attic where Alistair's black family lived. Alistair wrote that 'Ella didn't like the attic quarters for Kate and the children. She thought it was too good for them and didn't understand why they couldn't sleep on the floor in the back hall. The beds were soft with feather mattresses. There were sheets, blankets and pillows. I made sure they had several changes of clothing and a small fireplace they could use to cook and keep warm. Ella was outraged. The bitch begged me to hire a Spirit Breaker."

"What's a Spirit Breaker?" Carl asked.

"A Spirit Breaker," Trixie said, "would come and beat the independence out of slaves, literally beat them into submission so they would never think of rebelling or talking back to their owners. Slaves would be reduced to the equivalent of cowering animals who would live in constant fear, programmed through carnal punishment to work until they dropped dead in service to their masters. When Ella asked Alistair to do this the only response she got from him was a cold stare that terrified her."

Carl got up and walked over to the window while Trixie continued. Running his hands through his hair, Carl wanted to pull his hair out. "Ella kept a diary also that Madeline found. This is an excerpt from hers".

(Date unknown)

I keep overhearing house slaves whispering about how Kate and Alistair spend nights together in some bedroom I can't find. I have spent hours walking through this house trying to find the bedroom where they spend nights together, sharing thoughts and affection he never expresses to me. I want to tell someone what's going on out here, but I don't dare. He still works the land once or twice a month picking cotton just like those savages. No one even thinks about getting in a fist fight with him either. His physical strength is amazing. May God forgive me, but I often think about killing him. After our son, Patrick, was born I became invisible. I wake up in the middle of the night and Alistair's gone. He's with her. I know it. He told me yesterday that he wants us to have separate bedrooms. He's taking the room at the end of the hall that's closer to the back stairs that lead to the attic."

Alistair wrote, "Ella got so mad one day she pushed Ruth, the house slave who did the laundry, down the stairs and broke her back. Ella thinks I don't know what she did. She had two slaves from the stable take Ruth out, and ordered the Overseer to kill Ruth and bury her in one of the back fields. Marrying Ella was a mistake. But I couldn't marry Kate."

Madeline whispered something to Trixie that led Trixie to putting her arm around Madeline's shoulder and kissing her on the forehead before handing Madeline the papers. Shifting in her chair, Madeline said, "Alistair's relationship with Kate started years before Ella arrived, about a year or two after Marie died in childbirth. One night, Alistair climbed the stairs to the attic. He wrote..."

"I didn't know how much longer I could control myself. I took one of Marie's robes, went up to the attic where Kate slept and stood at the door for several minutes before knocking. I walked in and said, 'Kate.'

"Master?"

"Kate, I want you to come with me," I said standing at the foot of her bed.

Kate quickly got out of bed and reached for her dress to put on over her dressing gown. I handed her Marie's robe and told her to put it on."

"Master, what is wrong? Has something happened? Is someone sick? Baby Elisabeth?" She took the robe and then realized that it belonged to Marie. Kate hesitated.

"Put it on, Kate. Everything's fine, and yes, something has happened."

I took her hand and led her down the hallway to a storage room. It was still crammed with cartons, old furniture, some trunks, dust. I stepped over the trunks to the rear wall, pushed aside an old dresser, bent down and pressed a floor board. The wall turned and revealed a bedroom. Kate's posture stiffened. I took her by the hand and we walked in. She was awe struck. I had worked on this for months. I closed the wall and walked over to her.

Dropping her head, she said, "Master please..."

I told her that, "In this room, I'm not your Master and you're not my slave. You're not my housekeeper. You're a woman I'm deeply attracted to, maybe in love with, and I want to act on it." I put my hands on her shoulders and realized she was trembling. I told her to not be afraid, that I would protect her with my life."

She looked up at me, helpless. I unbuttoned my shirt, and told her that, "If I were a better man, I'd sell all this, free every slave I own, and leave this bloody country, take Elizabeth and you with me. We'd go back to Scotland. It's beautiful where I come from Kate. But I'm consumed with greed and ambition because the smell and taste of the poverty I experienced as a child will never leave me. I'm not a good man, Kate. I'm capable of terrible things but I do feel deeply for you. I'm guilty of wanting it all. I want you. I undressed her and we spent our first night together. She was so shy and so scared. I didn't know I was capable of being that gentle."

"And that's how it began," Madeline said. "A year later Sinclair was born. Two years later, Bridget came. Elisabeth was enthralled with Bridget and considered Bridget her doll until her father sat her down one day and said, 'She's not your plaything, Elizabeth. You look at Bridget and treat her like your sister, like family, because she is. If anybody gives you any trouble about that, you let me know.' Elizabeth was seven, too young to understand the import of what her father was saying. What she did know was she idolized him and would do whatever he said. That never changed."

Madeline turned to a page she had marked with a yellow sticky before continuing. "The best I could figure," said Madeline, "was Elizabeth had to be seven or eight when Alistair wrote the following.

'I took the children for a walk in the flower garden this evening. The sun was down and the air was cooling off. Elizabeth's started asking lots of questions. She's a watcher. She wanted to know why people were different colors. I knew that question was coming. I pointed out all the different flowers, especially the roses, to Elizabeth, Sinclair and Bridget. The roses were amazing. Red ones, white ones, pink ones, all looking like magical multicolored balls of cotton. I keep thinking that flowers are God's kisses. We stood right in the middle of all those roses. Elizabeth and Bridget were mesmerized by them.'

'So, you want to know why people are different colors, why your skin color is different from Sinclair and Bridget and their mother, Kate? We're different colors for the same reasons flowers are. You, and Bridget and Sinclair and baby Patrick, you're my mixed bouquet of flowers from God. Elizabeth's face lit up. Bridget grabbed my leg and I picked her up. We walked over to a nearby swing and sat together, side by side, Sinclair on one side and the girls on the other. I told them there were people out here, people we know, who would kill or steal Sinclair and Bridget because they're not the same color as I am or other white people. I told Elizabeth that it's important that she, and Patrick when he gets older, be very protective of Sinclair and Bridget. I told them they were to care for each other the way you would care for flowers.'

'They're bad people, Papa?' Elizabeth asked me. I thought for a moment and told her, 'bad is a big word in meaning. There are different kinds of bad. The people I'm talking about who would hurt Sinclair and Bridget are confused, scared and greedy. There's a little bit of badness in all of us. Just like roses have thorns, people have thorns. We all have to be careful.' When I told her that I was being bad owning all these slaves so they could work and make us rich, the look on her face almost killed me. She looked at me with those big, black eyes, and said, but Papa, I love you. I told her it was possible to love bad people and bad people had to do something to make it up to God. Sinclair's a very sharp little boy. He'd been listening to all this and asked me if I didn't have favorite roses. I told him Bridget was my favorite pink rose, and Elizabeth my favorite white rose, and he was my favorite red rose. That's why they're a bouquet. God made us all different so we could learn to appreciate how special we all are. Sinclair's face lit up. I left it at that and hugged them all. As we walked back to the house, I saw Kate looking at us from the library window. Our eyes locked for a moment as I picked up Bridget. One of the few times I've seen Kate smile outside of the confines of our room."

Carl looked at everyone and said, "I'm not sure I can take much more of this." He rubbed his eyes hoping no one saw that he was on the verge of tears. If he could've left he would have, but he couldn't. He knew it was only a matter of time before his secret would be revealed. Trixie wouldn't overlook that. She was too thorough. Carl knew this. It was just a feeling but Carl started thinking about what he was going to say. He chuckled to himself and thought, "What a karmic joke this is. Boy do we deserve it."

Trixie turned and looked at him, "You can't take much more of this? Is that what you said? Well... that's really too bad. All you have to do is listen. You didn't have to live any of this." Trixie turned and looked at Madeline, "Go ahead."

"One of the good things he did was teach Kate to read and write. Each Christmas he would buy her a dress saying he wanted his housekeeper to look proper for the holidays. By the time Ella arrived, she was almost an afterthought, something Alistair realized he needed like a good horse or a new rifle. As Mistress of the house, Ella was a prop to complete the look of the plantation for Alistair's neighbors and business associates." Madeline was fond of the word "prop." One way Madeline coped with the injustice of all this was to think of white people as nothing but props in a bad play called America. She had been waiting for this confrontation with the Capwells ever since she traced the blackmail payments back to them. With the patience and control of a ticking bomb, Madeline heard herself think, "The chickens have come home to roost, finally."

"Unfortunately, Ella realized this too late and made it hell for Kate, Sinclair and Bridget or, as she called them in her diary, the bastard children. Ella gave Alistair a son, Patrick, who would legally inherit the plantation and all that went with it. She was sure giving Alistair a child, especially a son, would increase her value to him. She gave birth to Patrick two years after they were married. Patrick was a happy little boy and almost an exact copy of Alistair. Patrick was curious about everything and completely devoted to his father and his siblings of both colors. Ella was sickened by the resemblance between Patrick and Sinclair and sickened by what was the undeniable ongoing and growing affection Alistair had for Kate. Ella's only solace was that Kate had no choice. Ella told herself there couldn't be any real feeling between her husband and this slave woman. Alistair didn't make love to this slave. She was an animal, a savage. He was raping Kate, and that made Ella feel very good every time she told Alistair. Of course," Madeline added, "Ella had no idea the danger she was in. Alistair had his limits."

The house was filled with the laughter of growing children, and the humid silence of Ella's burgeoning contempt for her situation. Her hate for Kate, Bridget, Sinclair and Alistair festered for what felt like several lifetimes. Her contempt for Sinclair and Bridget created a vicious tension with Kate. One day it exploded. Ella threw a pot of boiling water on Kate, but Kate was quick and managed to dodge it. Sinclair, who was twelve, saw it all along with Alistair who had just walked into the kitchen and was standing in the doorway.

Alistair looked at Kate. "Are you all right? Are you hurt in any way?"

"No sir. No sir, I'm not Master. I'll be fine," Kate said. She dropped her head remembering what was expected of her as a slave. She kept her head bowed for five seconds that felt like five years. Her heartbeat raced, her leg muscles tightened and she prayed that she and her children would be protected from Ella. Ella had a way of exacting revenge on slaves who displeased her. The fate of Ruth lived in every slave's heart and mind.

"Sinclair, leave us. Go in the library. I'll be there shortly," Alistair said.

The sound of Alistair's voice startled Kate and also relieved her fear.

"Yes Master." Sinclair reluctantly turned and left the kitchen but he glanced back at his mother. He was afraid for her as images popped up in his mind of what could happen, images of what he'd seen on the plantation. Would his father give in to his wife and have his mother beaten or worse?

Alistair walked over to Ella. Shaking, she started to say, "Alistair, you don't understand. She…"

He grabbed her by the arm, and said, "Not another word. Where's Patrick?"

"He's taking some riding lessons. Please, you're hurting me." Alistair never let go of her arm.

"Any of the other children see you do this to Kate?"

"No. Alistair, no. My arm, please." She was wincing in pain too frightened to look at him.

"You tried to damage my property, Ella. That's how you see them isn't it? Property. That's how everybody sees them. Well, what you just tried to do is punishable by law. You understand that, don't you? Men have been killed for less." Alistair was squeezing her arm so tightly, he felt the frailty of her bones. It wouldn't take much more effort for Alistair to snap her arm with the same ease one could snap a twig for kindling. Ella wasn't an especially small woman so much as Alistair was a huge man and dwarfs any average sized person.

"I don't know what came over me. I must've had some kind..." Ella didn't bother to finish the sentence. She managed to look into his eyes and saw an abyss. There was no reaching him now. She became cold all over and everything faded.

Alistair looked at her, assessing something Ella couldn't figure out, and then dragged her out of the kitchen. Ella tried to resist but it was futile. Kate stood there, praying, pretending not to hear or see anything while hearing and seeing everything.

As Kate was setting the dinner table that evening, Alistair walked in the dining room and said, "Mrs. Grant won't be joining us tonight, Kate."

"I see. Should I prepare a tray and take it up to her?"

"Prepare a tray. I'll take it up to her. The children and I will eat as usual in the dining room."

"The children, Master?"

He stopped and looked at Kate. "Yes, the children, all of them. Elizabeth, Sinclair, Patrick, and Bridget."

Shortly after that Ella became very ill. Alistair cared for her, refusing to let Kate near Ella. Within a month, Ella was dead. She didn't die peacefully according to Alistair's description in his diary.

It was a painful, loud death. The other house slaves were convinced Master Alistair poisoned Ella over Kate. He had learned a great deal about plants and herbs from several slaves, and the Cherokees. First the doctor vanished, and then Miss Ella died from unknown causes.

Alistair, with the help of Kate, raised his children. He wanted Sinclair and Bridget to be safe. Madeline took a deep breath before continuing. She told them that Bridget was sent to Paris to continue her education when she was sixteen. She lived with Alistair's brother and his family. They had done quite well, selling Alistair's cotton in Paris. Bridget ended up staying there and marrying a wealthy Frenchman. Her father visited several times, content that she was safe and taken care of, and took Kate with him twice to see their daughter. Bridget gave him three grandchildren that he adored. Elizabeth never married although she had many friends and suitors. She became one of the finest experts on horses in the area and started breeding them. She added to the family fortune and became a legend. Madeline said, "Look there's a lot of detail I'm leaving out, but I want you to get a sense of what went on. Just bear with me."

Trixie leaned over and said, "You've done enough. I can take it from here. Pour yourself some hot tea. We're almost at the end."

"Y'all need to understand that Sinclair posed a dangerous problem because he was a black man, regardless," Trixie said. "Y'all got that? Alistair went to great lengths to protect Sinclair including killing another man, sending him and Patrick north to finish their education, and paying off more than one slave trader to look the other way. Alistair used the law when it served him and his children, and violence when he ran out of options. I really understand that," Trixie said.

Carl and Tom cringed. Jeanette couldn't feel anything, anywhere at the moment. Frank and Wallace had dropped their heads swallowing their amusement over the Capwell's discomfort. John never took his eyes off the Capwells. He was feeling a range of emotions but amusement wasn't one of them.

"Sinclair and Patrick were more like twins than brothers," Trixie said, "even though they were five or six years apart in age. Alistair taught Sinclair and Patrick to run the plantation. It was a dangerous situation, but the truth is, ladies and gentlemen, the south often allowed for some realities to exist that defied logic, law and custom. The Grant family was one of those realities." By now, Jeanette was staring straight ahead. There was a remorseful look on Carl's face and the muscles on Tom's face sagged from fatigue and stress.

"Both young men were needed to run their father's plantation. Patrick understood strategic planning, and Sinclair had studied math. He had an expertise regarding the land and agriculture that was unmatched. The Grant brothers married, had children, and secured the foundation for the family business to evolve and grow right into the twenty-first century. This is how Grant Family Companies began, folks," Trixie said.

"Those who knew about Alistair and Kate never said a thing. Pay attention to this people. Word circulated that if you tried to 'mess with Alistair Grant's slaves, especially the house slave, Kate, and his two children he had with her, Grant would kill you with his bare hands. And don't you know that long before Alistair died he gave Kate, Sinclair and Bridget, their freedom along with some land on the plantation. Kate outlived Alistair by a decade. She stayed in the big house until she died. Elizabeth, Patrick and Sinclair buried her right next to Alistair, Marie and Ella."

"So, ladies and gentlemen," Trixie said, "Louis, the unusual looking black man with freckles, and his sister, Madeline, who reads and speaks Gaelic, are direct descendants of Sinclair Grant. I am a direct descendant of Patrick Grant, and Bridget's descendants? Still in Paris. We're going over to see them come Spring." Trixie put the papers down on the coffee table. Everyone was silent. They all knew that a very old score was going to be settled today, in the new Boston of the twenty-first century, on the top floor of a fancy hotel overlooking the harbor. This was the story that left Jeanette, Carl, and Tom speechless and finally frightened. The arrogance of confidence that the Capwells wore was gone.

Carl heard himself ask, "All this was in his diary?"

"Grandpa Alistair and all the Grant men kept detailed diaries and meticulous financial records. Every transaction, *every transaction since 1780,* has been recorded by my ancestors," Trixie said.

"Once we found the diaries and quite a few ledgers, it wasn't hard to piece this together," Madeline said.

Barely audible, Jeanette asked, "What does any of this have to do with us?"

Trixie smiled. "Oh, come on, Jeanette. You know. Stop playin'! But the truth is, we haven't gotten to the good part yet. Y'all want to take a break? Stretch your legs? We could order some more coffee and tea. Get refreshed.

Chapter Six:
The Problem

Trixie took Tom by the arm and they walked over to the window. Tom couldn't focus on anything. Boats, water, docks, the clear sky, none of it registered.

"Tell me, Tom, how long have you known about what we're going to go over?" Trixie asked. It was impossible to escape her eyes and it didn't matter if you looked at her or not. Her eyes made you feel as if you were always being watched.

"Ever since I've been working in the business. I heard rumors growing up," Tom said. Trixie let go of his arm so she could put her arm around his shoulder. He wished he wasn't so frightened of this woman.

"And you said nothing? You just let it go on?" and Trixie gave a little squeeze to his shoulder with her graceful hands to emphasize her point.

Tom sighed and swallowed. "I tried to... but not hard enough."

"No, not hard enough, but I appreciate your honesty when Louis called and during our meeting. I'm going to remember that." She took his hand and squeezed it briefly. "Go stretch your legs before we get back to it. And Tom?"

"Yes?"

"Don't ever, ever ignore a rumor."

"Yeah, I've learned that."

Jeanette walked over to Tom and said, "Take a walk with me, little brother."

They left the suite, took the elevator down to the lobby and sat in a corner.

"Tom, where is this going to end?" Jeanette asked.

"I don't really know."

"Yes, you do! You've spent more time with this woman than we have. I want some details now! What else happened at the car wash?"

"Look, I arrived early, so I decided to get the car washed before parking," and then he proceeded to lie. Tom's gut told him, "Lie. You know your sister's crazy. Save yourself and lie," and that's what he did to the extent he could and still live with himself. He continued to be puzzled by why Trixie shared with him her plan for this transaction. "Five or ten minutes later she showed up. We were standing there waiting for our cars and struck up a conversation. One thing led to another and I realized who I was talking to. I laughed. She laughed, and we had lunch right here, and talked about the company. Please don't underestimate this woman."

"What does that mean?" Jeanette asked. She started to bite her lower lip. Her eyes were staring into nothing, fixated on another faraway place only seen by her.

"It means that she knows the whole, sordid story, about all of us and there's no way out of this," Tom said. "That's the problem, there's no way out. She's putting a stop to his little arrangement our families had. C'mon Jeanette, did you think we could blackmail these folks forever?"

Paying no attention to her brother, Jeanette said, "We could find another buyer. Someone who doesn't know all of this. Tom, this is the family's business! Capwell Fabrics is the first company started. Daddy left me in charge. I was the oldest but I didn't have a penis. Nobody was going to listen to me so Carl and I made a deal negotiated in hell. I did this, and there's just got to be a way for me to turn this around."

Tom examined his sister's face and said, "Did you hear anything I just said? It's too late. You don't get it, do you? Focus! You are in charge, legally and psychologically. Jeanette, say something!" He placed his hand on her shoulder and gently shook it.

Jeannette stared back at him, her mouth slightly open, dissociated from her current surroundings.

Tom studied his sister's face for a moment. He had no clue what was going on in Jeanette's head. The only hint was that facial tic under her eye pulsating. "You know what I find fascinating?" Tom asked.

"What?" she asked weakly and looked around for a chair so she could sit down.

"You said nobody would listen to you if you took over. But people listen to Trixie."

"Different circumstances. Very different," Jeanette said. "You know what Father was like. I was his only option after Daniel died. You were off somewhere in Europe pretending to study architecture and living with that woman."

"I was going to marry that woman, Jeanette. The only reason I came back was because Rachel died and you know it, and I wasn't pretending anything. I'm a licensed architect." Tom held back from saying anything else. He was afraid he would say too much. Say things he couldn't take back or apologize for – ever.

She ignored her brother and asked, "What kind of options do you think we'll have? Will they at least give us a decent offer? Can we refuse and leave? What choices do we have, Tom?" Again, Tom noticed his sister was looking off into space. It worried him along with what she was asking.

"Choices? That's a joke! Look, what we'll determine is not if we take her offer, but which offer we take and there's only going to be one. C'mon, we should go back upstairs." Tom took Jeanette by the arm gently so he could help her stand. She pulled away.

Jeanette sat there continuing to stare into space.

"Please, c'mon. Let's go," Tom said. "Carl's probably going nuts." Jeanette slowly got up, sighed and followed her brother.

Before they got off the elevator, Tom said, "If there's going to be a sacrificial lamb in all this, it's going to be Carl. He's done."

"We've got to find a way to keep this quiet," Jeanette whispered to Tom, as if whispering now would help keep this a clandestine transaction.

"Good luck with that, sis," Tom said. "Like it or not, this is news. This is the Wall Street Journal, the business section of the

Times, a case study for the Harvard Business Review, some ethics classes, and a really interesting subject for history classes. There's no keepin' this quiet!"

Jeanette clenched her jaw and followed her brother back to the suite muttering under her breath, "Maybe you should've died instead of Daniel."

Eyes widening, Tom whipped around, grabbed her by the arm and asked, "What did you say?"

"Nothing. I said nothing," Jeanette pulled away from Tom and kept walking head held high as if she had won something.

Tom sidled up to his sister and whispered, "You're a bitch and a half! What the hell happened to you?" Jeanette's face turned red.

As they entered, Trixie looked at Tom and Jeanette and asked, "Well, is everybody refreshed?"

"We're good," Tom said while glaring at his sister. They sat down.

Carl took a deep breath and exhaled slowly as he sat down. He didn't look at Jeanette or Tom, but he did look at his watch.

Before Trixie sat, she said, "Well, now you know how Grandpa Alistair started our business. Wasn't he just something? Now we're going to tell you how y'all tried to destroy it."

"That's really an exaggeration," Carl said.

"Carl," Jeannette said, "please be quiet. Please."

Trixie sitting between Louis and Tom patted each one on the knee. "Madeline, let's get on with it. Wait! Has Peter arrived yet?"

"Who's Peter?" Tom and Jeannette asked in unison. Jeanette felt her heart jump.

"Peter, Peter Grant, he's my brother and the company's legal counsel. He heads it all up. We've got a smart legal staff. I told ya' that last night. Now you're going to meet the man who makes it all legit and proper, my brother."

"You really do keep it in the family, don't you?" Carl asked, the corners of his mouth turning up for a moment. He found himself admiring their loyalty to the company and each other.

"Absolutely. I know y'all didn't have such good luck with family but we did," Trixie said, her face beaming.

"Peter's on his way up. He just got in," Louis said.

"Okay. Let's all wait then," Trixie said.

More silence except for the faint sound of a clock ticking from somewhere, the soft whoosh of heat coming from an invisible source and the heavy, smooth descent of air swaddling all of them. Jeannette got up and walked to the window. There was nowhere else for her to go. Carl poured himself another cup of coffee while Tom reached for the Wall Street Journal still enraged by what he heard Jeanette say in the hallway.

Trixie, Louis and Madeline watched them. A small, careful smile slid across Louis' lips as he watched Jeannette. Carl gulped down his coffee, then pulled out a tissue and wiped his forehead. Madeline analyzed Carl's face. She too considered him a youthful looking middle-aged, dark haired man, with the kind of features that would wear well as he aged. But what was underneath that attractive exterior? Madeline couldn't figure out why he was with Jeanette. Was it all about the money, period? Meanwhile Carl continued to be fascinated by Trixie. He was intrigued by beautiful, intelligent women. Loosening his tie, he wished he had met Trixie and Madeline under different circumstances. Madeline was this visual enigma. The intensity of her blue eyes could force you to come to a halt and gasp for air. This was the woman who always got A pluses in school, aced every exam, and probably played field hockey with a vengeance. There was something about her jaw line and long, muscular legs that made Carl believe that. He wondered if all the Grant women had long legs.

The suite door opened, and Peter Grant walked in. Trixie jumped up to greet her brother with a hug. "I'm so glad you're here. Everybody, this is my brother, Peter Grant. And y'all need to know, he is the spitting image of Grandpa Alistair and almost as tall. If you were to put his portrait next to a photo of Peter, oh my God! It's genetic hopscotch."

Peter smiled at everyone and said, "I know who all of you are. Let's get started." He kissed his sister on the forehead, then pointed his forefinger at his cousins. They nodded and smiled back. It was a silent, masculine ritual of recognition.

As Trixie sat down again, Carl looked at Peter and asked, "So where did you go to school?"

"Harvard, undergrad, and Harvard Law, then the London School of Economics. I'm surprised you don't know that. I know just about everything about you."

Carl said nothing but clenched his jaw and tried to smile.

"Madeline," Trixie said, "tell the rest of this story for everyone.

Chapter Seven:
1641 - The Rest of the Story

Madeline passed around some additional papers. She looked at everyone and began. Carl wasn't sure he would make it through all this. It was too close to the secret he was keeping. His breathing was shallow, and a headache had worked its way from his neck and shoulders to the base of his skull. Jeanette held her hands to hide the tremor and leaned forward in anticipation. Tom leaned back and crossed his legs as he scanned the papers he was given. Frank, who looked like he had a gun because the outline of his shoulder holster forced its way through his suit jacket, positioned himself so he could watch Carl, Tom and Jeanette.

"Let's fast forward to just after the Civil War," Madeline said.

"Is it really necessary to go through all this?" Carl asked.

Peter stood up, put his hands in his pants pocket, looked at Carl and said, "It's necessary. Go ahead, Madeline." When Peter Grant stood it felt like the apocalypse had arrived. He was lean but massive like the two dark skinned men with braids running down their backs. All of them resembled each other. It was the difference in skin color that distracted most people from seeing that they were all "blood relatives."

Clearing her throat, Madeline looked down at her papers and began reading out loud to them.

"The Civil War took its toll on the Grant plantation," Madeline said.

"Wait a minute," Carl said. "Whose writing this now? How long did Alistair live? He wasn't immortal!"

Peter slowly walked over to Carl, looked down at him and said, "Alistair died when he was eighty, in 1845, roughly twenty years before the Civil War." Placing his hand on Carl's shoulder, Peter said, "This is an excerpt from Patrick's diary. Are we clear?"

Carl stiffened at Peter's touch and nodded his head. Peter sat on the arm of the couch, next to Carl. Madeline continued.

"During the war the plantation was reduced from five hundred to two hundred and fifty acres. After the war, the slaves had been freed but many of them stayed having no place to go and no other way of making a living than by working the land. Sinclair and I turned half the plantation into an agricultural pursuit leaving the other half for cotton right after the war. In 1879 we regained the land we lost through sheer determination and the spirit of Alistair. Some of his ways are stamped in us. We do what we have to do to protect and save our family, our land and our beliefs."

"Cotton didn't vanish after the Civil War. Manufacturers still needed it and we still supplied a large amount of high quality cotton to northern and European manufacturers. Because of its quality Grant cotton has become increasingly desirable and still demands high prices. Our cotton became synonymous with quality. Our wealth was rebuilt."

Sitting on the arm of the couch next to Carl, Peter stated that, "Before Alistair died, Sinclair started a correspondence with the Capwells to renew their business arrangement. Business is business. Our profit margin was large enough to 'accommodate' irregularities. This connection was maintained from one generation to the next, until Trixie took over." Peter clenched his jaw and stared at the Capwells.

Trixie leaned forward, looked at Jeanette and said, "Listen carefully because y'all lost your minds. Peter?"

Peter opened his brief case and pulled out a file. Louis already had a stack of papers in front of him, some were yellowed due to age. Madeline opened a box and pulled out two worn brown leather journals.

Carl and Jeanette, eyes cast downwards, were each lost in thought wondering how all this was going to end and who would be left standing. Tom thought about excusing himself to go to the men's room but realized he couldn't hide in there for the duration of the meeting. It was going exactly the way Trixie told him it would. He dreaded what was coming.

"Well," Peter began, "let me put it bluntly. You've been blackmailing our family since 1810, right through the Civil War and up until Louis discovered these mysterious payments being distributed to Capwell Fabrics a few months ago. Madeline?"

"Yes, and according to one of Alistair's diaries, a Capwell ancestor discovered that Sinclair and Bridget were Kate's children, and the blackmail started. Sinclair's grandson was reminded in the late 1800s, early 1900s, after the Civil War was long over that if the Grant's wanted to keep their business and not risk the lives of..." Madeline stopped and started to finger her pearls, teary eyed with flushed cheeks. Taking the diary from Madeline, Peter turned to the page with a blue post-it sticky.

Peter said, "Let me read this to you. It's an excerpt from Daniel Grant's diary. He was Alistair's youngest brother who came over here a few years before Alistair died." Peter paused and then began. "To keep our business and spare the lives of our family, particularly the descendants of Sinclair and his sister Bridget, we must give in to the Capwells of Boston and Lowell, who are blackmailing us. After all this time, it's shocking. We're a proud people, the Grants. The practice of family is strong. We won't sacrifice anyone of us regardless. Black blood, white blood, it's all red, made by God. We have to honor Alistair's standards. As Alistair's younger brother, I'm doing my best to guide Sinclair and his family and keep 'em alive. Patrick, became the legal head of the family when Alistair died. The Capwells are calling for a percentage of our profits, not just from cotton, but from everything or they'll expose us. There's a bitter, mean streak in what was the Confederacy. We barely survived the Civil War, and the bitterness down here is still on the tongues of those who've lost everything. The slave population, freed or not, is still fragile, vulnerable to hate. Reconstruction collapsed. Four blacks were killed last week, more like slaughtered, hung from trees like animals. I heard one was burned alive on what was the Johnson plantation. They'll never be seen as fully human, equal. Even President Jefferson, by far one of the finest Presidents this young country has had said in his, Notes on the State of Virginia, that 'black people are dull in imagination, inferior in reasoning to whites, and that the male orangutans even prefer black women over their own.' My God, how do you rise above that? Thankfully, here we're still protected by the legacy of Alistair to an extent, but these northerners are a different breed. Hypocrisy runs through their veins like water through a pump. We'll pay the Capwells but one day it'll come to a close and when it does, God help them." Peter closed the diary and handed it back to Madeline.

"That day has come," Trixie said.

No one said a word but the faces of the Capwells reflected collective agony, fear and frustration. They looked like alabaster statues. Tom with eyes shut hoped to stop tears from rolling down his face. Shoulders frozen, Jeanette's left hand covered her right one. She didn't want anyone to know how pronounced the tremor had become. Carl held back laughter at the absurdity of this while the thumping beat of his heart echoed in his ears. At that moment, he was ready to give the Grants anything they wanted. Carl had heard enough.

Louis stood, put his hands in his pockets and walked over to the window. While staring out at the harbor, he asked the Capwells, "Are you familiar with the census?"

"Of course," Tom said. "What kind of question is that?"

"I mean the census records from way back. And then church records and family bibles?"

"What are you getting at?" Jeanette asked. "What does that have to do with this transaction."

Louis sat back down. "Madeline, tell' em what you found out."

"We were really curious about your family given the blackmail... We found out your family had slaves." Madeline pulled out another folder.

"What?" Jeanette screeched and popped up from her seat like bread from a toaster. "How dare you? We have abolitionists in our family. It's recorded. It is a fact! The state of Massachusetts never had slavery. We never had anything to do with that. That was something southerners indulged in."

"No ma'am," Madeline said. "That's not true. Massachusetts was the first English colony to legalize slavery in 1641. Your ancestors actually donated one of their family bibles to some genealogical society in Boston, and there it was, the names of the slaves in your family back then."

"What are you telling me?" Jeanette asked as she slowly sat back down.

"1641. We're telling you that the illustrious liberal state of Massachusetts legalized slavery in 1641," Louis said. "I read somewhere that you never referred to them as slaves, but rather 'servants for life.' Granted y'all abolished it but your hands aren't clean in this either. The notion, never mind the actuality, of your family blackmailing our family because of black blood is ludicrous!"

Madeline scrutinized the Capwells, searching for some redeeming quality, while trying not to scream.

"It just seems to me," Trixie stated, "that all that the abolitionists in your family may have been trying to do is simply ease their guilt. Maybe they thought they could atone. I don't know."

Jeanette popped up again and said, "We don't have to take this."

Trixie stood up and faced her. "Yes you do! You will sit here and listen to everything we have to say because if you don't, we'll see to it that public ruination becomes your future. We'll make sure you're left with nothing including your dignity."

"You can't do that! This is absurd. You just can't do that," Jeanette said.

"Tell her, Peter."

"We can. We can prove in a court of law, blackmail, embezzlement committed by your husband, unfair labor practices, discrimination and Civil Rights violations. All those little companies you have in China and southeast Asia? Sweat shops by any definition in our courts. There were some irregularities over there with one very young woman who was abused in one of your so called factories. Don't worry about the statute of limitations on some of this because y'all didn't have the good sense to stop, or to be specific, Carl didn't have the good sense to put an end to all this.

He left a lot of loose ends and ill will. My God, man, and then you personally embezzled close to fifteen million dollars. Where did that go? Never mind the rest of it. Have you told Jeanette what you did with it?" Peter stopped long enough to let a big smile cover his face.

Carl sat there, his face turning red, his eyes tearing up. He said nothing. Jeanette eyeballed him searching for whatever it was Peter was referring to. That look and the fury behind it made Carl pray. The last time he prayed was when he rushed Jennifer to the hospital after Jeanette had beaten her.

"But, court, criminal court not civil court, would just be the beginning," Peter said. "We've already laid out a media plan. One based on reaching some agreement here privately, another based on your refusing our offer. And the plan is staggered. We will draw this out so it stays in the face of the public for a long time. You should know Carl that we have the hiring records from your tenure and before. We can also prove a consistent pattern of discrimination against women and minorities that goes back to the seventies. You see, that's what's important, proving a pattern. Your company is quite white. I know it's Capwell family tradition, but damn man… And, we've found some of those people you failed to hire. We have all the information on two recent out of court settlements you made, one with an African-American woman, and the other with an Asian man. Talked with them as recently as last week. We've talked with a total of ten people that you've discriminated against during the past five years.

Trixie raised one eyebrow as she looked at the Capwells.

"Carl, I gotta tell you, Louis and I were fascinated by all that money you embezzled. I kept wondering what you were doing with it," Peter said. "You didn't buy any fancy new cars, no big trips with Jeanette, no demons like gambling or drugs, nothing obvious like that."

Beleaguered, Carl froze in his seat and said to himself, "Please God…please."

"Madeline, where's that other folder?" Peter asked.

"I have it," she said and handed it to Peter.

He scanned the contents and smiled before handing it to Carl.

"What is this?" Carl asked.

"Look, and show it to your wife," Peter said.

Carl opened it and began to read. Overwrought yet relieved he examined the photos and memos.

Jeanette snatched the file from him and started to read it. Again, her breathing grew shallow. "You are beneath contempt," she told Carl. The tremor in her right hand was now uncontrollable.

Clueless, Tom asked, "What's going on? Somebody fill me in."

Trixie faced him and said, "I'll be glad to fill you in. Several million dollars that Carl stole from us went to supporting his second family."

"What?" screeched Tom. Jeanette was trying to grasp what she heard.

"Oh, darlin' yes. He has a second family living very nicely in Westchester, Scarsdale to be specific. Two precious little girls, Frederica and Nicole, aged six and four. Beautiful children! We know, personally, that when an inter-racial couple has children, those kids are often so beautiful."

Jeanette, slack jawed, looked at her husband and asked, "What is she talking about, an inter-racial couple? What is she talking about, Carl?"

Carl leaned forward and held his head in his hands for several seconds before straightening up and said, "She's... I."

"Oh Carl, let me help you," Trixie said. "Carl's other wife? A beautiful African-American woman. She's a medical doctor! A pediatrician, a pediatric neurosurgeon to be specific, down there who works at Montefiore Hospital in the Bronx. Wonderful woman. So, bless Carl's heart, he set up some trusts for all of them with that money, sends those little girls to some of the best schools. Jeanette, you had no idea, did you?"

"Why should I believe any of this?" Jeanette asked and realized she couldn't feel any sensation in her body.

Peter pulled up a chair, sat down between Jeanette and Carl and said, "Because we've got proof. Copies of the trust documents, the deposit slips, photos of Carl's credit card statements, and photos of Carl and his second family. Lots of 'em. We didn't want anyone accusing us of photo shopping. Carl really loves his little girls. Take a look at these photos." Peter placed a folder full of photos right in Jeanette's lap.

Jeanette's heart was racing as she struggled to find the right response. Several seconds passed in absolute silence as she looked through the photos. There was Frederica, age six, a serious looking little girl with long black braids, bangs and Carl's smile. Nicole, big brown eyes, short curly black hair, stood next to her sister. Nicole, at the age of four, had great potential to be an elf or a fairy. Her eyes roared mischief. There was another photo of Carl and his second family at Rockefeller Center ice-skating during Christmas. One photo showed Carl and his other wife loading their SUV with bag after bag of groceries from Whole Foods. Jeanette wanted to throw up.

Trixie stood, and coldness settled in Tom's stomach. She walked to a spot where she was directly opposite of Jeanette who was trying to digest this information about Carl without causing "a scene." Suddenly aware of Trixie's gaze, Jeanette said, "Now what?"

"Let me tell you the other thing I found so very interesting. Few people pay attention to your Mama's fortune. It's just always been there, like Mt. Everest or the stars. All that money so wisely invested from century to century. Where'd it come from, Jeanette?"

Tom leaned forward, wide-eyed. His eyes darted from Jeanette to Trixie and then to Peter. Carl realized he didn't know much about his mother-in-law's pile of money either.

"I, I don't really know," Jeanette mumbled. "We never talk about things like that. It's rude."

"Well, let me be rude and tell you, 'cause it's an interesting story." Trixie tapped Madeline on the shoulder. "Maddie, the last folder, please."

Madeline nodded her head and gave Trixie another thick folder.

"This won't take long. It's important because it wraps everything up in a nice, neat little package of historical irony. I love it!" Trixie walked back to her seat, crossed her legs and opened the folder. "Your Mama's maiden name was Katherine Douglas, Jeanette. The Douglas family came over here rich and then got richer. I guess you could say commerce was their business. They had a fleet of ships. Their most profitable cargo? Slaves, back and forth between here and Africa, down to the Caribbean and even down to South America, doing lots of business in Brazil. The Douglas family was so industrious. They'd snatch Africans, ship 'em over here, put 'em on the auction block, and the rest is history. Nobody had to be bothered by the sin of this because y'all were up here where evil is invisible unlike us where evil hangs from trees."

The pain of that reference spooked Carl and made him restless. He started thinking about his Catholic upbringing, the last time he went to Confession and what it meant to do penance. He wanted to get up and walk around but he didn't dare. Tom started to think that the Capwells were a bunch of candy-asses, hypocrites. He wanted nothing to do with them. Bad enough his father, Angus, was a first class whacko but his maternal grandmother descended from slave traders! He really didn't want to hear about this but he felt stuck and obligated to hear what his ancestors had been capable of. Better an ugly truth than a comfortable lie.

"Anyway, outta sight, outta mind in the north," Trixie was saying. "But the power of money is never really invisible especially if it's evil." Stopping to give what she was going to say the power and drama of silence for a second or two, Trixie said, "The Grants know about the torment of evil money. You can't wash the evil away. It just stays with you. The money all of us have disguises itself too often through good deeds. But you Northerners have turned it into an art form. Nobody seemed to care how the Douglas family made their money just so long as they had it. There was some information we found that documented Douglas contributions to their church. They were the go-to family when finances ran low. But, that's not the important thing. Y'all need something to drink?"

The Capwells were speechless. Carl managed to reach for a glass of water, as did Tom. Jeanette did nothing but stare at Trixie.

"Well, suit yourselves," Trixie said. "Here we go. I don't know what made the Douglas family do this but they branded the Africans they kidnapped. Maybe that was common practice. Anyway, Madeline found a picture of the branding image among some very old business documents and made a copy of it. Pass it around Maddie."

She pulled out a crisp white piece of paper with a copy of the symbol. Carl quickly glanced at Jeanette and whispered, "What is this?"

Jeanette shook her head from side to side and whispered back, "I don't know."

Trixie was thumbing through the folder and repeated, "It's the branding symbol your mother's family used on their human cargo... like ranchers who brand their cattle. Listen up, people. This is the last excerpt I'm going to read from Alistair's diary. Ready? Hold on to that copy.

"For the first time last night I examined the brand on Kate's upper arm. She told me she couldn't remember when the slave trader branded her except that she was still a child, long before I bought her. All she recalled was the pain, and that he kept her for a few years. The simplicity of the brand is burned in my mind, a large circle with the letter D inside and the rest of the letters across the diameter of the circle. I think it says Douglas. I vaguely remember talking to him when I purchased Kate. He always bragged about his family's big, fancy place up in Boston. Doing business with him was a necessary evil."

"Are you telling us that one of our ancestors sold Kate to Alistair Grant? Is that what you're saying?" Tom asked hoping his head wouldn't explode.

"Yes it is Tom. That's exactly what I'm telling you." Trixie looked at her watch. "Look, it's lunch time. Y'all probably need something to sustain yourselves."

"Yeah...lunch is a good idea," Tom said and ran his hand through his hair, while thinking to himself, "Who the hell can eat after this?"

"Just a minute," Jeanette said. "I want you to know I take great exception to the implication that the Capwell family is guilty of racist practices. We..."

Tom's mouth dropped open as he gawked at his sister. She didn't seem to be there. It was almost as if someone else was talking and Jeanette had left. Gradually she snapped out of it. Her eyes focused and she looked at Trixie, Peter, Madeline, Carl, Tom and Louis like it was the first time she'd seen them...ever.

Jeanette opened her mouth again, and words stampeded right over her tongue so everyone could hear. "You don't even know! You're fools. Africans enslaved their own people. We saved blacks with slavery right here! They were herded by their own so they could be killed. I read somewhere they even ate each other."

Now Carl's mouth was hanging open. Trixie just shook her head slightly from side to side never taking her eyes off Jeanette. Louis sat there seething. Madeline got up and left the room. Peter gave Jeanette the side eye and reminded himself about the penalties associated with homicide and manslaughter. Finally, Tom found his voice.

"What does that have to do with us, right now? Are you saying we're heroes! That we rescued those people by condemning them to a lesser evil? That we had the 'good' kind of slavery? Are you serious? You've been listening to that crazy radio nonsense, with all those right wing nut cases!" Tom was almost shouting. His face was flushed and if looks could kill, Jeanette would be dead.

Carl looked at Jeanette and said, "Jeanette, please. Just be quiet."

"Oh stop it," Trixie said. "We're all damned guilty! The difference is we know our sins. The Grants had to face the ugliness, and the conflict, and the flat out evil that slavery was, regardless, and try to atone for it all. We will continue to atone for generations! This southern family knows what it did. For our purposes, I don't give a damn about what happened to African people in Africa. Right here, right now, we're dealing with our sins that occurred in this country." Trixie threw down a teaspoon she was using with her tea. Tom flinched, and Peter folded his arms cross his chest watching the Capwells just as Frank was.

"Do you really want to sit here and review the hypocritical and shameful behavior that's gone on up here? You really want to do that? Because darlin' we did our homework. We know what y'all have done, and who you did it with, and to, Miss Jeanette. Your Mama's family made a fortune from slave trading. But lynchin' for lynchin' you know you can match us. All those sundown towns you have up here. How many black friends you got? How many? Your husband certainly has a close, damn it, an intimate affiliation with one black woman without a doubt. At least we've got black family we acknowledge, we embrace, we listen to, and trust me, it makes all the difference. So, Miss Jeanette, let's be clear, neither the Capwells nor the Grants would be rich if it weren't for the labor of enslaved black people working the land stolen from red people. So don't you talk to me about being free and clear of racist practices because we had a nicer form of slavery."

By now, Trixie was staring at Jeanette with such intensity Jeanette thought she was going to pass out. Or maybe Trixie was going to kill her on the spot the way Alistair killed people. Jeanette had to go to the bathroom badly but didn't dare move.

"You just say the word, Jeanette, and we can skip through the past three hundred years and compare records. We can spend the entire afternoon doing that. You Northerners knock me out! Bunch of fancy hypocrites."

Peter's eyes narrowed while thinking, "Trixie's just getting warmed up."

"Y'all are not the only hypocrites up here. Do you know what they found in New York City right down there in the Wall Street area? The remnants of a slave market! 40% of New Yorkers owned slaves before it was outlawed there. Um-hmm. New York City, one of the world's greatest cities, was also built on the backs of slaves. And look what's on Wall Street now. Makes you wonder about the relationship between America's wealth and slavery. I think about it a lot."

"You don't need to go on," Tom said. "We get the picture. Jeanette, Carl, let's go downstairs to lunch." Jeanette could barely walk and thought she might collapse when she got up. Her underpants were feeling a little moist. She really had to go to the bathroom. Nobody had ever talked to her the way Trixie had.

"We've reserved a private dining room for you," Peter said. "We thought you'd want as much privacy as possible to talk about this."

"You don't miss a trick, do you?" Carl asked.

"We try not to." Peter smiled at him.

Chapter Eight:
Lunch

Tom, Carl and Jeanette were seated in the private dining room reserved for them. It was tastefully decorated and quiet. The waiter came in with the menus and asked if he could take their drink orders. Tom asked for bourbon. Jeanette requested a vodka martini, and Carl ordered a gin and tonic. As the waiter left, Jeanette pulled out her cell phone.

"Who're you calling?" asked Carl still dazed by the information the Grants discovered.

"You stupid s.o.b.," she whispered. "I'm calling our lawyer. Something you should've done."

Carl raised his eyebrows, and said, "It's kinda late for that."

She put the phone down and slapped him so hard Carl almost fell off his chair.

The waiter walked in with everyone's drink order just as Jeanette slapped Carl. The waiter gasped and everyone turned and stopped talking. The waiter set down the drinks on the table. He turned and scurried out.

Still stunned by the strength of her slap, Carl blinked a few times and rubbed his jaw. Regaining his balance, he said, "What the hell is the matter with you? You crazy bitch." In a flash he thought he was going to become unglued, but he reigned it in.

Tom jumped up and said, "Jeanette, please... Carl, c'mon now..."

Picking up the phone again, she looked at Tom and said, "Please what? Take it easy? Don't get hysterical? We may lose everything. I mean everything and for what?"

"They can't take everything, Jeanette," Carl said as he continued to rub his jaw. He reached for his gin and tonic and gulped down a swallow.

"We have children. Have you forgotten our children? What are we going to leave them?"

"Relax, their trust funds are intact. Untouchable. They'll be fine and we'll be fine. Jennifer's married to this Wall Street guy. What's his name? I keep forgetting it but he's got enough money to buy her anything she wants. What's his name? John? Joe? I never liked him. Acted like he was doing us a favor marrying Jennifer. Anyway, Jennifer works. Harrison will be fine. His dissertation is coming up next month, and he's already been offered several positions. Our kids will be okay. I don't know about you." Carl stood up, backed away from the table and said, "You know something, you stay here Jeanette. You figure this mess out. I'm not going to sit here and try to create some kind of scheme to deal with the Grants. They've got us."

"You can't even remember your son-in-law's name? My God," Jeanette said. "What is happening to us?"

Carl stared at his wife, jaw clenched along with his fists. "He's an arrogant little snot," Carl muttered.

Ignoring Carl Tom said, "You snapped Jeanette. What the hell is wrong with you?" Tom looked at Carl and pleaded, "Please, sit down. Just sit down." Tom's eyes were wide with panic. Carl sat down but he pulled his chair several inches away from Jeanette.

Jeanette popped up from her seat like a Jack-In-The-Box, redialed, then sat back down while the phone rang. "Hello? Hi, this is Jeanette Capwell. How are you? I need to speak to Kenneth." She paused for a few seconds. "You get him out of that meeting. This is an emergency."

The waiter came in to check on their drinks and get their lunch orders. Carl and Tom ordered another round and gave their orders while Jeanette was on the phone.

"You're just a few blocks from us Kenneth," Jeanette said. "The New Harbor Hotel. We're in a private dining room. It's number three. We'll wait for you." She hung up and looked at her husband and brother and said, "We have to do something. Did either one of you order for me?"

"Yeah, traditional Caesar salad, no anchovies," Carl said.

The three of them embraced the safety of silence again. Each one was thoughtfully engaged with the numbing powers of alcohol hoping gin, bourbon, vodka and vermouth would help them get through the rest of the afternoon with the Grants.

Tom sipped his bourbon and looked at his sister over the rim of his glass. Ugly childhood memories ran through his mind of Jeanette trying so hard to be Daddy's best little girl while their mother was having a nervous breakdown. Depression so severe, Katherine Douglas Capwell ended up at McLean's Hospital in Belmont frequently. After a while, McLean's felt like a second home for her. He remembered how frightened Jeanette was every time their mother was taken to McLean's. There were lots of whispers about shock therapy that caused their father to rant and rave, often becoming violent, punching walls, throwing things, and almost always reaching for one of his rifles. He'd race down the front hall, out to the garage and take off in one of his many cars, if they were lucky. Tom snickered to himself thinking about all the times his father didn't run out the door with a rifle, and instead ran up the stairs looking for one of the children to torment either verbally or physically. Tom knew what to do. He would run to his room, lock it from the inside, and push any piece of furniture he could move in front of the door. Let him go after Danny, Tom thought. He can handle it. During one of these rampages, Jeanette would sit in the living room, hands folded on her lap and wait. She was the good girl and Daddy would never hit her.

Jeanette would never be touched physically. Her abuse was the sole domain of their mother who would beat Jeanette without a second thought. One time, she broke her daughter's arm. Another time, she slammed Jeanette to the floor so hard she ended up with a serious concussion. And the morning after? Everybody acted like nothing had happened. So much for "joy cometh in the morning..." Tom thought.

The waiter returned with their lunch orders. The three of them were still sitting in silence. Tom was staring into his drink while Carl lit a cigarette.

"You can't smoke in here," Tom said.

"Can you smoke anywhere today?" Carl asked. "What am I supposed to do?"

"Drink," Jeanette said. "You have a real talent for that."

Carl stood and headed for the door. Tom grabbed his arm and asked, "Where're you going, man? You can't leave."

"Can I go to the bathroom?" Carl asked.

Tom let go of his brother-in-law's arm. "Okay…but don't take too long."

Carl patted Tom on the shoulder and reassured him that he would be back. He looked at his watch and walked out. Carl went right past the men's room to the far end of the lobby. He found a chair in a secluded corner, sat, and pulled out his cell phone.

Holding it to his ear, Carl scanned the lobby every few minutes hoping to see Kenneth when he arrived.

Carl's face suddenly lit up. "Hi! How's my Princess doing? Are you feeling any better?"

"Hi Daddy," said this sweet little voice. "I'm not throwing up anymore," Frederica said.

"I am so glad to hear that. I wish I was there with you."

"Me too. When are you coming home?" she asked while wiping her runny nose with a tissue.

"Sweetheart, I will probably be home by the end of the week," Carl said. His face was beaming with joy. "If all goes well, maybe by tonight or tomorrow."

"But you'll have to leave again," she said.

"No, I think this will be the end of Daddy traveling back and forth. Daddy's coming home to stay."

"Really? You promise?" Frederica asked.

"I do. How's your sister feeling? She didn't sound good last night when I called."

"Nicole's okay. She didn't get as sick so she went to school today. Mom took her temperature and said she couldn't stay home."

"Okay. And Mrs. Franklin is with you?"

"Yup."

"Let me speak to her, sweetheart. I've got to get back to my meeting,"

"Okay. Daddy, I love you."

"Love you too," Carl said. "Feel better." He spent some time talking to the housekeeper about the girls and walked back to the dining room.

Jeanette was pacing until she heard the door open. She spun around and saw Carl. Her face fell, and she sat, looked at Tom, and asked, "By the way, who is that Madeline woman? She's like a little robot with all her facts and research," Jeanette said. "Who the hell speaks Gaelic anymore? They can barely speak English."

"Didn't you hear Trixie? Madeline is their cousin. She's Louis' sister," Tom said. "She's the baby, the youngest of all of them. Trixie's the oldest. Peter's in the middle, and there are two other brothers. Trixie told me one brother is a vet and raises horses somewhere. I think the other one is a medical doctor. I don't know." Tom looked at his sister and realized she wasn't listening to him.

Jeanette had fixed her eyes on Carl. "Do you have anything to say? I mean anything? I've known for several years you were having an affair, but a second family with additional children? And a black woman? Was being married to me so bad that you had to find somebody black? Say something?"

"I'm sorry," Carl muttered and thought to himself, "God knows I didn't want this mess."

"You're sorry. What were you thinking?" Jeanette said, her voice dropping a half octave.

"I was thinking that being married to a woman who tried to beat our children to death while they were growing up was more than I could bear," Carl said, and he readjusted his suit jacket. "C'mon, we don't love each other, never have."

Jeanette stared at her martini glass, and said, "What are they talking about, a pattern of discrimination? What have you been doing? Were they all black? Who's that Asian they're talking about?"

Tom looked at his sister thinking, "She's lost it."

"You didn't want 'those people' in the company. You made that very clear and I didn't hire them. It's your company and I do exactly what you say. But the law requires that I at least interview them."

"But you're sleeping with one of 'em. Help me understand that?"

Watching his sister, Tom frowned and finished his drink.

"We're a family owned company. We don't have to answer to anybody! We can do what we want. Isn't that what you said Jeanette?" Carl didn't expect her to answer and she didn't.

"Oh Jesus," Tom mumbled. "What did I tell you? You're living in a fantasy. We're not above the law. It's the twenty-first century. It's not enough to have black people in the mail room or sitting behind the receptionist's desk. The phrase is 'window dressing.' I'm amazed you gave the cleaning contract to those Brazilian people!"

"What more do they want?! They're loud," Jeanette screamed.

"Sis," Tom said, "C'mon, please. Bring it down a notch." She paid no attention to him and continued ranting.

"Their women are ugly to boot. Maybe not all of them but have you really looked at the rest of them? Some of 'em wear those dreadlocks or have their hair all braided up. Those people aren't like us. Never have been. The Asians at least are smart, but you can't trust them. Not really. You know what we went through setting up those factories in China. They're hard, relentless. No flexibility. No breathing room – nothing."

The waiter walked in and they stopped talking while he served them. Tom discretely glanced at him, wondering how much he heard of their conversation, if anything. Once he left, they resumed.

"That's the only thing they're qualified to do, isn't it? Serve us. Wait on us. That's what you think, isn't it?" asked Carl as he thought about the waiter who looked Latino. But he could've been black or both. All Carl was sure of was that the waiter was not white. He watched his wife take another sip of her martini and said, "You know, sometimes I think that you think they're less than human. You're a throwback to a very bad time in this country and I'm not much better," Carl said more to himself than Jeanette.

"Let me get this straight. You've had a serious relationship with a black woman for six years. You have two children with her, and you refused to hire black people for my father's company? Do you see how insane that is? Explain this to me. I'm not going to ask again," Jeanette said.

Tom stopped eating and stared at his sister. He was afraid to say anything but that didn't stop him. "Jeanette, you're contradicting yourself. You're talking like a crazy person again. Do you hear yourself?"

Jeanette ignored him waiting for Carl to respond who was also watching her.

"Denise is different," Carl finally said and took a bite of his turkey club sandwich.

"Is that her name? Denise? So, Denise is different. How? Why her? What can she do that I couldn't?" Jeanette wanted to throw her drink in his face but didn't and grabbed her knife instead.

Carl started to laugh and said, "You can't be serious."

"Jeanette, you're not making any sense," Tom said and swallowed hard while running his hand through his hair. "You've got to get a grip," he said. "Have you stopped taking your medication?" Tom asked.

She turned and told Tom to shut up, and then said to her husband, "You let this happen."

"Let what happen?" Carl asked. He wiped his mouth with his napkin and threw it down on the table.

"You should've done something," she muttered. "Hired at least one of them. One of them might have been okay, but just one."

"Listen, the ones I interviewed weren't qualified according to you," Carl stated while he kept his eye on the knife she grabbed.

"You can prove that? Those people they referred to, can you prove they weren't qualified. Were none of them qualified?" Jeanette asked, and she started tapping the table with the knife.

"Do you have any idea of how crazy you sound?" Carl asked never taking his eyes off the knife.

"He can't prove that," Tom said. "I interviewed the African-American woman also. Sharp as a tack. Went to Stanford and Harvard. Her parents were professionals. She's traveled, speaks Spanish, and Mandarin Chinese. If anything, she was over qualified! We should've hired her especially given the mess we're in over there. She was cute too, far from ugly."

"You barely made it out of college, much less grad school, Carl. Maybe you don't know what it is to be qualified," Jeanette snapped and slammed the knife down on the table. Tom jumped and Carl put his sandwich down.

"And what would happen if she really flew up the ranks? What if she wanted my job?" Carl asked still watching Jeanette, and keeping one eye on the knife that she had put down.

"We should've given it to her," Jeanette snapped. Tom noticed his sister's hands were now shaking. "Maybe we wouldn't be in this mess if she was running things." Jeanette picked up the knife again and started examining it. Carefully, with her hand still shaking, she ran her forefinger over the knife's serrated edge. "This knife isn't sharp enough."

"Sharp enough for what?" Tom thought. "Sis, you're not making any sense. Really, you've got to pull yourself together. Maybe you should go home, take a nap, take a pill, something!"

The door opened and a well-dressed, middle-aged man in a navy suit walked in. Jeanette turned to see their lawyer, Kenneth Heller. He kissed Jeanette on the cheek, patted Tom on the back and nodded at Carl before sitting down. He looked at all of them and said, "So tell me what the emergency is and why your legal staff isn't here. I'm assuming this is really bad."

Jeanette summarized what took place that morning. Heller sat there and listened, his face motionless. He just looked at them. "I can't believe this," he finally said. "What the hell have you been doing? You send me a very healthy retainer every month and this is the first I'm hearing of all this? I'll betcha' they've got a lawyer up there with God knows how many more in the wings."

"Yeah. There's a lawyer up there," Tom said.

"Who is he?" Heller asked. "Maybe I know him."

"His name is Peter Grant," Jeanette said.

Heller looked at her for a moment. "Peter Grant? Grant Family Companies? Tall, good looking guy, dark hair? That's who've you crossed?"

"Yes," Jeanette said. "Do you know him?"

"I know of him. He was a presenter at a conference I attended last year. He's a master designing and negotiating hostile takeovers. His middle name ought to be mergers and acquisitions. He can be ruthless. Nothing short of brilliant, devotes most of his time to their company. G.F.C. is legendary in some circles. Quite a history. They've got more money than they know what to do with. This is who you're up against?" he asked rhetorically. "Their timing is almost always evil in its perfection."

"We have a long history with them," Jeanette said. "We go back generations."

"That sounds about right because G.F.C. is known for having more patience than God! They'll lay in wait for you and then pounce. Whatever they're doing, they've played out all the possibilities. They've already foreseen everything that could go wrong. The sister is up there also? Charlotte or Charles, as she's known in some circles."

"Yes. What do you know about her?" Jeanette asked.

"Charlotte Alison Grant? The lady with the Midas touch. Unnerving ability to make money. Very few people outside of their company have actually met her. I understand she's quite formidable and not to be underestimated. The woman's got credentials that'll make your heart stop. Don't be distracted by that southern charm. That's all an act to distract you, and create a false sense of security."

"That's for damn sure," Tom muttered.

"What kind of credentials?" Jeanette asked.

Their lawyer leaned back in his chair. "You really don't know?"

"No," Jeanette and Carl said in unison.

Ken chuckled, shook his head and said, "She graduated from the University of Virginia with a double major in political science and contemporary American history, and then went to Harvard and got an MBA. She and her brother, Peter, were Rhodes Scholars. She's very big on history." He turned and looked at Carl. "Did you do no homework on these people when the offer came in?"

"A little. Not enough, but how did you find out about her and Grant Family Companies?" Carl asked. "We just didn't connect the dots."

"That's like someone from our generation coming to Massachusetts and asking who the Kennedys are. Look, the New York Times did a feature piece on them a year or so ago in their Sunday magazine. She and Peter were on the cover of Forbes three years ago. And when she took the company over four years ago, she was on the cover of Vogue. They're well known in the business world. Major players. Lots of power. Lots of money. You really should know that."

"We know who they are," Tom said. "We just didn't realize... We underestimated them. You need to know the whole story, Kenneth." Tom leaned back in his chair and pointed to his sister as if to say, "You better tell."

Ken frowned and looked at Jeanette, "What's Tom mean?"

"Oh," Jeanette said. "I can't believe we're in this mess. That company must be her life. She can't be married with any children," Jeanette said and stared off into space. "She's probably sad and lonely with nothing and no one else..." The three men pretended to ignore Jeanette as she continued to mumble to herself

"Okay, what else?" Heller asked. "I need to know all of it and I need some lunch. How do we get a waiter in here?"

Jeanette stood and said, "I'll go find him...just listen to Tom and Carl."

Tom and Carl briefed him, going all the way back to Alistair Grant, the blackmail and why it started, and the connection with Kate. Heller's eyes widened with disbelief while he watched Jeanette who was having trouble walking. But she managed to leave the room without falling.

Focusing on Tom and Carl again, Heller asked, "Are you shittin' me? This is a joke, right? What's Jeanette's role in all this?"

"Ken, it's complicated and it is what it is. They had, have black relatives back then and now. The Grants back then believed they had to pay. I think it was the law...and after watching and listening to Jeanette, she thinks it should still be the law." Tom drank the last of his bourbon when Jeanette returned with the waiter.

They were silent for a few seconds and looked at Jeanette, searching for something that would tell them she was okay. It didn't happen. All they saw was a blank, empty stare as she sat down. The three men looked at each other, eyebrows raised. The waiter gave Kenneth a menu and within a minute or two he gave his order asking the waiter if he could hurry the order. The waiter nodded his head and briefly looked at each one of them. Tom wanted to vanish. Carl and Kenneth pretended the waiter wasn't there but not Jeanette.

"What are you looking at?" Jeanette asked the waiter. If she was an animal she would be on the verge of foaming at the mouth. The hostile, hateful air she emanated was palpable.

The waiter and Jeanette locked eyes for a moment. Everything stopped. Kenneth's eyes darted from Jeanette to the waiter. Sensing something bad was about to happen, Kenneth got up, walked over to the waiter and put his arm around his shoulder. "Let me apologize. She's been under a lot of stress. She didn't mean anything by it." Kenneth walked the waiter out and slipped him a twenty. Kenneth whispered to the waiter, "Thank-you." Walking back Kenneth sat down and realized something was really wrong with Jeanette. Putting the napkin back in his lap, he looked up. "Okay – what were we saying?"

Tom took a deep breath and asked, "What's your best advice, Kenneth?"

He still kept one eye on Jeanette and said, "Without knowing anything other than what you're telling me, and assuming they can prove all that they say they can, take their best offer. We can stall for a few days maybe. I can tell them I need some time to look everything over...but that may be the best we can do. If this goes public, you will lose."

"Lose?" Jeanette said. "We can't lose, Kenneth." She had picked up her knife and was squeezing the handle and then loosening her grip repeatedly.

"This is a case where public perception plays a big role. This will be Christmas, Easter, and Thanksgiving for the media. A family fortune secured by the textile industry, bolstered by slave trade and later secured by blackmail going on for hundreds of years. Race, miscegenation, embezzlement, discriminatory hiring practices. There will be newspaper stories, magazine features, television documentaries and God knows what else. Hell, I could see a movie," Kenneth said and took Jeanette's hand making her let go of the knife. "Look, let me eat something quickly and we'll all go up together."

"Public perception. It's over isn't it?" Jeanette asked.

Still holding her hand Kenneth realized her eyes were filled with tears. "Unless something radical presents itself, I think so. You have nothing to gain from going down in flames." Kenneth took a deep breath, let it out, and looked directly at Carl. "This second family you have? Have you actually married this woman? Don't answer. Until this is over, keep your mouth shut, and pray that nobody has said anything. Bad enough the Grants have this information. Who finally received the payments from them? Whose hand did these payments end up in?"

Carl raised his hand and said, "That would be me, for roughly a decade or so."

Heller just shook his head from side to side and mumbled, "Amazing. Amazingly stupid. And before then?"

"I took it, invested it for Jennifer and Harrison," Jeanette said, "You've got to fix this. Make it all go away."

Carl was dumbfounded. Tom stopped everything he was doing and looked with total disbelief at his sister. The truth was, no one knew where the money had gone at that time. This would be Jeanette's secret.

Still holding her hand, Kenneth squeezed it and said, "Jeanette, this is beyond fixing. Let's see what can be salvaged. I don't want any of you publicly embarrassed. The fixing is keeping this as quiet as possible and controlling what story gets out, if we can. A story of this magnitude? Something will leak and who knows what the Grants have planned."

"I am not going to be humiliated, do you understand?" Jeanette asked and grabbed his other hand. "The Capwell legacy must be maintained."

"We understand," Kenneth said and gently kissed her hands. Tom glanced at Carl and Carl glanced at Tom, while quickly rolling his eyes, and finishing his lunch.

Jeanette looked at Tom, and remembered what he told her when they were taking a break in the lobby. There was no way out. Thinking about that made Jeanette gasp for air. She pulled her hands away from Kenneth and fell back in her chair. Who knew, Jeanette thought, that dinner with Trixie was the beginning of the end for her family. Jeanette looked at her Cesar salad and pushed it aside. She was no longer hungry.

Chapter Nine:
Lunch Upstairs

The Grants were finishing lunch in their suite, which resembled a three bedroom luxury apartment. You could hear the flatware hitting porcelain plates, some laughter, and the soft sound of jazz music floating from an audio system in the corner.

"How long has it taken us to get here?" Peter asked rhetorically.

"Over two hundred years," Louis said. "Hallelujah, the chickens have finally come home to roost," and he waved his hands in the air.

"Madeline, where did you find all those diaries?" Trixie asked.

"I went out to the big house and up to the attic. I always wanted to go up there and poke around. Just never had a reason until now. There was a small trunk up against a wall and something said, open it, and there they were."

"It's all there isn't it? All the stories," Trixie asked and then bit into her rare hamburger.

"It sure looks like it," Madeline said. "I apologize for choking this morning. I just got so mad…"

"Don't worry about it," Peter said. "You did fine. If it wasn't for you I don't know where our case would be." Sitting next to her he gave her a quick kiss. "Okay? You are our hero. Don't ever forget that."

Madeline looked at Peter, smiled and went back to eating her clam chowder.

"Grandpa Alistair," said Louis, "was something else! Did he write about Kate?"

"He did," Madeline said.

"Did he love her? Did he write that?" Peter asked. "I wish I could go back in time, meet him and really feel what everybody was going through. Just to be a witness... The diaries, Maddie, that's the closest we'll come. And Kate, wow."

"I haven't read all of his diaries, but...yeah, he did. He did love her. I don't know how that worked back then. How do you love a slave when they can't openly love you back and you own them? Maybe she did. It's complicated. I remember the passages where he wrote about the first time she smiled at him and the first time she kissed him back. There was another entry about the time he insisted she call him Alistair when they were alone. I think Alistair was at heart a poet. He was like you, Peter! You and your poetry. Anyway, he described her kiss once. Oh my God!" Madeline blushed. Peter laughed. Louis was just wide eyed, and Trixie got a little teary. Frank and Wallace said in unison, "Umph..." and continued to eat. John rolled his eyes and cut into his steak.

Madeline played with her pearls for a minute and then said, "I keep wondering where that secret bedroom is. I bet you it's right in front of us and we just don't see it. I want to find it. I did start to read something about two of his Overseers," Madeline said. "My

God, two of 'em were the devil incarnate. Sadistic bastards. Grandpa Alistair fired one of 'em and the other one…"

Trixie cut her off and said, "…mysteriously vanished?"

They all laughed. Peter took his fork and tried to finish the remainder of Madeline's salad, thinking she was through with it. She playfully slapped his hand and said, "Damn Peter! Where do you put all the food you eat? Steak, potatoes and now you want the rest of my salad after finishing your own! God!"

He grinned at her and said, "You never finish and I like salad! You barely weigh a hundred pounds."

Letting him eat her salad, Madeline made a face at him. "Okay, then I take your dessert!" She watched Peter smirk and then smile at her.

"Maddie, I'm a growing boy," he said and popped a cherry tomato in his mouth.

"Oh stop it!"

Trixie watched this sibling like interaction and said, "Madeline, you know you need to watch Peter! How many times have I told you that? If you think you're going to get his dessert…"

Madeline quietly groaned. Turning her attention away from Peter she said, "You know, I bet if I spent enough time going through all of Alistair's diaries we'd have an incredible story. My God, did anybody know about the long standing relationship the family had with the Cherokees back then? I ought to set my mind to it, and just spend a couple of months going through all of Alistair's diaries."

"Yeah Maddie, some of us know. We're part of that lost chapter," Wallace said and eyed his cousins who nodded their heads.

Finishing his steak, Frank nodded. "The way grandmother told the story, after Alistair, it was his brother, Daniel, who set that in motion...and here we are."

Trixie shifted in her seat and said, "You know what fascinates me?"

"Many things, cuz. Many things," Wallace said and finished his roast beef sandwich. They all laughed.

Louis leaned over and gave Trixie a peck on the cheek and said, "This woman is not to be messed with!"

"Y'all stop," Trixie said. "Seriously now."

Everyone settled down and focused their attention on Trixie. She had finished eating and that was her informal signal that it was time for business.

"Why is it that so many white folks, I don't want to say all because I know better. But why is it so many white folks just either don't or refuse to understand the depth of damage slavery has done, and continues to do to this country? I just don't get that. And I'll put good money on the fact that Jeanette is sittin' downstairs befuddled and bewildered by why we care so much, why we're going to such extremes with all this. Do they just don't know? Is it ignorance? Denial? What the hell is it?"

"Justice," said Peter, "They're afraid because justice is never restored painlessly."

Louis said, "Too many white folks in America, live in a state of deliberate ignorance. They don't want to know. That's a luxury that's going to end one day and when it does, God help us all."

"Naw…" Wallace said, "They know. They just don't want to face it. There's too much money to lose. They're in some kinda historic denial, cuz, like slavery was just a paragraph in US history. Frank, John and I live with the possibility that we could be killed for no other reason than being 'not white' in America. Only two races in this country, white and not white. It's just that simple. Tell 'em Frank, you still don't let your daughters or your wife go out alone after dark. Atlanta is one thing. Leave the city limits and that's another reality. Black folks still disappear, and this is the 21st century when the police just freak out and shoot anyone not white."

Finishing his lunch, John looked at everyone and said, "They don't know what to do about their guilt over all this. They can't escape it and yet they try to ignore it. All they gotta do is just look at us. Their crimes are in our blood lines and on our faces. They brought hell with them when they stepped foot on this land, and we're still livin' in it."

Everyone was silent letting the reality of what John and Wallace said sink in. John was the oldest of the three cousins who were black Indians. Leaner than Frank and Wallace, with curly blue black hair, John was Senior Vice President of Security for all of Grant Family Companies. He was a Marine and a college graduate with a Master's Degree in Business Administration. His great-grandmother, on his father's side, was a Medicine Woman from the

Creek Nation. John remembered his Cherokee grandfather telling him stories about the white man creating something called, The Five Great Nations, Cherokee, Chickasaw, Choctaw, Creek, and Seminole. The white man found these nations easier to "convert" to their ways, or so they thought. John had stopped eating thinking about all this along with the complicated blood relationship with the Grants. But they were his people too on his mother's side. At that moment, the way the light settled on his face made John look ancient. There was no trace of the forty-two year old corporate executive, with a wife and two sons. John took three days off to accompany this branch of his family to meet with the Capwells.

"Lies, secrets and silence, America's holy trinity of injustice," Peter said and finished drinking his Coke.

"Yeah," Trixie said. "The Capwell practice to blackmail us eternally is finished! Let's talk about how the afternoon is going to work. By this time tomorrow, I want all of this resolved. I want it done so we can get back home. John, the money is secure? It's all there?"

"It's there," he said and leaned back in his chair. "We're ready."

"Frank, I want this to go down without a hitch," Trixie said

"Nothing's going to go wrong. We're ready," Frank said.

"Okay," Trixie said. "Expect them to come back here with an attorney of some sort. I'm surprised they walked in here this morning without one. Damned fools! If they have any sense, they'll call their Communications Director."

"Who's that again? I forget her name but her file is right here," Peter said and showed it to Trixie.

"Yeah, her name is Gillian Anderson, sharp as a tack. We might want to keep her. Thank-you for setting up that meeting with her a few weeks ago. I needed to look her in the eye. This woman looks impeccable and chic at all times. She gives the impression that she never sweats! But more importantly, she has a mind like a computer and knows how to keep her mouth shut. Gillian is an asset. But let's see who they bring back with them," Trixie said.

"Kenneth Heller is who they will bring," Peter said. "He's their bag man. Cleans up all their messes. This is way beyond their corporate legal staff and my guess is the Capwells don't want their corporate team knowing any of this if possible. So enter Kenneth Heller."

"I'm sure bigamy will take up some of his time," Trixie said! "I wonder how he'll fix that. My God. I don't think Jeanette realizes Carl has married Denise."

"What's the worst case scenario?" Louis asked.

"Jeanette will lose her mind," said Trixie. "If she doesn't do it here, she will when she leaves, but I haven't finished with her. She loves this little company and all the fanfare that goes with it more than she loves anything or anyone, but we are going to take it all. She is done! The men won't have enough sense to go crazy. You watch. And Carl? He's already making plans to flee to Scarsdale permanently. I can just feel it. Tom is the 'x' factor. It could go either way for him. I hope he pulls through. But this is going to end badly for them regardless. It's going to hurt them in the worst way. The Capwell dynasty is over."

"But that's what we want," said Peter.

"It's exactly what we want," Trixie said.

Chapter Ten:
Afternoon

Jeanette, Carl and Tom walked in the suite with Kenneth Heller. Peter walked over, extended his hand and said, "Kenneth Heller, I'm Peter Grant." Peter was taller than Heller or at least appeared that way.

"Mr. Grant, pleasure to meet you. Your reputation precedes you," Kenneth said and swallowed hard shaking hands with Peter.

Peter looked at him for a second, turned and said, "I want you to meet the rest of my family." Pointing he said, "This is Louis Grant Bergeron. He's our CFO and our cousin, Madeline is Special Assistant to my sister. Madeline is Louis' sister." They all shook hands and Peter continued. "Kenneth, this gentleman seated by the credenza is John Wilson, another cousin who's Senior Vice President for GFC Security. The gentleman by the door is cousin Frank McRoy, and the very large gentleman in the hallway is Wallace McRoy. We all grew up together more or less."

Peter got so much enjoyment from the confused looks he would get when introducing Frank, Wallace and John as Grant cousins. People would look at the copper colored skin of the cousins, and then look at the Grants, and wonder how this happened. Louis and Madeline were easier to accept. They were lighter, and it was easier to see the Grant resemblance, but Maddie's blue eyes were incomprehensible to many. Kenneth was handling it fairly well. No outraged looks registered on his face. However, the apprehension settling in his stomach couldn't be denied or ignored.

Kenneth nodded his head in acknowledgment while Jeanette, Tom and Carl found places to sit. Trixie was leaning against the wall next to John, arms folded across her chest watching everything and everyone.

Peter sighed, looked at Kenneth and said, "The brain behind Grant Family Companies, is my big sister, Charlotte Alison Grant, or as the business world knows her, Charles A. Grant."

Kenneth tried not to stare. He found her both stunning and intimidating. She wasn't a big woman (without those heels) but she seemed mighty and powerful. She had a presence that scared him. Charlotte, or Trixie, stepped forward and extended her hand to his. It was a very firm handshake, and it just further unnerved Kenneth. She pointed to the sitting area and said, "I thought you'd come Mr. Heller." That charming southern accent sounded ominous now.

Once everyone was seated, Trixie said, "I don't think we need to go through the arithmetic of the Capwell debacle. I mean, we can if you want to."

"We have a clear idea of where you stand on the numbers," Jeanette said.

"What numbers are we talking about?" Kenneth asked.

"The embezzlement specifically," Jeanette said quietly.

"You worry about the embezzlement," Trixie said, "But the numbers we want agreed upon have to do with the blackmail that's been going on for over a hundred years."

"The worth of the Capwell parent company, however, may warrant some conversation," Kenneth said. "What you're talking about as blackmail is open to debate."

"No, there's no debate," Peter said. "The Capwells have been blackmailing us since the early 1800s. We have the documentation to prove this. Now, do you really want to spend time reviewing the decline of the Capwell parent company thinking you can razzle-dazzle us with some of that magic math they've been using?"

"I'm here to help insure fairness," Kenneth said.

"Fairness?" Trixie said. "Mr. Heller, we are way beyond fairness. Fairness isn't even in the ballpark. The issue is justice. The two aren't interchangeable." She looked at Jeanette and asked, "Didn't you tell him about our strategy, our media strategy? You shouldn't have secrets from your lawyer."

"They did," said Kenneth, "But this is still business."

"Now see, that's where you're wrong. This isn't business, and this isn't about being fair. This is settling an old score. Let's be clear," Trixie said. "Throw all your tricks and games out the window."

Silence settled among them like fog descending on a bridge. For a minute you had the sensation that every member of the Grant clan was breathing in unison.

Peter opened a folder and pulled out some papers, scanned them, and then handed the papers to Kenneth.

"What's this?" Kenneth asked.

"The terms of this transaction," Trixie said.

"Let me see those papers, Kenneth. Hand them over right now," Jeanette said. As soon as she read the first page, Jeanette looked up and said, "You have got to be kidding me. This is insane," and she handed the papers to Kenneth.

"Maybe," Trixie said. "Maybe not."

"I thought you just wanted our parent company," Jeanette said.

"Your parent company isn't worth very much anymore. It won't begin to cover the blackmail. Didn't you know that? Capwell Fabrics, your precious parent company is just a breath away from bankruptcy."

"My ancestors built all this. It's their legacy... I can't believe you want it all," Jeanette said.

"What goes around comes around, Jeanette," Trixie said. "Listen, first y'all have slaves and try to forget it. There was the little slave trading business on your Mama's side you tried to keep on the down low. Then y'all blackmail us because we have a black ancestor who had two children with Grandpa Alistair. Fast forward and you're running a lily-white company while your husband has set up housekeeping with a black woman, a black professional woman no less, and has two children with her. And to add insult to injury, he refuses to hire people of any color, red, yellow, black, brown on your orders Jeanette, while y'all look down your noses at us because we're Southerners. Are you serious?"

Jeanette was speechless. Her eyes were glazed over.

"Okay," Kenneth said with his heart pounding, "If I understand this, you want us to take an undisclosed cash offer for all of Capwell or you will launch a campaign and publicly disgrace the Capwell family, and all of its business enterprises before we even get to court. I don't quite see how you can do that."

Trixie laughed. "Okay, we do have a fantastic media plan. But more importantly, we have friends and contacts at every major network, including Cable, and newspapers here, in China, Japan and western Europe. A lot of people in high places owe us. And we have many, many friends on Capitol Hill and in the British Parliament. So, feel free to refuse, and by tomorrow morning I promise you a whole lot of reporters are going to be camped out on the Capwell lawn in front of those lovely iron gates. The weather will be irrelevant. Think about those live news feeds, Skype, all that stuff. And those charitable donations y'all gave, they'll be returning that money because there will be too much shame associated with it. Y'all gave money to Amnesty International, the NAACP, the Urban League, the ACLU! It's too perfect. Oh, and Mr. Heller, have somebody on your staff start looking at the stockholders of some of these media outlets and don't forget Facebook and twitter."

Heller covered his mouth with his fingers and shifted in his seat. He needed a glass of water or scotch.

"The money," said Carl. "How the hell do we know you've got any money or have any intent to give us anything? This is insane! It's untenable!"

Trixie shot a look at Carl, and said, "Darlin' please..." and then nodded to John. He walked over to where they were seated with a large metal briefcase and placed it on the coffee table. "Open it, John."

Lips pressed together, Jeanette noticed John's blue silk handkerchief in his suit jacket pocket and wondered, "What's he doing with a silk handkerchief?"

John unlocked and opened the suitcase, revealing what appeared to be endless rows of money.

"How much is in there?" Kenneth asked.

"You're not gamblers, are you? Blackmail is your thing, embezzlement," Peter said. "The questions you have to answer are how much is your reputation worth? How important are appearances, and saving face worth? What are you willing to sacrifice for all this knowing that you will lose in any court?"

Tom was desperately trying to estimate how much could be in the briefcase. There were stacks of hundred dollar bills. But he didn't know how many were in each stack nor did he know how many stacks were in the briefcase. He couldn't figure out if they all contained hundred dollar bills. Why was it in the movies somebody could just look at stacks of money and instantly know how much was there?

"John, thank-you. You can take it away," Trixie said.

"You can't expect us to make a decision like this right now," Jeanette said.

"You are so right," Trixie said. "You know what? I'll give you until tomorrow morning at ten AM. By then, we want an answer and the agreement signed. Show up and we'll finish this. Don't show up and we'll still finish it. The story will be on the six o'clock news tomorrow night if not before, and on the front page of the Wall St. Journal, the NY Times and the Boston Globe the next morning. Of course, there are all those Cable outlets. First thing tomorrow morning I'll have our communications people on twitter. Imagine what the tabloids will do with this, especially the Boston Herald right here in your back yard."

"I'm going to need more than overnight to look through this," Kenneth said.

"Overnight is all you have, Mr. Heller. They've been paying you all kinds of money to retain your services, your expertise. Tonight, you can demonstrate that."

Kenneth looked at his watch. It was 3:30 PM. "Okay, I better get started." He looked at Carl, Tom and Jeanette. "You need to be available this evening. This agreement is over twenty pages long."

Jeanette looked at him and said, "You're coming to the house with us. Call your wife. Tell her you've got an emergency." Jeanette sat there and tried not to wring her hands while the tic under her eye was almost popping off her face.

Kenneth looked at her and sighed, "Okay. I'm going back to the office to get some things. I'll drive out."

"Hurry so you can beat the traffic. Rush hour is starting earlier and earlier," Jeanette said. She looked at Tom and asked, "Where are our coats?"

"Oh Jeanette," Trixie said. "You're going nowhere. Let's you and I have a light dinner. Don't worry about getting home. I'll have the limo take you back."

"I have matters to look over. Decisions to be made. I can't stay here," Jeanette said.

"There is nothing for you to look over. Whether you accept it or not, this decision is made. Your lawyer is stalling. We understand. You need to stay here so we can talk, woman to woman, break bread together as two women who were loved by their Daddies. At least, I was."

Chapter Eleven:
Dinner With "Charlotte"

Jeanette took the elevator down with her brother and husband. Carl stood as far away from her as he could while Tom huddled near the control panel. Biting her lip, she said, "Listen, maybe I can salvage something. Maybe if I appeal directly to her, she'll ease up. Meanwhile you work with Kenneth and see if there's anything at all that isn't wrapped tight as a drum in that so-called agreement she wants us to sign." Jeanette stared at the elevator door and slowly rubbed her hands together as she continued to think.

Tom was looking down at his shoes trying not to breathe too hard. He looked up and said, "Look, sis, I think we need to figure out how we can best smooth this over. Trixie, or Charlotte, isn't going to back down. Did you see the look in their eyes?"

"You can't be sure," Jeanette said. She folded her arms across her chest, looked directly at Tom and said, "You have her ear. Maybe she'll listen to you. Maybe you could call later..."

Carl cleared his throat, adjusted his tie and said, "We've got enough money and real estate to retire on, Jeanette." Taking one step closer to her, he said, "So the Capwell dynasty will no longer be run by Capwells. Let it go, Jeanette. Worse things could happen."

"Like what?" Jeanette screamed.

"Jeanette, c'mon, lower your voice," Tom said.

Ignoring him, Jeanette told Carl, "You can say that. You s.o.b, you've got your second family in Scarsdale. This company is who I am. Daddy worked and struggled to make it what it is. He gave me the company. It's mine. Mine! Our children are gone. I will have nothing and it's all because of them. Slaves rising from the grave, rushing through time, reaching out to take everything from us. What am I supposed to do with my life?"

Tom and Carl stared at Jeanette as the elevator doors opened. They stepped out and Carl grabbed her by the arm and whispered, "The same thing you've been doing all these years. Hiding behind your father's craziness! Cowering! Making excuses for him and yourself! You were too damned afraid to stand your ground, to take charge, to use common sense, to really be somebody. You can't look at yourself in the mirror and you know it. You're not a stupid woman, just spineless and sick, and this is what it's cost you," Carl said and let her go.

"You dare blame me after all you've done?" She glared at her husband. The three of them walked in silence over to a corner in the lobby to continue.

Carl backed her up against a wall while all the color drained from Tom's face. "Go ahead, hit me again, if it'll make you feel better," Carl said. "Go right ahead." He paused waiting for her say or do something. Jeanette froze. "Do you see how messed up this is? All of us are messed up. Maybe this is supposed to happen. Maybe this is some kind of karmic adjustment. Let's accept it with some kind of damned grace, and move on. I'm tired of this. Not only do I want out, I need out, and I'm getting out." Carl stepped back and looked around to see if anyone was watching him. He noticed another couple that walked by who glared at them. Other than those two, no one gave any indication that they saw or heard anything.

"Sis," Tom said quietly and took Jeanette's hand while she was still looking at Carl, "don't do this to yourself. We didn't play the game well enough. We got sloppy and we got caught. It's good to know when you've lost. That's all there is to it. We need to spend this evening talking to Kenneth about the legitimate legal ramifications. That's it. That's all. Go back upstairs, have some dinner, look her in the eye and say. 'Well done. Well played. You got us."

Jeanette examined her brother's face searching for a clue and asked him "Why are you giving so much credit to your darling Trixie? What's she done? After all, who is she? First she's Trixie, then she's Charlotte. What the hell is that?"

Tom looked at Carl and he dropped his head, shaking it slightly from side to side.

"Sis, Trixie set us up, but Charlotte? Charlotte Alison Grant, the corporate head of GFC, descendant of Alistair William Grant, is taking us down. I told you, there's no way out of this."

The Grant suite was hushed, softly lit and held an unnatural silence. Everyone seemed to have vanished. The only one in the living room was Trixie. Now it was her turn to look out the window. It was getting dark earlier than she was used to, but that's the east coast in the dead of winter she thought.

"The damned east coast, what a piece of work," Trixie thought. She rubbed her hand across the back of her neck and turned around. Madeline had taken all the folders back to her room where she would finalize some details for tomorrow. John was in his bedroom keeping the money company. And yes, Frank did have a gun in his shoulder holster along with a permit to carry it. He was having a club soda in the hotel bar. He didn't need a gun. All he had to do was put one of his enormous hands around someone's neck and lift them off the floor. Wallace was still guarding the door with his meaty hands crossed in front of him. Every now and then he would think about Trixie's plan for the Capwells, and that produced a guttural chuckle from him.

"What a silly way to live," Trixie thought. Guns, money, guards and lawyers. Things weren't so different today than they were centuries ago when Alistair was doing business. "In fact," Trixie thought, "it might have been more honorable then than now." She shook her head from side to side and laughed a little at the absurdity of it all.

Wallace opened the suite door and Jeanette walked in scanning the living room. As she approached, Trixie just looked at her. Trixie didn't say a word and took in every detail of Jeanette as she assessed the Capwell matriarch. She wore boring, expensive clothes that didn't quite fit the way they should have. Jeanette would always look like she was wearing hand me downs from someone who took pity on her. The suit jacket was a bit too tight and the skirt an inch too long. "What a waste of money," Trixie thought. Jeanette's shoulder length brown hair was as dull and unremarkable as her clothing. "How sad," Trixie thought. "How very sad. A woman with no style and little substance to boot," Trixie thought. But Jeanette was fighting demons. Immune to Botox, every line on her face was possessed.

Jeanette stood by one of the upholstered club chairs waiting for Trixie to say something. For a full minute they stared at each other in silence. Lifetimes stood between them. Jeanette felt her mouth become dry, and there was pounding in her ears that increased as Trixie slowly walked towards her. The silence between them felt predatory. Taking her time, Trixie moved like one of those big cats Jeanette saw on Cable nature shows. Jeanette's fingers squeezed into the back of the chair with enough force to break one of her fingernails.

"Sit down, Jeanette," Trixie said and pointed to the chair. The impact of Trixie's voice was like thunder on a hot summer evening in the deep South.

Jeanette sat down and never took her eyes off Trixie while Trixie sat on the couch across from her.

Leaning back while stretching her arm along the back of the couch and crossing her legs, Trixie said, "So, what the hell happened, Jeanette? How did you let all this happen? By this time tomorrow evening, Capwell Enterprises will be owned and operated by Grant Family Companies."

With her heart creeping up her throat, Jeanette asked, "Why are you taking everything? All we wanted to do was sell the parent company, smooth over Carl's stupid mistakes and his...indiscretions. This is really a family matter. I know you understand that. Why are you doing this?"

"Because we can, and we know how to do it, and you don't. You are so painfully vulnerable." Trixie stopped for a moment and continued to study Jeanette. "You really don't get this, do you? See, this is what happens when you don't know your history or ignore it. You sure as hell don't understand it nor its ramifications." Trixie was now holding a pencil in her hand tapping the side with the eraser very firmly and rhythmically on a pad of paper that was on the left arm of the sofa. That tapping pencil caused Jeanette's body to tighten. The yellow number 2 pencil was being perceived by Jeanette as an automatic weapon in Trixie's hands.

"Do you know what this is going to do to us?" Jeanette asked.

"I know exactly what it's going to do to you."

"I can't believe this is really about what some of my ancestors did to your ancestors over some black people back in the 1800s. It makes no sense to me! And this transaction involves large amounts of money. What is it with you and black people? My God!"

"They're family, Jeanette. Family. We're all God's children, remember? And as you just said, there's a lot of money involved."

"Why can't we have civil conversations about all this? People have to learn how to talk about these things. You and I haven't done anything to hurt these people. They've created their own problems, ignorant, lazy. Every other one of them is a thug or they belong to a gang. All that slavery business was a long time ago and neither one of us had anything to do with it," Jeanette said trying not to hyperventilate. "We are not responsible for all this racism. You have to stop thinking that way."

Trixie raised one eyebrow and said, "Are you serious? You and I and everybody else in this country who's white, rich, poor and in between, have benefitted from the slave labor that built this country and continue to benefit from black oppression right up to this very minute. You want a civil conversation? Okay. Here's my civil contribution. Do you think Jim Crow is over? Well, it's not. Black people didn't create Jim Crow! They didn't lynch themselves either! Didn't give themselves inferior schools and they didn't choose to work for less pay... If that's too much for you to comprehend, we can go back to lynching!"

"Look, I don't even know what it means to be lynched. How can I have anything to do with that," Jeanette asked with her eyes welling up with tears.

Trixie tried not to gawk at her. She stopped tapping her pencil and became so still that Jeanette found her face wet with tears of fear and frustration. Inside, where nobody had access to, Jeanette knew she was fighting for her life.

"All I'm doing is honoring Kate and Alistair and the children they bore, regardless of what you and your family tried to do. Money talks." Trixie resumed tapping her pencil and never took her eyes off Jeanette. "You think it's an accident there're so few wealthy black people in this country? You think it's an accident that some black men with college degrees can only earn what a white male high-school graduate makes? The median white household in this country has roughly 13 times the wealth of a median black household? It's always about the money. But let's take money off the table for a minute. Hell, even Oprah had a hard time in Paris shopping! Little French woman took one look at Oprah and assumed she couldn't afford what was in the store. We've created some complex shit, Jeanette! And on top of it, we don't have the decency to just listen to them tell their stories. Damn girl! C'mon, you and I are sinners."

"What? I haven't sinned. I go to church, Christmas and Easter at least. We are God fearing people." Jeanette wiped her eyes with her hand.

"We're sinners, Jeanette," Trixie repeated with a smile and continued tapping that pencil.

"Now listen. You and I aren't all that far apart. In some other circumstance, we could probably be friends."

Trixie started to laugh. "Are you serious? There are no circumstances where we could be friends. Let's get something straight. The primary difference between the Grants and the Capwells? We own our sins, no matter how delicious and profitable they may have been. And Lord knows, it has been and continues to be profitable. We owe black people billions of dollars for their labor, not to mention the fact that they haven't killed every last one of us. The Grants know this. Now, the Capwells," Trixie said as she raised her right arm for emphasis, "I don't know what y'all know." Her right hand fell back down on the couch with a dull thud that caused Jeanette to flinch. Trixie stopped and looked at Jeanette whose eyes had grown wide. "I tell ya' what, girlfriend. Let's confess our sins to each other. You know what they say, confession is good for the soul."

Jeanette clinched her jaw. "Please... I have not sinned. My family has not sinned. We have nothing to be ashamed of. We owe those people nothing, yet we've done so much for them and they're still angry," Jeanette said. "I don't need to hear from any politician or sociologist and none of their so called church leaders. I'm done with all that. I'm just trying to live my life."

Trixie was watching Jeanette and started to think she had gone into some kind of trance. Her eyes were out of focus.

Jeanette looked down at her hands and said, "You don't need the money. Your great, great, great something Alistair had some children with a slave and we found out. So what? Now we have to pay for it with our companies? No! They're not worth it."

Trixie threw the pencil onto the coffee table, got up, and opened the bar cabinet. "Did you hear a word I said? You or Carl or somebody has benefitted from blackmail. Do you understand that? You benefitted from the crimes of your ancestors even though they started over a hundred plus years ago and so have I. Anybody in this country who's white has benefitted and I don't give a damn if they're rich or poor, young or old, immigrant or born in the USA. We won't get away with this. Now what is it about this that you don't understand? You just wait. It's coming for us, all of us."

Jeanette's eyes widened with some unknown fear she couldn't name but felt all over her tight body that was now having chills. Her breathing had grown shallow but she managed to hiss, "You dare condemn me. You've got that treasoness Confederate flag waving from every damned building and those statues. You're not even American!"

Trixie put down the glass of wine she had poured and slowly walked towards Jeanette. Trixie leaned over her placing one hand on each arm rest, trapping Jeanette in the club chair where she was seated.

"Now, let me tell you one thing," Trixie said. "I do not control the Confederate flag. I'm not an elected official. I'm not an appointed official. All I have control over is my family's company. That is my domain, and I'm going to do everything I can to clean this mess up, in a just, correct way, understand? I suggest you do the same. You're responsible for what you can control. Am I making myself clear? That's the very least I can do. Leave changing the world up to the politicians, the intellectuals and the preachers. We ought to fall on our knees every day, thanking God that black folks and red folks haven't gotten together and decided to slit our throats, considering what we did. Ya' with me? Can you understand that? Is that clear? Makes you wonder who the real Christians are, at least I do."

Jeanette was on the verge of tears again. For a moment, she thought Trixie was a shape shifter who had transformed into a deadly, drooling, big cat that was going to rip her to shreds. She looked into Trixie's eyes and managed to say, "But slavery is over. It's done. We need to forget it."

"Slavery, according to an activist I heard in Atlanta, isn't over. According to him it's just evolved. Look who has the wealth. It sure as hell isn't black folks. I repeat, not an accident, Jeanette." Trixie leaned back from Jeanette, stood up, stretched and asked, "Would you like a glass of wine? You look like you could use a glass. A martini, that's what you usually drink isn't it?" Trixie walked back to the bar and said, "God's gonna get all of us for this hell, but right now I'm ahead."

"A glass of wine would be fine." The tic under Jeanette's eye was pulsating and she was doing her best not to cry again in front of Trixie.

"We've also got a great French vermouth, Lillet Blonde. Wanna try that?" Trixie asked. "I really like it. I'm going to have some with dinner."

"Okay, that's fine," Jeanette muttered.

Trixie poured both of them a glass of Lillet, walked back to the couch facing Jeanette, sat down, handed Jeanette her glass, and said, "Let's talk about what you Yankees just don't get. You make sure you keep black folks at arm's length up here. Y'all smile and say the right things in front of 'em and the minute they're gone...well, it's a whole other story. Whether we like it or not, we're much closer to black folks in the South. I mean, these people have seen us in some of our worst moments, some of our most private moments. They clean for us, wash our clothes, know who's doing what to whom, what the truth of our lives really is. Hell, they've nursed our children, cared for us when we were sick, when we were drunk and puking our brains out, wiped our behinds and kept our secrets. And what do most of us know about them?" Trixie stopped and looked at Jeanette. "More than anybody else in this country, we know how truly human they are and how Christian."

Trixie took a sip of Lillet. She waited for the faint citrus flavor to work its way down her throat before speaking. Looking into her glass she blinked and then looked at Jeanette. "Let me tell you about the lessons from lynching; we saw the blood, smelled the skin burning, witnessed the tears and still hear the screams. Those screams are going to echo throughout time. We killed them for sport. White folks used to gather for a lynching like it was a picnic!" Trixie stopped. Her eyes were filling with tears. She leaned towards Jeanette and said, "You know I studied history in school, so all of this stays fresh in my memory. Our country knew what it was doing and what would be waiting for us also. Evil. That's what we did, Jeanette. We did evil and we've yet to atone for it. Let me give you a little refresher course."

"I don't want a history lesson."

"Well, that's too bad, 'cause you need some lessons. So sit back."

Trixie took off her shoes and folded her legs underneath her on the couch before continuing. "John Quincy Adams, somebody from right up here, knew we were 'exterminating' Native Americans. That was the word he used, exterminating."

"I don't need to hear this, Trixie. I really don't"

"You think I care what you want right now? Really? The least we can do is listen."

Jeanette got up and looked at the door. Wallace was standing in front of it blocking her exit. All he had to do was look at her and Jeanette sat back down.

"John Quincy Adams said we were exterminating them, 'with such merciless and perfidious cruelty as part and parcel of the heinous sins of this nation, for which I believe God will one day bring [it] to judgment.' I never forgot that. Yet we walked around and told ourselves they were less than human, savages, to justify the evil we were doing. We had to tell ourselves something, didn't we?" Trixie paused and looked carefully at Jeanette, noting the lines on her face were deeper now than they were this morning especially around her eyes. The lines in her forehead were creases getting deeper by the minute. Trixie said to herself, "Hmph," in recognition of the visible toll this was taking on Jeanette. "Listen, we're intimate with black folks in ways y'all just don't understand. An intimacy that allowed us to abuse them, treat them like dirt when it was to our benefit, kill 'em for looking the wrong way, and hope that God turned his head and would forget all that we had done. God forgets nothing. It's a moral mess, Jeanette." Trixie paused for a second. "You been to Washington, DC?"

"No, not recently. Why?"

"Well, if you visit the Jefferson Memorial I think you'll see a quote from him. Where ever the quote may be, this is it. Pay attention, Jeanette. 'I tremble for my country when I reflect that God is just: that this injustice cannot sleep forever.'" Trixie paused and stared into space for a second then looked directly into Jeanette's eyes and said, "Let me tell you something about my brother, Peter. He is one complex man. He's a fine lawyer, but he's also a poet. That's what he wanted to be for a long while and studied it in college. Daddy was worried. Made him promise to be a college professor if he really wanted to be a poet. Anyway, Peter was fascinated with Walt Whitman. Whitman was sort of a romantic, patriotic figure to Peter, representing America in all its glory through his poetry. And then Peter ran across a statement made by Whitman. Whitman wrote, 'The nigger, like the Injun, will be eliminated; it is the law of the races, history… A superior grade of rats come and then all the minor rats are cleared out.' That did something to Peter, something shattered inside him."

Jeanette's heart was racing and her face paler than usual. Exhaustion dragged her eyes downward and intensified the lines on her face.

"Am I making you uncomfortable?" Trixie asked. "I certainly hope so because you wanted a civil exchange. This is about as civil as I get."

"I still don't see what that has to do with us. All of that's in the past. It really is." Jeanette looked at her fingernails, so she'd have something to focus on other than her fear and panic.

"You cannot be that stupid," Trixie said. "What – thirty, forty years ago this city damn near exploded due to busing! We saw that on television and laughed. It's no wonder black folks don't want to come here! My God, woman! And you know what? Y'all didn't even have the balls to tell the whole story. Y'all have managed to cultivate a convenient state of deliberate ignorance on these things."

"Now what are you talking about?"

"You see, this wasn't just about busing, and some black kids trying to integrate white schools. The real story is about the money as usual. Pitting two very poor communities against each other, then using race to drive a wedge between them. Boom! And then light a bomb of violence. Y'all make me sick. Intra class warfare is what you started and after all this time, Boston's still got its head stuck in the sands of avoidance and denial. Please." Trixie rolled her eyes and finished her glass of Lillet. "What's it going to take, Jeanette? Who or what has to happen?"

The suite door flew open and a little girl ran in the room holding a stuffed Teddy Bear. Her eyes seemed to dance. "Mama! Mama! Look what I have." Peter followed her with an indulgent smile on his face.

Jeanette was in shock and confused. This little ball of energy had the presence of a fairy, but not a blonde one with blue or green eyes. This little girl had black eyes and olive skin. Jeanette wondered if the child was middle-eastern or mixed race. She certainly wasn't white. But the child's eyes reminded her of Trixie, eyes that smiled and at the same time looked right through you searching for your soul. It was unnerving. She wanted to know not only who this child was but what she was also. Her black, curly shoulder length hair made Jeanette think of lively music, like Zydeco from Cajun country. Carl played that music often after he came back from a business trip to New Orleans.

Trixie picked up the little girl and gave her a kiss. "Hey baby girl. Did Uncle Peter buy you that Teddy Bear so Mr. Bunny would have a friend?" Jeanette sat her and the Teddy Bear on the couch.

She nodded her head and then threw her arms around her mother's neck and hugged her.

Turning back towards Jeanette, Trixie said, "This is my daughter, Jacqueline. Sometimes we call her Jacq. Sweetheart, say hello to Mrs. Davidson."

The little girl looked at Jeanette and said very confidently, "Hello."

"Hello," Jeanette said. "You're a very pretty little girl."

"Thank-you," Jacqueline said. "Do you ski?"

"No. No I don't. Why?"

"We went skiing before we came here. I love it."

"Jacqueline, I want you and Uncle Peter to have dinner and I'm going to come in later. I picked up some books for you and I thought you could choose one and we could read it together. Chloe will be back real soon. Is that okay?"

"Yes. Where're you gonna be?" she asked while looking at Jeanette.

"I'm going to be right here having dinner with Mrs. Davidson."

Jacqueline looked at Jeanette and asked her, "Why are you so sad?"

Trixie raised her eyebrows, and said, "Jacqueline..."

"I'm sorry, Mama. But she's sad. She has sad colors all around her."

"I know. Look, go with Uncle Peter and have some dinner."

Peter walked over and extended his hand to the little girl. She grabbed it and he helped her stand. As he picked Jacqueline up, he looked at his sister and asked, "Everything okay in here?"

"Things are fine," Trixie said. "As a matter of fact, we're going to order dinner, so Jeanette can get home."

"Okay. We'll be down the hall," Peter said. "I think we're going to do room service. Chloe had to go to a museum for something."

"Okay, but Peter, y'all order a decent meal, understand? Jacq needs to eat more than cake and French fries!" Peter smiled and left with his niece.

"I didn't know you had any children," Jeanette said. "Who's Chloe? Peter's wife?" Jeanette's face was a map of confusion and curiosity.

"There's a lot you don't know, Jeanette."

"Is she yours?"

Trixie glared at her. "What?"

"I mean, is she yours? She's beautiful, but she's different from you. I mean..." Jeanette was struggling. "And what did she mean about the colors around me?"

Trixie began to grin enjoying Jeanette's discomfort. "Well, Jacq is gifted in many ways, but go ahead, say it. She doesn't look white. And that's important to you because what, you're a naturally curious person?"

Jeanette closed her eyes with regret. Opening them, she took a deep breath and asked, "Where's the bathroom?"

Trixie pointed to her left. Jeanette got up and almost ran. She slammed the door shut, locked it, and then turned on the faucets. As the water ran, she collapsed to the floor hoping the running water would muffle the sound of her crying. When she was cried out Jeanette stood up, wiped her eyes and looked in the mirror.

"Don't you let that bitch get the best of you, Jeanette Capwell. You're not a bad person and you've done nothing wrong. You certainly haven't participated in this racism nonsense. Go back out there and fight, fight for what's yours!" Jeanette bit her lip, threw her shoulders back and prepared to continue the battle after splashing water on her face.

When Jeanette returned, Trixie was reading the menu. She looked up and thought Jeanette was going to jump out of her skin.

"Here's the menu. Order anything you like," Trixie said. "By the way, do you know your eyes are all puffy and red?"

Jeanette took the menu, ignored Trixie's observation, and sat down. As she read the offerings, she was aware that Trixie was watching her.

"So, tell me how this happened to you. I mean, we are two women who've had, and still have some extraordinary privileges and a lotta money. How the hell, did you let your business get run in the ground by two men with compromised balls?"

"No one would listen to me. No one took me seriously."

"Then you make them listen to you. If you take yourself seriously, they will take you seriously."

"The business was supposed to be taken over by my older brother…"

Trixie interrupted her. "Oh, I know, your older brother, Daniel Capwell. The war hero who went to the Middle East and got killed on his second tour of duty. Your Daddy was devastated. Your Mama had another breakdown. I know all that. What I want to know is what happened to you?"

"I don't know. I don't know what happened. I was surrounded by men who didn't…"

"I was surrounded by men all my life! My daddy was larger than life. The shadow of Alistair Grant was huge. Peter didn't want to run G.F.C. He discovered the law after his love affair with poetry and Walt Whitman ended, and fell in love with it. Thank God. I have two other brothers. Liam's a vet and raises horses in Kentucky, and Conner is an oncologist in New York City. That left me, and I love making money and making deals and ruling Grant Family Companies."

"In case you haven't noticed, we are very different women, Trixie."

"I can see that."

"I loved my father. I tried to do everything he wanted me to do. I learned how to shoot, go on safari, read annual reports. I even wanted to go to business school, but he told me women didn't need to do that. He told me he would teach me everything I needed to know. I ended up marrying Carl because my father thought it was a shrewd decision. I believed everything my father told me. Everything. And then my brother, Dan, died. Tom wanted nothing to do with the business. He really wanted to be an artist and become an architect, but Dad eviscerated him for that. You know, Tom stood up to him, defied him and got his architecture degree from Harvard. Imagine that. My baby brother told our father to go fuck himself. Tom left. The only reason he came back after his fiancé died..." Jeanette paused and swallowed. "I begged Tom to come home and help me. I just didn't know how to take over and Carl was there, ready..." For a moment the two women sat in absolute silence. "Is there anything I can say to change this?" Jeanette asked. "Anything I can do or promise you?"

"Not one thing." Trixie studied Jeanette's face but then said, "Jeanette, justice and fairness have an uneasy, often painful relationship, and deep down you know it." Trixie felt sorry for Jeanette but it didn't change anything.

Jeanette sat, her eyes brimming with tears again. "I refuse to believe this is about some ancestors of ours. We can't let black people take over, and they will. The truth is they're dangerous, Trixie. My father told me all about them."

"Dangerous? Your daddy told you they were dangerous? You want to know what dangerous is? You are looking at one of America's most dangerous individuals, a white, southern, liberal, progressive, feminist who's filthy rich, and powerful. Now that is dangerous. So yes, this is about black people and revenge. I am not ashamed to say that. 'Vengeance is mine' says the Lord. Well, I'm helping him out. I don't want my baby girl inheriting this much of a moral mess when she's grown. I've got to do all that I can."

"You even went so far as to adopt one of their children. That little girl...I mean, what are you trying to prove?"

"You make some predictable assumptions, don't you? Jacqueline isn't adopted," Trixie said. "She's mine. I gave birth to Jacqueline."

"Did you marry a black man to prove a point? To make a statement? My father told me about people like you. He did! What, who are you, really? I feel like I'm in some political satire, and none of this is real!" Jeanette threw up her hands and they fell right back into her lap like wet rags.

"This is very real. For the record, I am not married to any man, nor living with, nor having a relationship with a black man or any other man of any color." Trixie watched Jeanette and tried to hide her amusement. "You need to order something to eat. As my grandmother would've said, 'You're looking a little peaked.' You need some food."

"You know, I don't think I'm hungry. I've lost my appetite."

"Order something," Trixie said, never once taking her eyes off of Jeanette. "Seriously, you look like you're going to pass out."

The suite door opened and a very striking woman, who looked like she was in her thirties, with curly dark shoulder length hair and olive skin walked in. Her fur jacket was open revealing a beautiful off-white cable knitted sweater. She wore faded jeans and a pair of simple, black, highly polished, over the knee, flat leather boots.

"Trix, I just wanted to let you know I'm back. Where's our little girl?" the woman asked while glancing at Jeanette.

"She's with Peter probably eating cake! Chloe, I want you to meet Jeanette Capwell Davidson of Capwell Enterprises."

Chloe turned around and faced Jeanette. "I've heard a lot about your family," Chloe said, and she took off her jacket and threw it on the couch.

Jeanette tried to smile. "I'm sure you have," she said.

"Chloe is my wife, my life partner, Jeanette. We've been together for almost ten years," Trixie said as she walked towards the phone, "It's all nice and legal."

Jeanette's mouth fell open. She quickly shut it.

"Trix, you're tormenting this woman," Chloe said with a slight accent that Jeanette couldn't identify. "I can tell. Shame on you!" Chloe's eyes sparkled as did her smile. She looked at Jeanette and said, "Don't let her get to you," then winked her eye at Jeanette.

"Look, I'm going to order dinner," Trixie said. "Y'all talk. And Jeanette, I'm going to order for the both of us. We might even have some of those tiny little chickens..." A big grin spread across Trixie's face.

Chloe sat down on the couch across from Jeanette. "Is Trixie giving you a hard time?" Chloe crossed her legs and placed her arm along the top of the couch.

"You could say that. She drives a hard bargain," Jeanette said and tried not to stare at Chloe. She was wearing an exquisite pair of perfectly cut, dazzling diamond stud earrings that caught Jeanette's envious eye.

"Yes, she does," Chloe said while studying Jeanette's face. "You're wondering, aren't you? You don't have to say anything. Trixie told me what a curious person you are. So, let me help you. Our daughter, Jacqueline, is the result of having one of my eggs fertilized by someone we know and respect. But Trixie carried Jacqueline for nine months. You understand?"

Jeanette nodded her head afraid to say a word.

"Okay – that mystery is solved." Chloe looked at her and smiled, her face gleaming.

"Just one more thing. Where are you from?" Jeanette asked.

"Michigan."

"No, I mean..." mumbled Jeanette. "Your heritage? You look foreign."

Chloe smiled again and said, "It's been nice meeting you." She stood up and looked around. "Trix? Where are you?"

"Yeah babe." Trixie walked back into the living room of the suite.

"I'll be with Peter and Jacqueline. So, take your time with Mrs. Davidson. By the way, she thinks I look foreign."

"Of course! As soon as we finish, I'll call." Trixie lightly kissed Chloe on the cheek before Chloe left.

Trixie turned and looked at Jeanette. "Any more questions?"

"No, none," Jeanette said. Her eyes were still wide with confusion. So many questions ran through her head that she was afraid to ask. Why couldn't someone answer her questions about these people?

"About Chloe, perhaps?"

"She just doesn't look American that's all," Jeanette said.

"And Americans look like what, Jeanette?"

"Please...I'm not a bad person."

"This isn't about good or bad. It's about right and wrong, the courage to face ugly truths and do something about it. It's about guts, Jeanette. You need guts, my friend. And then you need to pay and pray. I keep tellin' you that we're all sinners. You think I said that for dramatic effect? Good people can do had things and not even know it half the time."

"My God..." muttered Jeanette. "You just don't know... I've already paid."

"Not enough. Not enough," Trixie said. "None of us have. You know what they say, the sins of the fathers shall be visited upon...well daughters don't get a free pass."

Jeanette raised her hand to stop Trixie and nodded her head while staring into space.

"Okay – well the food will be up shortly. We'll eat and talk about tomorrow. There's a lot to discuss given this transfer of power and ownership. You think you can handle that kind of conversation without 'the boys'? I want to make sure that you, Jeanette Capwell Davidson, are clear about what's happening and why. I don't give a damn about your husband or your brother or your lawyer who couldn't take his eyes off you for more than a minute."

Jeanette closed her eyes and wished that this was a very bad movie that would end soon.

Chapter Twelve:
Back in Weston

The men were in Carl's study. His desk was covered with papers, files and ledgers with an opened laptop right in the middle of it all. There was no overhead lighting, only table lamps were lit giving the room a Rembrandt aura. It was definitely a masculine room, dark brown leather furniture, built in cherry wood bookcases, a few tasteful, original prints from contemporary artists, and several black and white photos of football and baseball players with an antique radio dominating one end of the room. It was a comfortable space that welcomed decision making, cigar smoke, fine brandy and expensive Scotch. Women were not part of this room's design.

Tom was stretched out on the couch, his eyes covered with his forearm. He was trying to ignore the cabinet on the other side of the room that held his father's gun collection, everything from muskets to AK47s and a few hand guns that made Tom nervous. He remembered his father going on and on about the craftsmanship used to create "beautiful rifles." There was something called a Beretta Field Rifle that his father would talk about. Tom remembered his father trying to teach him how to shoot a rifle as a young boy so they could hunt together. The first time Tom pulled the trigger was his last. Shooting a rifle is an interactive event. As the bullet flies forward, the rifle often jolts back into your shoulder. It frightened Tom, and he dropped the rifle. He almost threw up. His lunch raced up his throat but he knew he couldn't throw up in front of his father and brother, Dan. The big brother, the tough guy who could do no wrong. Dan loved rifles! He loved all guns! Big ones, little ones, handguns, automatic weapons, all of them delighted Dan. Just being around guns gave Dan a rush.

Tom remembered too well that his big brother also loved killing. He made it look fashionable. That's why he signed up for a second tour of duty in Afghanistan. It had nothing to do with patriotism and everything to do with having the power to kill. That lust for killing was juxtaposed to Dan's good looks. It was hard for Tom to believe that someone that good looking would enjoy killing. Dan was every girl's heart throb growing up. Tom considered himself an average looking guy with a great smile and a thick head of hair. He saw Dan as a blonde version of their father who had a streak of Scandinavian blood. Tom wondered why he was in this family. How did that happen? Maybe he was an orphan adopted by the Capwells! Tom chuckled to himself.

Kenneth, seated behind Carl's desk, was drinking a cup of coffee, and finishing a sandwich while Carl sat in a leather club chair in front of his desk finally able to smoke. The rest of the house was quiet and still and as unnatural as a silent forest.

"Your personal trusts are fine. You won't lose that, nor will your children. You'll still be very, very rich, folks. The profits directly earned from Capwell that you've invested elsewhere…gone. The problem is the Weston house," Kenneth said.

Tom sat up and turned so he was looking at Carl and Kenneth. "What about the house?" Tom asked.

"Well, Carl has the house and its contents owned by Capwell Enterprises, so it's an asset of the company. The Grants get the house, the furniture, the paintings, the rugs, all of it, because it's an asset. They want it vacated in thirty days."

"What are you saying?" Jeanette asked.

The men looked up and found Jeanette standing in the door. Tom jumped up and went over to her while Carl just lifted his glass of red wine and saluted her in mock fashion.

"For God's sake," Kenneth muttered. "Knock it off, Carl."

"We are going to lose the house and everything in it? The house I grew up in? The house my children grew up in? Jennifer was married here. No!" She stomped her foot for emphasis. The rage coming from her eyes was palpable.

"Come on, Jeanette. Sit down and let me get you something," Tom said. He led her to the couch and went to fix her a drink.

"What can you get me that's going to fix this?!" Jeanette looked at the men, wild eyed. "We're going to be homeless," she whispered. "I've just spent hours with this bitch only to come home and find out she wants the house also? I'll be homeless!"

"Stop with the drama, Jeanette," Carl said. "There's the country house in the Berkshires, and the apartment in Manhattan. Buy yourself a condo in Boston."

"Look, everybody stop," Kenneth said. "Let's all breathe. I know I can work something out."

"Work it out so we can keep the house?" Jeanette asked.

"No, but so you can have more time," Kenneth said.

Jeanette got up and walked out of the study leaving Tom holding the drink he had prepared for her. She walked up the stairs working hard not to trip, went in her bedroom, and began to slowly undress. Standing in her underwear, she found herself in the bathroom looking in the mirror. Her body was showing all the signs of middle-age betrayal, breasts slightly sagging, skin drying making way for those sneaky wrinkles settling in her face and neck representing stories no book would ever be able to adequately express. Not too long ago, she overheard some friends talk about how dry her skin was, how she was aging right before them while some black women they knew seemed to never age, never wrinkle. It had something to do with the melanin in their skin. Jeanette wanted to know why they should have this melanin and she didn't. It wasn't fair. At this stage of her life, she had to work to look attractive. Lately she chose not to work very hard at it.

She placed her hands on her hips and tried to squeeze them. They were still firm but the muscle tone was beginning to give. Her waist needed elastic to accommodate its ballooning girth. She wasn't limber anymore either. Bending down, doing squats, twisting for a Yoga position were all things of the past. Jeanette saw herself fading from everything and everyone.

She let tears slide from her eyes and slowly roll down her face for what had to be the third or fourth time in one day. As her reflection taunted her, all she could think about was how good Trixie and Chloe looked. How could such beautiful, stylish, sexy looking women be gay, Jeanette wondered? She thought it just wasn't fair and found herself wondering how old they were. They had to be in their late thirties or early forties, Jeanette thought. She had just turned fifty and had been thinking about getting a face lift.

She leaned against the vanity feeling light headed. What did these women do in bed, Jeanette wondered? Who played the male and who played the female? That's how it worked, Jeanette thought. Or, maybe not. Maybe it was different. Why couldn't things be simple? Her father told her how things should be and in his version of life there was no room and no need for complexity: men married women, blacks stayed in their place and served us, swarms of immigrants, including Jews, were prohibited, Christians ruled under white leadership and everything would be fine. There were no black Presidents, no women running for President, no accommodating homosexuals, no interracial marriages, no Indians protesting about their land. Everything was being upended.

Things weren't fine, and Jeanette was terrified of the realization that maybe her father was wrong because everything was complicated now. Blacks didn't stay in their place, immigrants were everywhere, Christians had to share heaven with Muslims, Catholics, Jews, Buddhists and who knows what else? Her children were complicated. Her marriage was beyond redemption and everywhere she went there were people who didn't look like her, didn't sound like her, didn't even eat like her. Seething, she couldn't admit who or what had thrown dust in her eyes with all these delusions. She stood in front of the mirror and watched her reflection vanish.

Jeanette snapped out of it, stood up straight and washed the face she saw in the mirror. With no makeup she looked weaker, paler, plainer, and older. She wanted to know more about melanin. How could she get some? Could she get a prescription for it? Jeanette walked into her dressing room and saw a pair of slacks lying on a chair. She put them on, found a shirt and sweater, a pair of shoes, and slid her feet into them.

Walking back into the bedroom, she flopped down on the chaise lounge. There were some photos of Jennifer and Harrison on a side table. One was of Jennifer on her wedding day. She had just gotten married last year. It was a big wedding held on the grounds of the estate. No expense was spared. Anything for her daughter. Next to that photo was one of Harrison. He got all the looks. There he was, sitting on one of the stone fences that surrounded their property out in the Berkshires. He looked like a fashion ad for the all-American boy. Harrison was her baby, the youngest, the brightest of the two from Jeanette's perspective. But he walked away from the family business and buried himself in graduate work at Yale in environmentalism. Jeanette knew that Harrison had walked away from her and everything associated with her. She didn't mean to hurt him while beating him for misbehaving and crying so often as a little boy, but Jeanette didn't know what else to do.

She favored Harrison as evidenced by four photos she had of him compared to the two photos of Jennifer. Jeanette never bonded with her daughter who now lived in New York City working as an Urban Designer. Jennifer's husband ran a start-up investment firm on Wall Street. Jeanette sighed as she looked at another photo of her daughter seated next to Carl in the breakfast room. Jennifer looked more like Carl, dark hair, beautiful cream-colored Irish skin. Jeanette tried to push away memories of the years of abuse she inflicted on her children. But those memories were always hanging around in the back rooms of her mind, ready to attack her at any moment. She was convinced that her children had ruined her marriage to Carl, and they had to pay for being born and "interfering" with her life.

Carl's ancestors came from Ireland. They fled to the United States when the potato famine started. She remembered her father being suspect of Carl because of his Irish roots. Her father and grandfather believed that "no Irish need apply" for anything, ever, not even as domestics if possible. But the Capwells believed that Carl was "an exception," not like the others. Carl was clean, smart, with a well-dressed polished demeanor, and his family had earned a fortune. The Capwells didn't care how Carl's family made their money. The fact that they had money was enough.

Carl knocked softly and slowly opened the bedroom door. He stuck his head in and saw Jeanette on the chaise lounge holding one photo of their daughter. "You okay?" he quietly asked.

"Am I okay? No. No, I'm not. How could I be okay? Are you finished?" she asked referring to their meeting.

"We're taking a break. I just wanted to check on you. Jeanette, we're all worried about you." He walked in and shut the door. "I know things have been difficult. Not just this but I mean between you and me. It's been bad, very bad."

"Ya' think? You with the second family in Scarsdale? That is difficult. How did that happen? You owe me some kind of an explanation," Jeanette said. "Dinner with Trixie, no two dinners with Trixie, and my life is destroyed including our marriage."

"C'mon, our marriage has been dead for years and you know it."

"I want some answers. Who is she?" Jeanette demanded and threw her daughter's photo on the chaise lounge.

Noting that, Carl said, "Look, it just happened. We met at one of those charity balls in Manhattan."

"You mean I was with you when you first met her?" Carl and Jeanette always went to charity events together, a united front on behalf of the Capwell legacy.

"Yeah. And she was introduced to you too. You blew her off," Carl said. He paused for a moment before going on. "You were so rude to her I went over later and apologized. Denise is a real person, gracious, kind, and a brilliant doctor."

"So that's it. She's real and brilliant? I remember her now. I know exactly who she is. Did you notice she was black? Or was that it? Is she some exotic creature who gives you sexual treats you've never had?"

Carl grabbed his wife by the shoulders, lifted her to her feet, and said, "She listens to me! She cares about what I really want in life. We share stories. We have fun. We have actual conversations about all sorts of things including race!" Carl realized what he was doing and let go of his wife. Jeanette fell down on the lounge, trembling and hoping Carl didn't notice.

"I've got a lot to work out about race and racism, but knowing Denise is making all the difference. Listening to her stories, how and why she sees the world the way she does. I never knew. There's a lot to learn, Jeanette." He walked back to the door, turned and said, "Denise and I have a relationship, a real relationship. She treats me like her equal, not some substitute for the real thing, and now I have the chance to be the kind of father I wanted to be with Jennifer and Harrison. A father who can spend time with them and not worry that their mother is going to beat them senseless. I had to send Jennifer and Harrison to boarding school to protect them from you Jeanette. With Denise, I get a second chance. I'm a man in love! I can be a father who loves my children's mother."

"What do you want me to tell Jennifer and Harrison? This is going to kill them," Jeanette said as if she hadn't heard a word Carl said.

"No, it won't. They know. I introduced them to Denise right after Nicole was born. They're not stupid, Jeanette. They figured most of it out. And stop pretending that you talk to them on a regular basis! C'mon."

"How? How did they figure it out?" Jeanette started to cry again. She stood up, ran her hands through her hair and started to pace like a confused animal.

"How? Well, once they were in college I was gone every weekend. On most holidays I'd take them someplace, anyplace other than here. You and I took separate vacations, and the fact that you and I sleep in separate rooms was a big clue!"

"Lots of couples sleep in separate rooms," Jeanette mumbled and wiped her eyes.

"Not ones who love each other! It's a joy sleeping next to Denise whether we make love or not. Look, Jennifer and Harrison have met Denise and the kids."

Jeanette's face fell. "What have you done? You've turned my own children against me."

"Stop, don't do this. You're embarrassing yourself. You alienated them with the beatings, your coldness, treating them like they were some kind of social ornament to trot out at the appropriate time, so please. It broke my heart when I had to send them to boarding school. Do you have any idea how much I missed them?"

Jeanette looked blankly at Carl, and then shrugged her shoulders. "I don't know what you mean."

"With all this going on, it's time you and I did the right thing, and got a divorce. It's one thing I'm talking to Kenneth about.

We're going to end all this foolishness. I'm leaving tomorrow...for good." Carl turned and quietly closed the door behind him.

Jeanette needed a martini.

Chapter Thirteen:
The Long, Dark Night

The impact of what Carl said paralyzed Jeanette. A divorce? Her children have met this Denise woman and the other children. Jeanette stared into space. "What will people think?" she asked herself. "What am I going to do? Where will I go?" She wanted to call someone but there was no one. She looked at her wedding ring and finally realized the charade was over. She didn't have any real friends, and she had no genuine interests anymore, and soon she would have no house, no place she considered home, and why? Her mind became a kaleidoscope of rage continuously spinning away from any form of truth.

She got caught up in this perverse fairy tale of wealth and power, only there is no happily ever after. "How will I ever get through this?" she asked herself.

The idea of building a new life was preposterous as far as Jeanette was concerned. How do you do that at fifty years old? She graduated from Wellesley College, got married to a good-looking Harvard man, Carl Davidson, and thought everything was going to be perfect. Envisioning a life that would sizzle, a life that would be featured in up-scale publications, she would have only the best for herself and her family. She'd have perfect, brilliant children but none of that happened. The children cried and made demands of her. They had needs she couldn't fulfill. Jeanette sank into a life of anonymous, old money, and wealth peppered with boredom, isolation, compromise, disappointment, adultery, and narcissism. The world Jeanette knew radically transformed when she wasn't looking. Its complexion literally changed, and so did the rules. But nobody told her about this new reality. She felt a headache reach into her brain squeezing her head and then twisting, mercilessly, her neck muscles. The pain pulsated with the rhythm of a drum in a marching band.

Carl and she had been sleeping in separate rooms for over a decade. "Why did I accept that?" Jeanette asked herself. "If I had only known he was off in New York with that black woman. How did that happen? How did it get so serious that he stole money from my family's company, and gave so much of it to her? And now there're children? He's going to be one of those late middle-aged men, with hair graying at the temples, a young wife hanging off his arm, and a second family of children who could be his grandchildren!" Jeanette laughed and muttered, "Well, maybe I'll find some young hunk. I could do that! I'm not dead yet."

Jeanette finally got up and walked back to the bathroom. She stared at herself in the mirror again and said out loud, "She can't be as good as I am. It's got to be the sex thing. They're all oversexed anyway. I remember father telling us that. That's why he wanted Dan and Tom to avoid them. He said they could play with these women on the side but it could never go any further." She flipped her body around with a burst of unexpected energy and stomped down the hall to Carl's bedroom.

"He must have a photo of her somewhere," Jeanette mumbled. "Where would he keep it?" She started searching his room, opening drawers, and then his closet, going through pockets of his pants and jackets. She saw a garment bag on the bed filled with his suits. She looked through stacks of papers on the desk. Nothing. She was growing more and more frustrated and started swearing. "What does she look like?" Jeanette screamed. "The black bitch! She can't be as good as I am. She can't. No matter what she does or has done, she'll never be as good as I am. None of them are! Never! Dad told me I was superior!" Jeanette's nostrils were flaring, her face was burning red, and she could hear her heart pounding in her ears.

"You're right. She's better," Carl said.

Jeanette twirled around and found Carl standing in the door. She didn't know what to say but she was afraid her body was going to explode.

Carl reached in his back pocket and pulled out his wallet. "You want to see a picture?"

"You carry it in your wallet? It's with you all the time?"

"Here," Carl said and handed her two photos, one of Denise, and one of his two other daughters, Nicole and Frederica.

Jeanette's eyes widened. Denise was beautiful maybe in her early to mid-forties, and the children were cute. It was obvious by their features that Carl had fathered them. One of the little girls reminded Jeanette of Jennifer. Jeanette's face twisted with a frown and pursed lips. Just as her hand was getting ready to tear up the photos, Carl grabbed them.

"Don't even think about it," he said.

"How could you do this?" Jeanette asked trying not to pay attention to the pounding in her ears.

"Do what? Find happiness? Change? That's what you want to know?"

"Yes, that's what I want to know."

"You really don't get it, do you? I fell in love. It's that simple and that complicated. Nothing short of a damned miracle. Come downstairs. Kenneth wants to talk with all of us." Carl stood in the door and waited for Jeanette. Looking at her, he said with an authority he'd never demonstrated in their marriage, "Pull yourself together, Jeanette. We've got to make the best of a very bad situation." As they walked down the stairs he mumbled, "This may be the best thing that's happened to us."

"I don't know how you can say that. The best thing... I don't understand you anymore. What is there to go over anyway?"

"A time-table, scheduling of events," Carl said as they walked down the stairs. "Sooner or later you and Tom have to get out of here. There's the press. How do we tell all the people that work for us? We have to get a handle on this before we meet with the Grants tomorrow, then there's Jennifer and Harrison. We have to call them tonight. I don't want them reading about this in the paper or hearing it on the radio. I don't care how late it is," Carl said.

"I can't give up this house. I just can't," Jeanette said as she clutched Carl's arm. "We'll be out on the streets. What am I supposed to do? Move into a hotel? Get a condo at the Ritz like all those older women who have nobody? What will people say?"

Carl stopped walking down the stairs and looked at Jeanette. "You know, the truth is we're going to be just fine. You can buy another place tomorrow if you wanted to. You're not losing many of your privileges if any, and neither am I. It'll be embarrassing for a while but we won't be destitute, not by a long shot. So please stop." He tried to pry loose her fingers that had sunk into his arm.

"We don't even know how much money they're giving us! What is wrong with you?" and shook his arm for emphasis.

"Look! We're very rich. No one should have as much money as we have. We'll just be a little less filthy rich." He chuckled. "I finally have a life, Denise, and our two kids. That's what I've got, a life waiting for me. Now take your hand off me."

Jeanette's eyes widened and she stood there. Not removing her hand, Carl peeled her fingers from his arm one at a time, and then continued down the stairs as she watched him. The night was just beginning for the Capwells.

It was two AM and Trixie had crawled into bed. She was rubbing her eyes. "It has been one hellish day," she said and finished buttoning her pajama top while Chloe took off her terry cloth robe and got in bed, naked.

Lying right next to Trixie, Chloe looked at her and said, "I know. You look tired but still beautiful! How do you do that? Work all day and still look…good enough to eat?"

"I'm more mentally exhausted than anything else," Trixie said and felt Chloe's delicate, soft hand run down and then up her inner thigh.

"I know it's late but how tired are you?"

"Never too tired for you, never," and Trixie slid out of her pajama bottoms.

Chloe smiled and said, "Then lean back and let me do the work."

"Revenge is such a terrible but satisfying thing," Trixie said while feeling her body respond to Chloe. "What was it Shakespeare said, or somebody, something like 'revenge is a dish best served cold'? Was that it?" Trixie groaned quietly with satisfaction. Among other things, Chloe was a master of sensuality. She touched Trixie's body the way one touched a beautiful flower or fine crystal and Trixie's body responded with appreciation.

"My God, where did you learn how to do that? You always surprise me." Trixie's face was flushed and a smile sat on her mouth. "Bless your heart, bless your little fingers…umph."

With her head now under the sheet, Chloe laughed and asked, "Is it worth all this?"

"What?" Trixie mumbled distracted by conversation their bodies were starting.

"Revenge. It's a lot of work to pull off," Chloe said and pulled Trixie's body closer.

"Um-hmmm. Worth every bit of it."

"Why? We don't need any more money. Our lives are wonderful. We have a beautiful little girl. Maybe we'll have another one," Chloe said now kissing Trixie's neck.

"I know. We're lucky, very lucky. I appreciate all that we have, Chloe, and I thank God for our good fortune."

Chloe pulled the sheet back, exposing both of them, and asked, "But what else? Hmm? What else? What's missing?"

"The truth? It makes me feel really good to destroy these people. Not as good as you're making me feel right now, but they've been trying to suck us dry, black mailing us since the 1800s. It's over now." Trixie looked at Chloe who was still lying between her legs, kissing the area around her navel and working her way back up. Trixie pulled Chloe up to her face, smiled and kissed her back.

Looking into Trixie's eyes, Chloe asked, "Did you ever consider just forgiving these people? Why can't we all just forgive each other?"

Trixie sat up in bed and was silent. Chloe could almost feel Trixie thinking. She ran her hand down the side of Chloe's face and said, "Forgiveness is tricky."

"What do you mean?"

"Too many people associate forgiveness with sanctioning or excusing the behavior that's caused the pain. It's like a 'get out of jail free' card. I think forgiveness works only when both sides play fair, and how likely is that in this situation?"

"Isn't that why we have things like repentance and lament?"

"Oh darlin'! Tell me how we repent for slavery? What would that even look like? Most white folks can't or won't begin to grasp how they perpetuate all this. It's not their fault, that's what they'll say. They don't understand! They don't understand because they don't want to understand. It hurts too much."

Chloe looked right into Trixie's eyes and said, "Maybe you decide together what forgiveness looks like."

Trixie grabbed Chloe's hand and squeezed it. "Chloe, I just read online that some white friends of a little eight-year-old, biracial boy tried to lynch him. Do you understand that? Thank-God, the little boy managed to free himself but his mother took pictures of the rope burns around his neck. He had to be rushed to the hospital. Where did those kids learn about lynching black folks, and what made them think it was the thing to do?"

"I don't know. I don't know how we repent. You know what they say, to err is human, to forgive is divine."

"Chloe... I am so far from divine!" They both laughed. "And you know it! When the women's movement was roaring, a bunch of women poets emerged. They were fabulous. One of 'em wrote this poem on anger. I memorized it because I just loved it. My favorite passage is 'a good anger acted upon is beautiful as lightening and swift with power. A good anger swallowed, clots of blood to slime.'*** I have no intention of swallowing my anger. You get migraine's that way!"

"I've come to know that! You've got a lot of your grandpa Alistair in you," Chloe said as she unbuttoned Trixie's pajama top. "You're so strong. Look at your legs, your arms. And then there's your heart," and Chloe placed her left hand between Trixie's breasts. "What would Alistair do if he were here?"

"Get ready to have a long conversation with God! I am not a perfect person and never will be."

"I know what you're capable of and you still find a way to sweep me off my feet. You have courage regardless of what it may cost you. I've watched you all these years reach out, speak brutal truths, and fight for what you believe in all the time. The patience you have with Jacq – explaining complicated things to her – and you respect our little girl. That's all amazing to me. So, my love, with all of your so-called flaws, I'm still in awe of you."

Caressing Chloe's bare back, Trixie said, "Don't be, Chlo. I'm not all that. You know I can be bad, low down if need be. The only reason I don't kill every last one of the Capwells is because it's illegal, and I would hate prison, and miss y'all too much. I couldn't stand being away from you and Jacq."

"So, you're doing this instead." Chloe kissed her on the neck again.

"Anyway, this is going to hurt 'em more than flat out killing 'em, especially that dried up bitch, Jeanette, who let this mess continue. I want her to suffer and know her life is over. They've had hundreds of years to feel morally superior. Not anymore." Trixie gave Chloe another kiss that took her breath away and flipped Chloe over on her back so she could lie on top of her. After another deep, powerful kiss that gave merging new meaning, Trixie said, "Turn out the light, Chloe. To hell with sleep."

Chloe turned it off.

It was almost 3:30 AM and Kenneth, Carl and Tom were wrapping things up. All of them looked weary and older than they were when the day started. Kenneth stood holding some papers in his hand. His tie was loosened and his shirt collar was open. He was tired, exhausted by the magnitude of events.

"Kenneth, thanks so much for doing all this," Carl said.

"It's what I'm supposed to do so no thanks needed."

Tom swallowed the last of his drink and said, "Look, I'm going to bed. There's nothing more I can do here."

"Oh no, no," Carl said. "We've got to get Jeanette to sign these papers."

"Yeah, tonight," Kenneth said.

"Well, good luck with that. It's not going to be me," Tom said and walked out.

Carl and Kenneth looked at each other. Kenneth reached for a pen and handed it and the papers to Carl. "You go, Carl. Get her signature. We can't wait. Come morning she won't want to do this and you know it."

"You really think I have any influence after all this? You go upstairs. You do it. I've got a headache."

"I don't want to do this, Carl. You should..."

Carl cut him off and looked up at him. "I should do what? Seduce her into signing away everything that means anything to her? Here's the bottom line, we're giving the Grants just about everything in exchange for saving face. Look, the two of you have been sleeping with each other for what? At least a year, maybe more. I don't know and don't really care. But you're the one to ask her. Denise is waiting for me to call. I don't want her blindsided by all this madness."

Kenneth stood there speechless, eyes not blinking at all.

"What? You thought I didn't know? I do know. I'm glad she found somebody she could respond to, show some affection for without it being part of a deal to maintain the damned family fortune. Go upstairs. You know where her bedroom is. By the way, it was one of your monogrammed shirts I found in the laundry she forgot to hide or maybe she didn't."

Kenneth, blushing, turned and walked out of the den. "What a fucking mess," he mumbled to himself as he went up the stairs to Jeanette's bedroom. He knocked softly on her bedroom door.

"Come in," Jeanette said.

The room was dark, and it took a moment for Kenneth's eyes to adjust. When they did, he saw Jeanette sitting up in bed. Her knees were pulled up to her chin. The silhouette she saw in the door wasn't Carl's nor Tom's.

"Jeanette?"

"Kenneth? Thank-God it's you."

Closing the door and walking over to the bed, he said, "Yeah, it's me. Can we turn on a light? You've got to sign these papers."

"No."

"No what?"

"Don't turn on the light,"

Kenneth sat down on the edge of the bed and placed the papers next to an empty wineglass on her nightstand. "Jeanette, you've got to sign these. Don't make it worse than it already is. The Grants play hardball. This is as serious as it gets." He scooted closer to her and felt his hand against her face that was damp from crying.

These were hands she'd come to know intimately. "You're going to get through this," Kenneth said.

"No, I won't." Silence sat between them like a soldier on watch. Kenneth didn't know what to do so he kissed her, and she kissed him back, pushing her tongue into his half-opened mouth. The next thing she knew she was unbuckling his belt, unzipping his pants, pulling them down along with his black jockey shorts, and reaching between his legs. Barely breathing, Kenneth lifted her nightgown above her breasts, and with some difficulty, managed to place himself between her legs without kicking off his underwear and pants.

Jeanette's hands were searching for romance, for passion, for something deeply felt, steady and real, for anything other than what it was, a carnal exchange of body fluids masquerading as love or compassion, with every muscle in their bodies playing along. Kenneth became hard and penetrated Jeanette instantly. There were no sounds of satisfaction, just a few rough grunts. The next few minutes were out of his control, and nowhere near romantic or even erotic, just some choreographed, indifferent reflexes programmed by nature. When he finished, he fell over on his back seemingly exhausted, naked from his waist to his ankles where his clothing was bunched up around the awkward presence of his shoes. She felt one of her thighs lying in the wet spot he left while goose bumps popped up all over her chest and arms. Deflated from despair, she grabbed his arm on the verge of throwing up but the sensation passed. Kenneth was silent realizing that he could have gotten more pleasure from a sex toy than Jeanette. With all the kissing and touching and grabbing and thrusting, Jeanette's heart felt nothing. She sat up in bed, turned on the light and said, "Give me the papers to sign."

Chapter Fourteen:
The Next Day

Jeanette had not slept. It was almost six AM. Carl had been going up and down the stairs for at least a half hour. Jeanette didn't know what he was doing until she heard the sound of wheels rolling. Why, she wondered would he be pulling a suitcase? That's what it had to be, a suitcase. She refused to believe he was really leaving and didn't think any more about it. She turned over facing her clock radio on the nightstand. "I'll get up in a few minutes," she thought. "Take a shower... Breakfast would be good." Then she heard Tom's muffled voice as he passed her bedroom door, but she couldn't make out what he was saying.

Annoyed, she sat up, turned on the light, and looked around the room. "How will I ever get this place packed up?" she asked herself. "Maybe I won't have to. Maybe something will happen. Maybe... because I can't leave." Absentmindedly, she picked up the empty wine glass on her nightstand and started playing with it while staring off into space. She stopped turning it around and squeezed the bowl of the glass. In less than a minute, the glass gave way to the pressure of her hand leaving shards of glass all over her bed. She gasped as the glass fell silently followed by several streams of blood from her hand.

Looking at her bleeding hand, she winced while biting her lip as anger rose from some deep spot inside of her like lava spilling silently from a dormant volcano. Every muscle in her face tightened. She picked up one of the larger shards and considered cutting her hand to pieces but changed her mind, and then thought about slashing her wrists. But suddenly she had a better idea. Tranquility washed over her body.

She got out of bed leaving a trail of blood smeared by her feet as she walked to her bathroom to shower. Jeanette barely felt the water on her body. Blood rushed from her hand onto the tiled floor and out the shower drain. For some reason she refused to understand, she was angry with Kenneth. Where was a man when you needed one? Where was her father when she needed him? If only her father were still here.

As she stumbled out of the shower, she finally admitted that she wanted to kill Denise and the children she had with Carl, and she wanted them dead now. Jeanette muttered while drying herself with tomato red blood running down her hand. At first, she didn't understand how to stop the bleeding. The blood fell onto the white marble floor of her bathroom forming a puddle. It was the kind of image you saw in a horror movie, not in anybody's real bathroom.

"Somebody's going to pay for all this and I know who's the blame," Jeanette muttered. She bent down to wipe up the blood with her white towel, her hand still dripping rivulets of blood starkly highlighted against the white marble. It took on a sinister, prophetic quality that made Jeanette nervous. The more nervous she became the faster she tried to wipe up the blood.

Trixie opened her eyes, propped herself up on her elbows and looked at her daughter who was about to leap into her arms, "Good mornin' baby."

"Mama! Mommy! Get up! C'mon," Jacq said. "I wanna eat breakfast, please." Jacq managed to jump right in the middle of her parents' bed, landing with a soft whooshing sound made by down comforters.

"You want breakfast already?" Trixie picked up her watch from the nightstand and looked at it. "Sweetheart, it's 6:30, and you want to eat? Now?"

"Yes, I do. Right now. Is Mommy going to wake up?"

"I'm awake Jacq," Chloe said pulling the sheet up around her bare chest.

"You should wear something, Mommy. You'll get cold," Jacq said while looking at her mother's bare shoulders. "This is the North! It's not like home."

Chloe sat up and reached out to her daughter. Jacq crawled into her arms and Chloe asked, "What do you want for breakfast?"

"Whatever you and Mama are having," Jacq said, her curly dark hair seemed to be having a party on her small head! "What about waffles?!"

"Jacq," Trixie said, "Y'all decide. I'm going to see if Uncle Peter will join us." Trixie got out of bed and walked down the short hallway to Peter's room. She knocked three times and heard her brother's voice.

"Come in, Trix!"

"How do you always know it's me?"

"You always knock three times." He extended his arm and motioned for her to come over and she did. Putting his arm around her he said, "Did you wake-up with that frown?"

"No!"

"Don't start worrying. We're ready for whatever they do or don't do." Peter faced his sister and cupped her face in his hands, looking more like a movie star in his navy silk robe and light blue pajamas, and not one of the shrewdest and toughest lawyers in the country. His bare feet added vulnerability to this well-built man who gave the impression that he was afraid of nothing. Like his dark hair, Peter had a very dark side to his soul that was devoted to keeping his family powerful, prosperous and safe.

"Okay. I'll calm down," Trixie said. "Let's have breakfast and no talkin' business in front of Jacq. She doesn't need to hear about the Capwells at four years old. She's already smart way beyond her years. Stick to the news. We can explain that to do her."

"I got it. But what happens when we're on the news? What'll we tell her?"

"We tell Jacq the truth, gently, but the truth so she could understand. I'll order breakfast. The Capwells better be here by ten o'clock. I'm running out of patience with these people." She walked out of his bedroom yelling, "I know what you want for breakfast, Peter. I'll order it."

Jeanette, Carl and Tom were standing in the foyer putting on their coats, hats and gloves with silence tickling their discomfort.

Jeanette said, "I'll be right back," turned and ran into the study. "I forgot something."

"Forgot what?" Tom yelled, "Don't take too long. We don't want to be late." He turned to Carl and asked, "What the hell could she want? I've got the all the paperwork." Tom then whispered to Carl, "What happened to her hand?"

"Whaddya mean?"

"She's got a large bandage around her right hand. What the hell happened?" Tom heard the click-click-click of Jeanette's heels on the hardwood floor as she walked back. They stopped talking.

"Who knows? Look, I'm going to drive my car," Carl said. "Take Jeanette's car."

"Why?" Jeanette asked as she approached. "What's wrong?" she asked while closing her tote bag. "Why can't we all go together in one car? We can save gas."

Carl took a deep breath and let it out slowly, "I'm leaving after our meeting. I told you that last night."

"Leaving? Leaving for where?"

Tom dropped his head. He dreaded what Carl was going to say.

"One more time. I'm driving to New York to be with Denise. Don't act like I didn't already tell you this. I've packed most of my clothes. What I can't take with me today, I'll send for in a few days."

Jeanette's mouth opened slightly. "New York! How can you do that? How can you leave now? This is not true, none of it!"

Carl put on his black leather gloves and ignored her.

Tom touched her elbow and quietly said, "C'mon Jeanette. Let's get in the car." He could feel her trembling. Her mouth was tightly closed and she jerked her elbow away from Tom.

"I'm fine."

Tom stepped back from her, threw up his hands and said, "Okay. You're fine! We're all fine!"

"No drama, Jeanette," said Carl. "I'm outta this. You'll find a formal letter of resignation from me recommending that Tom take over. Talk to Kenneth. I had a conference call last night with the company's legal people and senior management. They know what to do. I'm falling on the sword. Blame all this on me. I really don't care anymore. See you at the hotel."

Jeanette looked like a little child abandoned by her family. She didn't know where to go nor what to do. Her world was swirling, getting farther and farther out of reach.

"Sis, come on, let's go. We can sort this out later," Tom said. "I've already called all those that Carl didn't. As we speak they're telling our employees. I talked to Jennifer and Harrison at length. Everybody knows. Nobody will be blindsided."

The two cars left, and within minutes they were on the Mass Pike. The traffic was heavy, and bottle necked right before they reached the Newton toll. They came to a stop while the radio was giving a traffic report telling them what they already knew. A mid-sized, relatively new, graphite gray, Volvo S60 with an African-American couple, on the passenger side, almost cut in front of Jeanette and Tom. Jeanette turned her head and looked at the couple. They were aggravated also.

Staring at them, Jeanette hissed, "It's their fault. Look at what they just tried to do."

"What are you talking about?" Tom asked while looking straight ahead. "Whose fault?" He slowly maneuvered their car into the EZ Pass lane while the Volvo moved into an adjoining lane.

"Black people. See what they just tried to do to us... trying to get ahead of us. They're the reason we're losing everything. Look at them. They have everything and we're going to have nothing."

Tom felt his heart race. He looked in the rear-view mirror and saw Carl right behind them in his car. "Jeanette, you gotta stop thinking like that. You sound crazy."

"Am I? I don't think so. I'm not going to let them take everything away from us, Tom. I'm not. We have rights in this country. We worked hard for what we have. We made this country. All this nonsense about slavery. The nerve of them to ask for reparations. Slavery's over." She looked down at the large bandage she had put on her hand and started picking at it.

Tom shook his head and said, "Yeah, well maybe slavery's over but the impact of it isn't over. I read..."

Jeanette cut him off. "I don't care what you read. I think South Africa had it right. Father and I had a long talk about it just before he died. We agreed. Let them out to go to work and by a certain time they would have to be back to their area. That way we wouldn't have to look at them and we would be safe. I certainly don't want to have anything to do with them. Then we could keep our money and live the life we were meant to live as intelligent, civilized white people. Otherwise, we're going to be penniless. They'll take it all."

They went through the EZ Pass toll and Tom pulled over to the side in the break down lane while Carl sailed right past them. Tom stopped the car, turned on the hazard lights, and said, "Jeanette, look at me." She didn't move. "Jeanette! Look at me!"

"What?"

"You've got to get a handle on this. First, it's not like we're going to be penniless, okay? We will have more than enough money left. I know I will. And this fixation on blaming black people...it's sick. You're sick. Ever since this started you've been making these asinine, ignorant remarks. Hell, some would say they're racist and with good reason. My God! Jeanette, we did the blackmailing. We're guilty!"

"I am not a racist. I've never been a racist. We don't lynch black people. The Capwells haven't thrown any stones at them or burned any crosses on their lawns. We give to their organizations. You even play tennis with some black people."

"C'mon, you know and I know there's way more to it than burning crosses and hiding under those damned hoods! Every day we all do something to add to this madness. I know I'm guilty."

"Didn't you understand what Daddy taught us about those people?"

"Dad was a nut, Jeanette. That's what drove Mom to an early grave."

"Listen to me, those people have been given opportunities. Everything's been handed to them, and still they're not satisfied. As for our mother, she was weak Tom. That's all. She didn't know any better and filled your head with a lot of nonsense. Those people would do God knows what to us."

"Jeanette, you don't even know any black people," Tom shouted! "It helps to know different kinds of people. It really does. Red ones, brown ones, black ones...You gotta know people. You live in a world that no longer exists, Jeanette. This is the 21st century, and this shit is complicated!"

Jeanette continued ranting oblivious to Tom. "My God, Barack Obama is President! He's half black, but see, his mother was white that's why he became President. He's half white, not black. Tom, slavery's an excuse for the rest of them now. That's all it is, an excuse, and they have to push it aside. Get over it like the Jews got over the Holocaust. They're fine. It doesn't bother them anymore. I don't know why more people don't admit that. Slavery was a way of life in ancient Greece and Rome..."

Tom cut her off. "Rome fell! My God, Jeanette." He shook his head hoping he had imagined what his sister was saying, but he knew better.

Jeanette looked blankly at Tom and said, "What?"

He looked at the side view mirror, preparing to get back in traffic, and said, "I don't think we're ever going to get over slavery. We participated in an ugly truth, and we've got to own that. I don't like thinking about it but that's a luxury we can't afford. It's a dangerous luxury! Walkin' around like all's well! Like we aren't responsible for this mess. I don't know what you're afraid of unless it's the brutality of the truth. The Grants nailed our asses and well they should," he muttered.

Jeanette just stared straight ahead as if in a trance. "They're everywhere. I hate going into Boston because of them. They're all over television now, on magazine covers, even fashion magazines, and now one of 'em is in Carl's bed having his children like that damned slave, Kate! You have to watch the women, with their insatiable need for sex. Daddy told me they could reduce strong willed men to a whimper with their sex drive. It's almost like they're some kind of drug. We're in this mess because some slave woman wouldn't keep her legs closed and tell Alistair Grant, no. No, I won't sleep with you. Why didn't she do that?" Jeanette turned her head and waited for her brother to answer.

Tom gripped the steering wheel and continued driving. "Like she had a choice, Jeanette. You need to forget everything Dad taught you. Reduced them to a whimper! Please. Makes you rethink who's the weaker sex... Do you really think she was on equal footing with Alistair Grant who literally owned her? I mean, c'mon, think about it."

"And now, Carl is having some tawdry affair with one of them," she muttered. "Maybe he's our own Alistair Grant. Two of those children – both of 'em had two of those..." Jeanette bit her bottom lip barely breathing now and almost whispered, "What did they call those kinds of children blacks have with whites? Father told me. Mulattoes? Quadroons? Half-breeds? That's what they are, mongrels, good for nothing. Defective. Mentally impaired... They must be."

"Jeanette, stop it! Carl is not having some tawdry affair! It's way beyond that if it ever was. They are a family! God! Jeanette, face facts. It's time." Tom honked at the car in front of him out of building frustration.

She squinted her eyes at Tom and asked, "Did you know? Did you know he was with this woman?"

"Yeah, I knew."

"Oh my God. My own brother has been poisoned also. You haven't met her, have you?"

Tom hesitated. "Yeah...sis, I've met her. I had to go down to the New York office and the three of us had dinner. Yesterday when the photos were presented I was..."

Jeanette cut him off. "Dinner? Where? Where did you go?"

"Well...it was at their Scarsdale house...I had no idea then that Trixie's people would...the photos. I'm sorry. I didn't want you to know."

Jeanette was silent. Her lips parted and she said, "I keep telling you... Why won't you see it? I'm trying to save you

Tommy… They're robbing us of everything. They're robbing me…of my life. The Grants deserved to be blackmailed. All of them. Blacks are trying to take over. And now… Denise… she has a house. Look what she's done. It's their fault…"

"Jeanette, this mess is our fault. Some fool ancestor thought blackmail was a good idea, and we didn't have the good sense to stop it. It just went on and on and on, and here we are. Carl and Denise? A whole other thing." Tom blew air through his lips, almost whistling, and continued. "We are almost there. If you can't pull yourself together I'm not going to let you walk into this meeting." Traffic had slowed down to a crawl. Tom fell back in the seat, hands white knuckled on the steering wheel wishing he could just vanish. He was feeling very old and he wasn't even forty!

Given that traffic had dramatically slowed down, he wondered if there was an accident ahead. The Mass Pike was never big enough or wide enough to handle rush hour traffic as they approached Boston proper. It was cold and that mitigated the impact of exhaust fumes floating out of one car and into the vents of another. The temperature this morning was in the single digits. It was better than sitting in traffic on a hot, sticky day with the humidity at some God-awful measurement and people sticking to the sidewalks. That's what Tom told himself. He wondered why the weather couldn't freeze his sister's mouth shut! He realized that Jeanette was still talking. So early in the day to feel weary, worn down, defeated, his eye lids were already heavy and whatever energy Tom had was gone.

"I don't associate with black people because they're ignorant and dirty. And then they hate you because you have things and they don't, except for Oprah. She's different. But that's just the way things are. Daddy always told us to be watchful around them, especially if they show up someplace they're not supposed to be, the men in particular. That's why Dad would never let us associate with any of them, Tom. They'd rob us blind. That's why they don't earn anything. They've already taken it from us." She paused and then muttered, "All that singing and dancing, that's all they can do... although they are good performers... Father loved Sammy Davis Junior and Duke Ellington."

Traffic finally stopped. Tom closed his eyes and prayed. But he knew he was really begging. In the middle of his plea to God, he heard police sirens approaching. His eyes snapped open and looked in the rearview mirror. Two cars were trying to pull over to let the police car through. There was nowhere for Tom to go. He was already in the far right lane. The only other place to go was into a stone wall! This section of the Mass. Pike had three inadequate inbound lanes. He felt trapped by traffic outside of his car and trapped inside by a crazy person who happened to be his sister.

"Did you hear anything I just said?"

Tom started to deliberately take more deep breaths hoping it would calm him down and prevent him from saying things he could never take back.

"And they have all kinds of benefits they abuse. It's our money they're living off," Jeanette said. "We're supporting black people."

"Keep this up, and I swear I'm going to leave you right here on the Mass. Pike. Got it? Or I'll get off at Copley Place and leave you at the library. Read something! Get a clue, Jeanette!" An ambulance siren blared past their ears. Tom could almost feel the rush and vibration of air as the ambulance flew by.

"You wouldn't," Jeanette said, as she looked at her younger brother.

"Keep it up. This is going to backfire on you, badly. I can just feel it. Reign it in! We're supporting black people... Are you serious? If we are, we're doing a damned poor job of it. Do you know anything about these people other than some pathetic, ignorant stereotypes that Dad pounded into your head? Black people have some real problems they've got to face, every damned day! Problems we couldn't begin to grasp. They didn't enslave themselves! We did that! What is it about that that you don't get?!" Traffic started to move again and Tom let out an audible sigh of relief. His head was pounding.

"This country has bent over backwards trying to help our black people and look at them! They must be genetically inferior like I read somewhere..."

"Jeanette, shut the fuck up!" Tom turned up the radio only to hear the following.

"... some breaking news from the corporate world. Although none of this is confirmed just yet, reliable sources have told us that by the end of the day, one of New England's oldest corporate giants will be changing hands. Grant Family Companies of Atlanta will be acquiring Capwell Enterprises based here in Boston. Capwell Enterprises..."

"God! Why would they do that? We should sue them!"

"Oh yeah, that'll work. Please Jeanette. Please. This is for real." Traffic picked up and within ten minutes they were pulling up to the hotel entrance.

Tom, Carl and Jeanette stood with several other people waiting for the elevator. Tom made a slight jerking motion with his head to get Carl's attention without Jeanette noticing. Tom was unsuccessful. He wanted Carl to know that Jeanette had flipped out in the car. Tom decided he would pull Carl aside before the meeting started to let him know.

When the elevator arrived, the three of them stepped in first. As Jeanette turned around, her knees weakened. Her breathing grew shallow. She grabbed Carl's arm for support, and he pulled away from her. Tom couldn't figure out what prompted the wide-eyed expression of horror on his sister's face until he looked at the other people in the elevator. They were black, three men and a woman, all dressed in business attire with the woman carrying a leather tote filled with paper files and a laptop computer. Tom thought the men looked like they stepped off the cover of some men's fashion magazine. They made him feel a little out of it and shabby. He'd been wearing the same tweed overcoat for over ten years, and it looked like it. The coat was one of the last things his mother purchased for him before she died. At least his black wing tipped shoes were polished. Tom's attention went back to his sister who now looked like she was going to faint, scream, or both. Thankfully they arrived at their floor before Jeanette collapsed. She almost ran off the elevator and whispered to Tom, "That black woman was dressed better than I'm dressed. Do you see what I mean? How can they afford to do that?"

Tom glared at her and said, "Maybe she has more money than you do or better taste."

Jeanette's nostrils flared at the possibility. She was stung by his response.

Carl heard the exchange and was alarmed by the sound of Jeanette's voice. It made his blood feel like frost on a cold morning. As the three of them walked towards the suite Tom suddenly understood how his nieces, Nicole and Frederica, felt when they were convinced monsters could live anywhere.

Jeanette looked at her brother, confusion twisting her face and outrage leaving her mouth half-open. She started to say something but stopped. Instead, under her breath she said, "Maybe I should go back and ask her how she can afford those clothes. Welfare checks probably plus affirmative action...that's how."

Carl heard her and became more uneasy and fearful. He couldn't shake the sensation that wrapped itself around him like a cold wind.

The three of them walked down the hall, and saw the very large cousin, Wallace McRoy, wearing a perfectly cut dark grey suit and a pale blue patterned tie. As usual, he was guarding the door to the Grant suite.

"Good morning," Tom said.

Wallace said nothing, looking at each one of them, unsmiling. He bore holes into them with his black eyes, and finally opened the door.

Chapter Fifteen:
Rendering Justice is Never Painless

As they walked in, Trixie, Peter, Louis and Madeline were waiting for them with Frank standing in a corner and John seated near the couch. None of them were smiling.

"Well," Trixie said. "Let's dispense with the niceties. What's it going to be? Where's Kenneth?"

Bursting through the door, Kenneth said, "I'm right here." He tore off this coat and threw it on a chair, joined everyone, and said something about traffic and missing the elevator.

Trixie stared at him before continuing. "Okay, all of you get settled. I've ordered us some coffee and tea. It'll be here in a moment." Trixie cleared her throat and said, "I know I gave y'all this deadline and I'm going to honor it. What's your decision?" and she looked at Jeanette.

Carl and Tom looked at Kenneth, something Trixie and Peter caught.

Trixie shifted in her seat and asked, "Jeanette, cat got your tongue? You can't answer? You waitin' for the boys?"

"Look," Kenneth said, "the Capwells have asked me to speak for them on this matter."

"Speak," Trixie said and gestured at him to begin.

Kenneth reached in his briefcase, pulled out the agreement and handed it to Trixie. "I think this is what you're looking for."

She immediately turned to the last page looking for Jeanette and Carl's signatures. Finding them, Jeanette flipped through the agreement, making sure there were no changes, and then handed everything to Peter for his approval.

"Now that that's done," Tom said, "Will you tell us exactly how much is in the suitcase? This is an odd situation."

"Frank," said Trixie, "bring the briefcase over."

Frank placed the large metal briefcase on the coffee table, opened it, and stepped back. Rows and rows of hundred-dollar bills neatly wrapped with narrow, tan colored, paper bands were exposed.

Tom leaned forward and said, "We still don't know what the amount is."

"You can count the money later," Trixie said. "Think of it as a surprise."

"We want to count the money now," Kenneth said and stood up. In an instant, Frank stopped Kenneth with one look. Another bad feeling settled in the room. The word hoodwinked ran across Kenneth's mind.

"You want to count the money now. My, my," Trixie said. "Frank, Peter, take Mr. Heller down the hall so he can count the money." Peter led the way with Kenneth followed by Frank, who had the money and a gun.

Trixie looked at all the Capwells. What a sorry bunch, she thought. What a very sorry bunch of people. "You know what? Now that they're counting the money, Jeanette, why don't you tell me about those fancy relatives of yours who came over on the Mayflower? I mean, that's what you've been telling people for God knows how long. Let's hear that story. We told you our story. You found your voice yet?" Trixie asked and pulled out her cell phone from her suit jacket pocket and started pressing buttons.

"I don't know what relevance that has," Jeanette said.

"Oh, but Jeanette, it's part of the story you've been telling. Part of the allure of the Capwells. Part of the image you've been selling for as long as y'all been in business. Pardon me for just a minute." Trixie started to speak into her phone. "Yup – you can use the release I approved last night." She paused. "That's right. We plan on leaving late afternoon and will be available this evening." She paused again and noticed that Jeanette was glaring at her. "Start with the Boston papers…well then start contacting the other outlets. That's right, for the evening news and social media too. Okay, thank-you."

"You're sending out a press release, so soon?" Jeanette asked.

"This is how it's done, Jeanette," Trixie said.

"Somebody has already leaked the story. We heard it driving in."

"And you're surprised, Jeanette? What is wrong with you?"

Carl cleared his throat and said, "Well, I'll call our media people. It would be good to have a copy of your release."

Louis looked at him and said, "You haven't called them yet?"

"I'm doing it now. Tom made some calls but I need to call especially with the news leak. Is there … I'll go out in the hall," Carl said. He took out his cell phone and left the room thinking that he wanted to give Tom a break from handling so much of the fallout.

Louis crossed his legs, and leaned his chin into his hand, trying to hide a smile that was edging its way across his face. "This is going to be something," he thought. More silence. Louis looked at Jeanette wondering what she was all about, exactly how someone like her came to be. What was really behind the hate, not to mention the free-floating fear that oozed from her entire being? This was one of those times he was grateful for having been raised abroad, far away from the United States.

"Okay, I understand. You don't want to talk about this, but we're going to talk about it anyway," Trixie stated. "Madeline, tell 'em what we found out. This is so interesting. I love history. You know what I learned early in life? It all depends on who's telling the damned story. Remember when Jesse Jackson was running for President? One thing I remember him saying was one man's terrorist is another man's freedom fighter. So true." Trixie crossed her legs and leaned back. Her eyes were sparkling like those of a mischievous child. "Madeline?"

"Yes. Let me hand out some things," and Madeline passed around another set of papers, neatly stapled and numbered, titled, The Truth About the Capwells.

Everyone started scanning the pages. There were lists and copies of very old documents and newspaper articles interspersed.

"My God," Tom said, "how long is this?"

"It's long enough," Jeanette said as she flipped from page to page. "I've never seen some of these articles."

Carl walked back in and Madeline handed him a packet. He saw the title on the cover sheet and groaned silently. He fell into the couch and reached inside his suit jacket for his glasses. He wanted to read every bit of this.

"If this gets in the wrong hands, it could be devastating," Tom said as he scanned the pages. He kept seeing the words, thief, stolen, fire and criminals along with the word treason. "Oh God," he thought, "when is this going to stop?" All he could see were potential headlines making the Capwells look like fools at best, along with ruthless, hypocritical, and crooks at the other extreme.

"Madeline, tell 'em," said Trixie.

"Well, the first fact we uncovered was your ancestors didn't come over on the Mayflower, Mrs. Davidson."

"How dare you," Jeanette exclaimed. She jumped up and announced, "The Mayflower is Capwell heritage."

"Umph," Trixie said. "Y'all sure do lie a lot! Sit down, Jeanette."

"The documents you've been using to prove this are forgeries. Good ones, but forgeries," Madeline said.

Tom grabbed his stomach, got up and left the room. Louis's eyes followed him. Carl was reading and didn't notice Tom's departure.

Madeline looked into Jeanette's eyes and said, "I have all the documentation showing how we traced this. It's amazing what you can find out on those genealogical websites now. It was like opening Pandora's Box. So, your ancestor, Joseph, and his wife, Ruth, came over four years after the Mayflower. We found the manifest of the ship they took. They did have a tailoring business but got in some kind of debt in the U.K., and had to leave. One article I found led me to believe that had they not left the country they would've gone to jail. Another document speculated on treason. Based on what we discovered in some additional articles from London newspapers, their lives were in danger. Somehow, they managed to scrape up enough for passage on a ship heading for the so called, New World, the colonies. It was evident how hard they worked. Their success is proof of that. But some trouble started when additional relatives came over from England. Theft was an issue again. What your ancestors couldn't buy, they stole or hoodwinked from people, especially land, which meant they swindled Native people."

"The land was free," Jeanette exclaimed. "Those red people didn't even have deeds! What did they know about owning property?!"

Carl put his hand on Jeanette's arm. "Just be quiet, please."

Puzzled, Jeanette looked at him but she did stop talking.

"Mrs. Davidson, your ancestors did some harsh things while building their businesses. After the war of 1812, they acquired more properties to open additional textile plants. They bought cotton from several plantations in the South but eventually the Grants became their primary suppliers for their mills north of Boston. By the time the Civil War started, they would've sold Jesus Christ to the devil if that would or could increase their wealth. Harsh, they did very harsh things."

"What do you mean by harsh?" asked Jeanette motionless.

Madeline stared back at her and responded. "You really want me to go into that?"

"I want to know."

"Your ancestors were ruthless, cold-hearted and miserly. They had these factories and the conditions were horrible. Many people died working in your family's textile mills. Some were children. There were no child labor laws at that time. And then there was this huge fire. If you turn to page ten of your packet, you'll see a copy of a newspaper article about it. Twelve people died under what we would call suspicious circumstances."

"I never knew this," Jeanette said and rubbed her eyes. "I never knew any of this. Daddy never told me."

"How could you not know, Jeanette?" Trixie asked. "Based on what Madeline found out that was a major event for y'all. Y'all did some questionable things to rebuild and expand after that. More stealing, more lying, working people to death for little to no money then and now! That mess over in southeast Asia...wow. Seems to be a Capwell tradition." Trixie shifted in her seat so she could look directly at Jeanette. "Either that or y'all are what I call practitioners of deliberate ignorance."

Jeanette leaned back in her seat, suddenly weary. "Okay, we weren't perfect people but neither are you," she said.

"No, we aren't," said Trixie. She leaned forward and looked into Jeanette's watery eyes. "The difference is, we own it, Jeanette. We've had to face it. Bridget and Sinclair? Family. Wallace, Frank, and John? Family. Alistair Grant was a helluva man. We're doing what he didn't do. If he were alive today, he would've married Kate, paid people living wages. I know that in my heart. But y'all...ooo-Lord. You know what you did and have continued to do. I read something really interesting and want to believe it. The word 'Yankee' comes from the Wampanoag. The loose translation? Yankee means thief." There was a pregnant pause in the room. "Y'all spend so much time puttin' on airs as my mother's people would've said. The pretense is astounding. Today it ends. All of it!"

They sat there in lethal silence for what felt like hours.

"About the house in Weston," Jeanette finally said. "Is there nothing we can do?"

Trixie smiled. "There may be something. Y'all have it as an asset of Capwell but I know it's your home. Home is important. What's that saying? Home is where you go when there's no place else to go? Even though you've got that cute little farm out in the Berkshires, the place in Aspen, the condo in Manhattan, and that beautiful house up in Nova Scotia you tried to keep hidden... Weston is home."

At that moment, Peter, Kenneth and Frank returned to the living room. Kenneth was not smiling. He turned to Trixie and said,

"What you're doing to these people is criminal. You know that. You're giving them four million dollars for the entire Capwell empire including their home." Kenneth looked at the Grants with pure contempt and then sat down next to Jeanette.

"I don't care what you think," Trixie said. "So, have you counted the money?"

"Yes," Kenneth said. Tom walked back from the bathroom, pale faced.

"Jeannette is asking if there's something we can do so she can keep the Weston house," Trixie told Peter. "I'm not heartless. I understand. You've got a connection to that land, and you don't want to leave it the way we all forced Indians to do hundreds of years ago. Let's see what we can do."

Jeanette relaxed a little and almost smiled, oblivious to Trixie's stinging comparison. Seated next to Jeanette, Kenneth held her hand and noticed they were ice cold.

Trixie stood up to stretch her legs. "How about this? We'll take the money in the suitcase in exchange for your house. You can live out the rest of your life there if it's worth it to you."

"You can't be serious! They will walk out of here having given you everything you wanted with nothing to show for it. This is beyond ridiculous," said Kenneth.

"Oh please. Jeanette and her family will have what they cherish most. That house will help them save face, hopefully, if they play their cards right. The public need never know about the hypocrisy of the great Capwell family of Massachusetts. Now you know that's what this is really about." Again, Trixie tried not to smile, but it ran across her mouth the same way Jacq ran in the bedroom that morning.

"You'll have the house," Peter said. "According to realtors and several appraisers we talked with the house is worth roughly three point five to four million today."

Jeanette gasped! "That house and the land is worth twice that."

"You know how real estate is…three point five to four million." Peter said.

"We just counted four and a half million dollars," Kenneth said.

"Well, it's up to y'all," said Trixie. "Make up your mind because we'll be leaving here in a few hours. It's not like you're gonna be sharecroppers or live in a cardboard box in downtown Boston. Stay in Weston since it means that much to you, or not, but make a decision."

Kenneth looked at Jeanette. "It's up to you. Do you want the house that badly?"

"Yes," Jeanette said. "I have to have it."

"Well, it's a done deal, isn't it?" Trixie said. "Peter, did you draw up the papers for this?"

Pulling out the documents from a file of his, Peter said, "They're right here ready to be signed."

Eyebrows lifted with surprise. "You had the papers drawn up? How did you know it would come to this?" Jeanette asked.

"I'm very good anticipating what people will do," Trixie said.

Chapter Sixteen:
Loose Ends

The Capwells left the hotel, grateful they still had the house that meant so much to Jeanette. Tom didn't give a damn. He knew it was time for him to move out, find his own place, finish healing from having lost the woman he loved to a fatal disease. It was overcast outside. A cold north wind was blowing. Tom knew snow was on the way.

"What a silly life this is," Tom muttered to Jeanette as they drove back to Weston. "There's a lot of work to do, Jeanette. Peter is coming back next week. Senior management and I are meeting first thing tomorrow, breakfast meeting at 7:30 AM in the Capwell Dining Room. It would be good if you were there." Tom glanced at Jeanette. "Are you listening to me? Have you heard anything I said?"

"It doesn't matter, Tom. Capwell Enterprises is now a property of G.F.C and Madam Trixie. We're done."

"We're not done! Jeanette, look, it's going to take some time for this transition to happen but after that, we're free! You can do whatever you want now without constantly thinking about the Capwell image. You can be you. I can be me." Tom was almost giddy. All the tension had left his neck and shoulders. His stomach had calmed down. He exhaled and wanted to wrap things up. The anticipation of freedom was overwhelming to him.

"And who are you, if not a Capwell? What am I supposed to do? Make quilts? Knit socks?" Jeanette asked while looking out the passenger window.

"Expand your circle of friends, Jeanette! You could start there. Those women you hang out with are downright silly! Get to know some new people." Tom zipped down the Mass. Pike, oblivious to the threatening sky, thinking about new friends he was going to make, and the new life taking shape in his mind. He thought this might be an entrée to happiness, something he let go of when Rachel died.

"I don't want any more friends, Tom. I know what you're really saying."

"I'm the man who let himself be consumed by grief and get sucked into this family insanity. I've got a second chance now. I can go back to architecture, try real estate development. I could go back to my painting. I have a friend up in Maine who's been trying to get me to join his firm for years. I talked to him last night."

The sky gave way to some kind of drizzle, not quite rain but not quite snow either. The precipitation had a devious quality making the roads slippery and dangerous. Tom slowed down and continued to day dream about the possibility that awaited him.

"Haven't you been busy. You're going to leave too?" Jeanette could barely be heard but Tom managed to make out what she said.

"Yeah, I'm leaving, not right away but soon. I worked a deal with Peter. I'm going to stay on for sixty to ninety days, and that's it. Heading to Portland. I've always loved Maine."

"I see. I guess I better make some plans too."

"A plan would be good, sis. Maybe you should think about some serious therapy again."

"I don't need therapy. I'm fine. Why would I need to sit in some office with a shrink for more than five minutes?"

"Jeanette, you're crazy. Get some help," The drizzle was turning into tiny white snowflakes that looked like crystals floating down from the sky.

"I told you. I'm fine. I'll resolve this. I have a plan. I do. We'll get you back to the house and then I'm going shopping."

"Retail therapy, Jeanette? That's your plan? Really?" Tom shook his head from side to side. "Don't you think both of us should go in and talk to our employees?"

"No." She was too calm.

Trixie and Chloe were gathering their luggage. Jacqueline was skipping and twirling around at the prospect of going home. Madeline and Louis were already in the lobby with Frank and John. In a few minutes, Chloe, Trixie, Peter and Jacqueline walked into the lobby followed by Wallace, a bellhop pushing their luggage and skis on a cart.

"Jacqueline," Trixie said, "I want you to get in the first limo with Uncle Peter. Mommy and I will be just a minute and button up your coat. You can do it!"

"Okay," Jacqueline said and quickly buttoned her coat with alarming dexterity for a four-year-old.

"Jacq, put that hat on. It's in your coat pocket," Trixie ordered. Jacqueline reached in her pocket and pulled out a multicolored, knitted hat. She pulled it over her thick curly hair and smiled triumphantly. Holding her Teddy Bear and Mr. Bunny, a small, fluffy, pink bunny with long floppy ears, Jacqueline ran to the limo, dodging snowflakes, with her uncle following close behind. The driver opened the door for her and Peter. Jacqueline lifted her small legs and got in the car clutching her stuffed animals and prepared to sit as close to Uncle Peter as possible. She adored her uncle and he adored her.

Chloe got in after Peter and flopped down in the back seat. There was a jump seat waiting for Trixie who arrived within the next minute. Wallace was already in the front seat. Everyone settled in. The first limo pulled out with the second one following. The light snow was on its way to becoming a storm. Logan airport was close to the city of Boston, and twenty minutes later both limos pulled up to Butler Aviation where private planes departed from and arrived. In less than a half hour, the G.F.C private jet took off for Atlanta, leaving the cold, damp winds and portending snow storm of Boston behind them.

As soon as they reached cruising altitude, everyone let out a collective sigh of relief, except for Jacqueline who was absorbed with drawing, and talking to her Teddy Bear and Mr. Bunny in a nearby seat.

Peter sat down next to his sister and said, "Well done."

Holding Chloe's hand, Trixie said, "Thank-you. Amazing how much saving face means to some people."

"It is," said Peter. "The fear of being labeled racist rather than doing something to eradicate it... I don't get that... Maybe it's us... But, big sister, this is one for the books though. You got the Capwell empire and didn't pay a dime for it." Peter grinned at his sister. With his long legs stretched out in the carpeted aisle of the airplane, he said, "I'm going back in a few days."

As they flew towards Atlanta, Peter and Trixie talked about the upcoming transition and some future plans, long term, and short term for a half hour plus. Wallace, Frank, and John were playing cards. Chloe was reading some magazines, and Jacq was still focused on drawing. She had a frown on her little face and her small lips were pressed together. Jacq's Teddy Bear was her sentinel, imbued with all the powers and charm from her uncle. Mr. Bunny was her version of Yoda, full of guidance and wisdom.

"You know what?" Trixie said. "We deserve a fabulous meal tonight. I mean a fabulous, down home meal."

"I thought you would want that," Chloe said. "I've talked with Bell. She's going to prepare all our favorites."

"Thank-God for Bell," Peter said, "because we don't want Trixie cooking!" Peter laughed and playfully hugged his big sister.

"Oh, stop it. My cooking isn't that bad!"

"Mama makes good cereal, Uncle Peter," Jacqueline turned and said.

"Thank-you, Jacq," Trixie said.

"Hey Louis, did you hear that? Jacq said Trix makes good cereal," Peter said. He leaned forward resting his elbows on his knees, grinning at Trixie.

Turning around in his seat so he could see them, Louis said, "She does, so long as it comes in a box. All you need then is a bowl and some milk! That's my cuz'! A business genius! A culinary disaster! Can barely boil water!"

"Y'all need to stop, right now. I can do more than that."

"Cuz, you can burn water! C'mon," Louis said and laughed. "Not being able to cook has got to be some kind of Southern sin!"

Trixie picked up a pillow and threw it at Louis stating, "You better watch out!"

Jacqueline put down her drawing and walked over to her mothers. She sat right between them. Chloe kissed her on the forehead. "You are our precious girl, Jacq. We love you. You know that, yes?"

Jacqueline looked into Chloe's eyes, grinned and said, "Yes, I know Mommy."

"Good. Don't ever forget it, no matter what."

Jacqueline looked at Trixie and said, "Mama?"

"Yes baby."

"That lady you were with? The one with the sad colors around her?"

"Yeah, I know who you're talking about." Trixie shut out the world to focus on her daughter.

"I think something bad is going to happen to her. I think it's going to be very sad, Mama. I think she has a lot of thorns."

They were all quiet for a few seconds.

"Jacq, what do you mean by thorns?" Trixie asked.

Looking up at Trixie, Jacqueline said, "A long time ago, Papa Alistair told me that all people had thorns, like roses. The thorns were the bad things in us. Some people have more thorns than others. That lady yesterday has more thorns."

"Jacqueline," Chloe said, "Where did you hear this?"

"Papa Alistair told me."

"When?" Trixie asked.

"A long, long time ago. My name was Elisabeth and I had hair like Mama's, and Uncle Peter was there, only that wasn't his name. Mommy was there too but her name was Kate."

"What was my name, Jacq?" Peter asked.

"It was Sinclair. You were part of the bouquet of roses. Cousin Louis was named Patrick." By now Madeline and Louis had joined them. Everyone was dumbfounded.

"Do you think there's anything we can do about what's going to happen to Mrs. Davidson, Jacq?" Trixie asked.

"No. It's just going to be sad. I made a drawing of what's gonna happen."

"You did," Trixie said. "Can we see it?"

"Yes." She jumped down and ran to where she was drawing and brought it back.

Chloe looked and handed the drawing to Trixie and Peter who examined it very carefully.

"Jacq, tell us what's going on in this drawing," Trixie said.

"This person," said Jacqueline as she pointed to a figure, "is the sad lady you saw, and these people over here, are the people she shoots."

Peter put his niece on his lap and asked, "Why would she shoot these people?"

"She's mad," Jacqueline pointed to the people shot. "She shoots only brown people. See. The first one she shoots is a pretty woman."

"Hopefully, that won't happen," Trixie said.

"It's going to be very sad, Mama. What'll we do?"

Trixie kissed her daughter and shot a look at Peter. "Well, we'll just have to be ready. Sad things happen to people, baby. It's all a part of life. Good people are sad sometimes and bad people can also be sad sometimes. Often you can't change that. But, if we weren't sad some of the time, it would be hard to know what happy feels like, you know?"

"I know," Jacqueline said. All the adults looked at each other for a few seconds. Peter sat Jacqueline down between her mothers and he sat across from them so he could really study this special little girl he was so proud of and loved.

Frank walked out from the cockpit. "Cuz, we should be landing in about half hour, forty minutes. We left the bad weather in Boston."

"Okay. Thank-you."

Jacqueline was suddenly tired and put her head in Chloe's lap. Anyone could understand how traveling would tire out a four-year-old. But it wasn't the travel that drained Jacq. It was the drawing and what it took to produce it. Within minutes, she fell into a deep sleep. Half of Jacq's face was covered with a veil of her dark curly hair.

Chloe looked at Trixie and said softly, "Don't you wonder about our little girl sometimes?"

Gazing at their daughter, Trixie said, "I wonder all the time. She's not an average child. We have a special little being here. Did you look at the rest of her drawing?"

Chloe nodded her head. "What do you think?"

"We'll find out. I'm going to get a blanket for her."

The Grant gang finally arrived home. Peter carried Jacqueline who was still half asleep with her Teddy Bear and Mr. Bunny held under his free arm.

Bell, their housekeeper, greeted them in the foyer. "It's good to have y'all back. It's been too quiet."

Bell was an imposing woman, not someone to be toyed with at all. Wide but not overweight, her brown face was home to eyes seasoned by witnessing all kinds of historic, demeaning slights she and her people still endured on a daily basis in the 21st century. These were encounters that made her sick with rage most of the time. And then there were other things, like not driving alone after dark, making sure you never got lost, knowing what outlying areas that circled Atlanta still embraced Jim Crow and descendants of the KKK. The KKK wasn't dead. White sheets and hoods had been folded up and placed on the top shelves of closets everywhere. Now, they often wore suits with white shirts and ties, and too often police uniforms. The only way you could identify them was by the hate in their eyes. Not ordinary, garden variety hate born of everyday frustrations over something inconsequential, but the kind of hate that wanted you wiped off the earth for no other reason than a blend of heinous contempt, deep fear and total ignorance. And then there were those "good white people" who endangered your life because they were just plain stupid and lazy. They refused to learn about any reality other than their own especially if it was going to make them uncomfortable. Bell had to always remember these things and be able to spot people like this. Her life depended on it along with anyone else who looked like her.

It was hard to know what Bell really thought but among the Grants she was "home." There was a sense of safety to a degree. These were white people she trusted not because of their legacy but because of how they acted. More than anybody Bell knew, this generation of the Grants walked their talk, regardless. They'd call anybody's bluff and link arms with you to face the lions of

America's original sin. They would help you when nobody else would and not ask a question. They didn't have to! The Grants would never desert you, and Trixie was their leader. Bell, and her mother who worked for the Grants, watched Trixie grow up. Trixie's father, David Garrison Grant, was tough, brilliant and a non-conformist. He was still a Democrat and loved his only daughter regardless of her sexual orientation. Trixie's mother, Margaret Hamilton Grant, was fearless. She didn't give a damn about what anybody thought. She followed Jesus, and dragged her four children through His teachings, both traditional, and especially the non-traditional lessons he left behind in works like the Gnostic Gospels. She read all of these lessons, including the more recent books of Thomas and unauthorized accountings of Mary Magdalene that made the Vatican nervous. It wasn't long before the children willingly followed their mother. "Don't be afraid to think," Margaret told her children. "And don't be afraid to love." Bell chuckled to herself. She often said, when no one was around but the spirits of past generations, "Look what y'all have produced!"

"It's good to be back," Chloe said and hugged Bell.

"I'm taking Jacq upstairs," Peter said.

"I'll go with you," Trixie said. "C'mon Bell, lookin' forward to your meal. Thank-you."

"I figured I'd save y'all from Miss Trixie's cereal cuisine! Dinner will be ready in a few minutes. Where do y'all want to eat? The kitchen, the dining room?"

"Let's eat in the kitchen," Chloe said while laughing. "Frank, John, are you joining us?"

"No, I'm going to take care of this," Frank said nodding at the briefcase full of money, "and then head home before my wife kills me! But Wallace and I will check the grounds before I leave."

"John?" Chloe asked.

"I gotta get home too. I've got that meeting in London next week. Gotta get ready. I'll call you and Peter before I leave so we can go over some things. Good work, Trix! Love 'ya!"

Louis and Madeline were taking off their coats. "Bell, is there anything I can do to help?" Louis asked.

"No sir, Mr. Louis. But you and Miss Madeline got some phone messages. I put them in the den. I don't know why they didn't call you on those cell phones y'all have."

A small hub-bub of activity started. People going up and down the stairs, phone calls being returned, Trixie putting Jacqueline to bed, Chloe and Trixie changing into more comfortable clothes, Louis and Madeline in the kitchen teasing Bell, and Frank hovering in a protective fashion before leaving. Cousin Wallace stayed at the house, live-in security.

They had a large house on ten acres of land located outside of Atlanta, six bedrooms, six bathrooms and a two-bedroom guest house with a breezeway connecting it to the main house. Within the main house was a one-bedroom apartment with a separate entrance where Peter lived. Louis had a condo right in Atlanta near the G.F.C. building but rarely stayed there. He preferred staying at the house with the family. Madeline also resided at the main house. Being part of this family was her life. She wanted nothing else.

This house had been in the family for almost a hundred years, undergoing many renovations to keep it updated. Comfortable was the word that best described it along with stylish and happy. Open spaces, bright colors, lots of natural light, plants, books, family portraits, framed historical documents and Jacqueline's toys were scattered almost everywhere. This was the family base. Further out was the plantation, the big house that Alistair Grant built, now designated as a historical landmark. When trouble erupted, that's where they all went.

The adults gathered in the kitchen. Bell served them dinner over the din of television. The table was crowded with an array of southern dishes and two desserts. Fried chicken was the featured main dish. There were collard greens, snap beans, warm potato salad, mashed potatoes, a green salad, crackling corn bread and sweet potato pie along with hand cranked vanilla ice-cream. Right in the center of the table among the plates, wine glasses and food, was a baby monitor just in case Jacqueline needed something or had a bad dream.

All you could hear was the television spitting out national news from a cable network and people eating. Eventually everyone settled down and a hush fell over the table. It was the hush and contentment of culinary satisfaction.

"Well," Louis said, "This is a tribute to the cook. When silence sets in because people are eating, it means the food is good."

"Indeed, it is," Peter said and reached for another piece of fried chicken.

"Miss Bell," Wallace said, "You got this thing going on. Love ya chicken, love ya' greens... have mercy!"

"I so love southern cooking," Chloe said.

"You'd never know it by lookin' at you," Bell said. "You're thin as a switch!"

"Her metabolism is a gift from the devil, Bell," Trixie said. "She's got me exercising every day. I so hate it!"

"But it's good for you," Chloe said. "Anyway, the Grants are lean, strong people. Lean and mean!"

"Aww, shucki, shucki," said Louis and laughed.

Wallace laughed and finished his glass of wine. It was an expression that implied agreement, adoration, and encouragement depending on the tone and emphasis one used. And sometimes it was used as a verbal goading device!

"I thought once she gave up modeling and focused on her art and running her gallery, we could forget all that exercise stuff," said Trixie. "Did I mention I really hate exercise?" Trixie repeated.

Everybody said, "Yes!"

"Aw right! I got it. No need to get rowdy!"

"You are a true original, Trix," Peter said.

"I'm just grateful to walk in her shadow," Madeline said with a mouth full of collard greens.

"Hey! I'm not worthy of that, Maddie. Don't even go there. C'mon now."

"Stop with the false modesty," said Madeline.

"Maddie is right. You are an extraordinary woman," Chloe said.

"Look, I'm not perfect, and I'm not an angel. Every one of you at this table knows that."

Bell muttered so everyone would hear, "I know that's the truth!" Laughter followed.

"It's not the perfection we admire," Peter said and winked his eye at his sister.

Shattering their contentment and satisfaction, they heard, "We've just received some breaking news. We're going to join our reporter on the scene in Boston, Kim Soto. Kim?"

Everyone stopped talking and looked up at the television.

"Good evening. I'm standing here in front of Mass General Hospital where four people have been admitted with life threatening gunshot wounds. All hospital officials would say is that three victims are in critical condition and one is in grave condition. Their names have not been released pending notification of their families. The police have ruled out terrorism. Earlier today, a woman matching the description of Massachusetts business icon, Jeanette Capwell Davidson of Capwell Enterprises, drove into downtown Boston, parked her car somewhere in Government Center, walked over to City Hall Plaza, and allegedly began shooting black people. There are several eye witnesses who are being interviewed by the police. Prior to this incident, we received word shortly before going live that a woman had been shot at point blank range in Sak's Fifth Avenue. The police have reason to believe that the shooter is the same person who shot these individuals in Government Square."

Everybody stopped eating. Peter wiped his mouth with a napkin and threw it down on the table. Trixie leaned back in her chair, arms folded across her chest, listening intently. Chloe had tears in her eyes, and Bell was the picture of stoicism. No one could tell what Bell was thinking, and Trixie's face right now was the definition of concentration.

With snow falling heavily, the hatless reporter continued. "We now have additional information linking Mrs. Davidson to the shooting earlier in Saks Fifth Ave. According to eye witness testimony, a woman matching Mrs. Davidson's description was buying some cosmetics when she turned, saw a woman of color making a purchase, engaged her in conversation, then pulled a gun from her handbag and shot the woman at point blank range, killing her instantly. The shooter escaped before security arrived. The manner in which this shooting was done is troubling to the police."

"What do you mean, Kim?" the anchor asked.

"According to witnesses at Sak's, the shooter smiled at her target, actually chatted with the victim, then shot the victim hitting the carotid artery. The victim died within minutes."

"Oh my God," mumbled Madeline. "She really is a crazy person."

"Nothing crazy about her," muttered Louis. He took a sip of wine. "She's not out of control. She knows exactly what she's doing."

"This same woman," said the reporter, "roughly an hour later, was seen running by several witnesses into a nearby garage across the street from City Hall." The reporter turned and pointed to Boston City Hall, a stark, modern, concrete building partially obscured by falling snow. "The irony is the police station is right on the other side of City Hall Plaza and the Kennedy building."

The reporter put her right hand up to her ear, listened for a second and said, "There are incoming reports from precincts in the South End and Roxbury that have many blacks and Latinos, that a white woman driving a late model, dark colored Mercedes sedan was seen driving through Dudley Square targeting black and Latino women. A car matching the same description was seen not much later with a woman shooting black and Latino people along Columbus Avenue."

The reporter paused, listening to her producer through the ear piece, and continued with, "The Motor Vehicle Bureau has confirmed that Jeanette Capwell-Davidson drives a navy-blue Mercedes sedan. It's not known at the moment how many people have been injured and admitted at Boston Medical Center, the nearest hospital to the South End and Roxbury. Let me make it clear that the identity of this woman has not been confirmed by the police."

The news anchor asked if there was any speculation on the motive.

"All we know right now is what you know. This afternoon around one PM there was a formal announcement that Capwell Enterprises was now part of Grant Family Companies, a family conglomerate based in Atlanta under the leadership of Charlotte A. Grant. Speculation from a source inside Capwell Enterprises believes the family was coerced into making the deal and Mrs. Davidson became distraught."

"Kim, coerced? Why? How?"

"We don't know yet, but we just got word that Thomas Capwell, acting CEO, as of this afternoon, will be holding a press conference later this evening. So, it would seem that Jeanette Capwell-Davidson has something to do with all this."

"Kim, thank-you for that report." The anchor turned his attention to viewers. "We will keep you informed as we receive more information on this very bizarre and puzzling story. Today on Wall Street..."

Silence hit the kitchen. For a few seconds no one said a thing. Peter drank some more wine. Trixie stared off into space, and Chloe was fixated on the baby monitor. Bell shook her head slightly. Everyone was adrift in their thoughts.

"Chloe, where's Jacq's drawing she did on the plane?" Trixie asked.

"I'll get it. I think I put it in the living room."

"This is what I don't understand," Louis said. "What kind of police force do they have in Boston? I get this picture of Capwell running all over town, shooting up everybody, and the police are ...where? Eating donuts? Taking a nap?"

"Who the hell knows," Trixie said. "I'm afraid it's going to be a long night. The final act has begun." The images of blood splattered on snow began to play on a screen in Trixie's head. She wrinkled her nose and thought to herself, "I so hate weak people. That's unkind, but I can't help it."

Bell was leaning against the stove, watching this family she worked for all her adult life as did her mother and so many others in her family. "Lord Jesus," Bell thought, "Somebody has felt the wrath of Alistair Grant, some kinda way."

Chloe walked back in the kitchen and handed Trixie the drawing. She looked at it carefully and then handed it to Peter. "Tell me how many bodies you see on the ground in Jacq's drawing."

Peter carefully looked and said, "I see eight."

"I wonder where Jeanette learned to shoot?" Chloe asked.

"Her father was big on hunting, especially safari hunts, big game hunting. He taught all his children how to shoot. Tom didn't do well according to one servant I located who had worked there at the time. Anyway, there was a story in the Boston Globe about him taking the family on a safari one summer when Jeanette and Dan were teenagers," Madeline said. "Tom was still a kid. I mean very young, ten or twelve."

"Really?" Trixie said. "Hmph! Is there anymore wine, Peter?"

"Yeah." He reached for the bottle and poured her some. The telephone rang and everyone jumped.

"Bell, if that's a reporter refer them to our Communications' Director," Trixie said. "They shouldn't be calling here anyway…"

"Yes ma'am," Bell said and answered the phone.

Trixie's cell phone rang and then Peter's. He got up and walked in the living room while Trixie answered hers at the kitchen table.

"Hello," Trixie said. "Tom?"

"Trixie? Yeah. Tom Capwell." His voice was unsteady. She had the feeling that she was talking to a scared animal and was ready for him whimper at any moment.

"I know. I recognize your voice. What the hell's going on up there?" Trixie asked.

"You may have already heard…" Tom said hoping his voice wasn't shaking.

"I heard some woman matching Jeanette's description went through Boston shooting up black people. What the hell is that?"

There was a pause. "I wanted you to hear it from me. It's worse than that. She killed four people earlier today, wounded three or four others, all of them black or Latino. Two are in grave condition and it's too early to tell about the others. And all of them were women."

"And what was that going to do?"

"She's angry. She's been angry for days and blames black people for all this. I heard the accounting from one of the clerks who witnessed the shooting in Sak's. The clerk described it as...demonic. That's the word she used."

Trixie was silent for a moment and then said, "I am so sorry, Tom. Where is she? Did the police just pick her up?"

"We don't know. She's missing. I want to find her before the police do. Gotta call Carl, Jennifer, Harrison before the press tracks them down, if they haven't already. I've got to issue a statement later tonight, in time for the eleven o'clock news. Maybe by then I'll find her or she'll give herself up. Everybody's going to be asking about the motivation."

"You could walk away from this right now, Tom. Nobody would blame you. Have your Communications Director handle this. Don't do this to yourself."

"Yeah, I know. Maybe I will. But I've gotta find Jeanette. I'll call you back as soon as I know more."

Trixie turned and looked at everyone, "Well, it's on now. Madeline, see if you can get me the names and addresses of the people this fool woman shot. Get me as much information as you can. See what we can do for them. They may need help with funeral expenses, hospital bills. It's going to be a long night."

Chapter Seventeen:
What Jeanette Did

Tom hung up the phone, grabbed his coat and rushed into the kitchen where the servants were cleaning up. Alejandro was putting things away in the butler's pantry when Tom found him.

"Excuse me, Alejandro, I'm asking..." and Tom stopped. He ran his hand across his forehead, took a deep breath and started again. "Alejandro, can you stay here until I get back?"

Trying not to stare at Tom who looked like he was either on the verge of tears or about to scream, Alejandro responded, "Of course, Mr. Capwell. That is not a problem. Sir, are you alright?"

"No, yeah – I'm going to be fine. I've gotta find my sister," Tom said as he hastily put on his coat and buttoned it. "If she comes back... do whatever you have to do to keep her here... don't let anybody in either."

"And if anyone calls?" Alejandro asked while watching Tom's hands shake as he finished buttoning his coat.

"Take a message, and don't get in any kind of conversation with them. There're two or three TV stations already at the gate. As it is, I've got to sneak outta here through the back. God..," Tom turned and walked out. He rushed to the garage and entered through a side door. Slipping into his silver SUV, he let out a deep breath and realized he couldn't turn on the headlights until he made his way out of the garage and off the grounds. If he did the reporters would see him leave. He found himself wondering if anyone would hear the garage door opening. You couldn't see the garage from the front of the estate. Tom never thought about whether or not anyone could hear the automatic door opening until now. It was important that nobody follow him, especially the police. One patrol car was already parked in front of the gate.

Once he was on the back-road driving away from the estate, Tom turned on the head lights, ignored the falling snow, slammed his foot down on the gas pedal, and practically slid to the Mass Pike straight to downtown Boston. He never noticed the unmarked police car following him.

Tom had a hunch his sister would be at the Capwell Headquarters. Parking in the underground garage, Tom ran to the elevator and went up to the executive floor where he, Carl, and Jeanette had offices. He didn't notice that Jeanette's car was parked underground also.

When the elevator doors opened, Tom stepped into comparative darkness in the dimly lit hallway. He breathed from one moment to the next while his eyes adjusted. With some hesitance, he made his way to Jeanette's office. The office that had been their father's was still intact almost a decade after his death. It was a memorial to him and it always gave Tom chills whenever he walked by. As he approached it, he saw light creeping from underneath the door.

"Oh God," Tom thought. "What the hell am I doing? Why can't I just walk away from this the way Carl did? Damn family." He placed his hand on the lever that opened the door to his father's office. Tom smirked remembering why there was a lever instead of a door knob. His father developed a severe case of arthritis in his hands. Turning a door knob became almost impossible for him, along with shooting and hunting.

One of the few conversations Tom ever had with him had to do with replacing the door knobs with levers. Given the arthritis, it would be easier for his father to open and close doors. That was the one time that Angus Capwell had ever listened to his youngest son.

Tom slowly opened the door and found Jeanette seated behind their father's desk. Tom didn't know what to say.

She looked up and smiled. "Hey Tom! I knew you'd find me. You're the only one that gives a damn. The only decent soul left in the Capwell family. Everybody's left me but you. Welcome to Daddy's office." She waved her hand around in a grandiose fashion. "It's like he just left it, and it will be tomorrow morning, and forever."

Tom slowly walked in and sat in the chair opposite the desk facing his sister. "Jeanette, what've you been doing? Did you kill those people?"

"What people?" she asked and leaned forward with her head cocked to the side. "I don't know what you're talking about." She grinned. She knew she was lying and enjoyed it.

"The black people, Jeanette. Did you shoot them because the police are looking for you?"

"Oh Tommy, they're not people. How could they be? They cause so much trouble. Look what they've done to us!" She fell back in the chair and bent down to reach in her bag. In a flash she held up a handgun equipped with a silencer. Pointing to it, she grinned again and said, "They can't hear you when you use this. Everything's polite and quiet. I'm so glad Daddy taught me how to shoot. He said..."

Tom cut her off and said, "Our Father was fuckin' nuts! A borderline personality at best. Drove Mom to a breakdown that had nothing to do with Danny's death. That was some crap he made up. She flipped out because of him. Don't you get that?!" Tom leaped up and started to pace in front of his father's desk. He unbuttoned his coat and threw it across the room to the couch.

Jeanette looked at him, clapped her hands when his coat landed on the couch, and continued right where she left off. "Daddy said I had the potential to be a sharp shooter. Said I was a natural!" She glanced at the gun again and then said, "This is such a beautiful little gun. It's prettier than I am Tommy! Daddy told me these were designed especially for women."

Looking at it, Tom stopped pacing. His eyes were large with fear and memories of Angus Capwell trying to teach him how to shoot. It was a disaster. Tom focused. He didn't know what Trixie was going to do. "Where'd you get that?" Tom asked.

"From Daddy's collection at the house," Jeanette said firmly. "I took it just before we left this morning to talk with that Southern bitch and her mixed-race brood of God knows what!"

"Look, sis, listen to me, there's all kinds of speculation. What have you done? Maybe you shouldn't tell me, but we've got to get you a good criminal attorney, regardless." Tom couldn't take his eyes off that gun and worked at breathing evenly.

Eyes gleaming, she looked at her brother and asked, "Why? This'll blow over. It will. Nobody cares about those black women. I mean, seriously. What value could they have to anyone? Don't worry. Kenneth takes care of all my needs." She smiled, closed her eyes and rubbed her hands down her torso stopping a second to caress her own breasts as if she were alone. Then her hands slid down between her thighs. She made a soft groaning noise. Opening her eyes, she looked at Tom, whose mouth was hanging open, and asked, "What did you say?" Not waiting for him to speak, she licked her lips as if she was tasting them and, said, "Sometimes Kenneth can really make me feel so good. I need to feel good every now and then. They say a woman has her personal needs and they are so right. And Carl has never fulfilled any of my needs even though he's so...virile"

"We've got to call Kenneth and have him find you the best criminal attorney money can buy. But I'll need to tell Kenneth what you did...please," Tom said still eyeing the gun that was slightly out of his reach. "Jeanette, you know guns scare me. Let's put your gun somewhere else. Maybe in Dad's safe over here." Tom pointed to a large painting that hid the office safe.

Jeanette ignored him and said, "We deserved some justice. I had to eliminate... no, exterminate. That's what we have to do, exterminate them like roaches. I took out as many of the women I could. So, I did go shopping, looking for their women. I found myself next to one of 'em in Sak's. She was buying the same brand of cosmetics I buy probably with our money. They've taken so much from us. But we got in a conversation, and she actually seemed literate. She looked so clean. I just don't know how she afforded her clothes and jewelry, but there she was dressed like a dream, like she had grown up wearing those kinds of clothes. She laughed when I asked her what she did that allowed her to buy these things. That's when I did it."

"Did what, Jeanette?" Tom's forehead was damp with perspiration. He sat back down, weak from expecting the worst, and searched his pocket for a tissue.

"Shot her right in the neck and just walked out, looking for more of 'em. I blended into the crowd going through the Prudential over to Copley Plaza. There was another one coming out of Tiffany's of all places! I managed to walk right next to her and put my little gun into her rib cage, pressed it hard so she'd feel it through that fur coat she had on. Then I said, very quietly, act like anything's wrong and I'll blow you away right here."

Tom was frozen with shock. He was looking at someone he didn't know. His sister's face was contorted, her breathing was on its way to becoming a pant, and her eyes were dead. He'd never seen anything or anyone like this, and heard himself think, "I am scared."

"So, we walked right out of the plaza and onto the street. It was really snowing by then, but I didn't care." Jeanette went on to tell Tom that she and this African American woman walked over to the public library and found an unlocked storage room. Jeanette shoved the woman inside, barricaded the door with boxes that were in a corner, and told her to sit down. There were no windows and no vents. There was one chair and a dim overhead light that came on when they opened the door.

Leaning against the door, Jeanette squinted, her eyes looking at this woman with caramel colored skin and short jet-black hair for something she couldn't articulate. Jeanette's mouth opened, and her lips started to twist but nothing came out for several seconds.

"Why can't you go away?" Jeanette asked as she gave her the once over. "You don't belong with us. So, why are you here? You make me uncomfortable, nervous. I don't want you here."

"Look lady. I don't know what's wrong with you, but..."

"Stop! There's nothing wrong with me. It's you people who've made this a third world country. You shouldn't even be in Tiffany's! Have you stolen money to shop there? What do you do? Answer me!"

"I have my own public relations company."

"You have a company? Well, how about that! I had a company until this afternoon when some southern, nigger loving bitch took it away from me."

"I have nothing..."

"Who said you could talk?" Jeanette walked over to her while putting the gun's silencer on. "Are you scared? You should be. I'm terrified of your kind, and I don't like being terrified. Take off your coat."

"Please, I have a family."

"Your coat."

The woman took off her coat and handed it to Jeanette.

"Put it over your head."

"What?!"

Jeanette pressed the gun barrel against the woman's forehead, then covered the woman's head with her coat and shot her. The woman slumped to the side absent of life.

"So, Tom, I left. I walked right back through Copley Plaza and to the garage. Police were everywhere. None of them stopped me. Who would stop a white woman like myself? Jeanette Capwell Davidson, they're not going to arrest me. I hopped in my car and drove to Government Center. They like those government jobs we're paying for. That's how they take our money too. Government jobs. I knew I'd find a few and I did. Two walked out of City Hall and I fixed my eyes on another one leaving the JFK Building and pop!"

Jeanette picked up the gun, pointed it at Tom and laughed. He stopped breathing. He realized his sister was now capable of anything, and there wasn't much he could do but think of ways to protect himself.

"By the time people realized they were shot, I was gone, gone before they hit the ground, before anybody could take a good look at me, you know? Then I found one in the parking garage. I wanted to get really close again, so I walked right up to her, pointed my gun at her tummy hoping to hit all those female organs. She tried to fight back! She almost grabbed the gun from me, but I persevered. Decided to blow her brains out instead. You should hear a gunshot in an underground garage with a silencer…it's remarkable. One muffled poof! Anyway, she fell down between the cars, looking like a bundle of old rags. Blood stained my shoes," Jeanette said. She reached down, picked up her blood-stained shoe, and said, "Tommy, see? Blood all over them. And these are expensive too. I should've worn my boots this morning, snowing and all… Oh well…" and she threw the shoe down on the floor.

All the color left Tom's face. His skin resembled that thick white paste elementary school students used. "Okay, look Jeanette. We've got to get you some help, right now. Give me the gun, please." Tom extended his right hand thinking, "She's fucking crazy!" She dragged the gun back towards her, out of Tom's reach.

"Oh no, I can't do that. I need my gun. We need our guns for protection. They're coming for us. That's why we can't let the government take our guns. I know those people have plans."

Tom had dropped into the chair in front of his father's desk. The office was exquisite, absolute perfection. Tom remembered when the Oriental rug was delivered to his father's office. He had been around ten years old. His father gave more attention to that rug than he did Tom. There was an original Andrew Wyeth hanging on the wall along with his father's diplomas and awards. And now his only daughter was sitting behind his desk playing with a gun as if it was an infant or a sex toy! Tom hated this office.

"You're not protecting anybody! Jeanette, you've killed people!" In a flash, he stood up and lunged for her gun.

But Jeanette was faster. She grabbed it and pushed back from the desk. Her face twisted again and seemed to change: squinting eyes accentuated by crow's feet, cheekbones too prominent highlighted with rouge, mouth twisted, lips screaming with bright crimson lipstick. Her eyes widened, and she resumed that heavy breathing, the kind associated with crank calls from teenage boys!

She yelled at Tom, "Why didn't you listen to our father? Danny and I did. But not you!" She jumped up from behind the desk and walked over to Tom, standing just inches from him, still holding her gun. He tried to back away from her, but the chair didn't have wheels and he knew better than to make any sudden moves.

"You challenged him at every opportunity you got, called him a bigot. How dare you! Who do you think you are, Martin Luther King? JFK? Our father was always looking out for us. He wanted us to be safe that's why we couldn't have anything to do with those people. They're trying to destroy us even from the grave. See what they did to Carl? He's run off with one of 'em. I had to stop it or at least try. If I killed their women, it's a twofer. No children will come from them, that's why they all had to be women. You want to destroy a race, kill the women." She turned and sat back down behind her father's desk. She cuddled her little gun and held it close to her chest. Tom was waiting for her to start singing it a lullaby!

Tom was in some kind of shock but he was aware enough to hear the elevator door open and the rapid approach of footsteps. He stood up and turned around to see three policemen from a SWAT team standing in the open doorway.

Jeanette stared at them and held her breath to the point where she felt every organ inside her was going to explode. She exhaled, resigned to some kind of confrontation. Everything stopped for Jeanette. There was no past and no future. She couldn't feel anything except her shallow breath keeping her alive. The police lost their individuality and all Jeanette saw was a wall of opposition. She was not going to let them win.

"Mrs. Davidson, put the gun down," the first officer said. "Mr. Capwell, we need you to step out of the office, now." Tom slowly backed away from Jeanette. The first officer repeated, "We need you out of here, Mr. Capwell." The second officer, a black female, scooted in, reached for Tom, and firmly pulled him out of the office and into the hall. Tom saw the look on Jeanette's face. It was a scrambled mass of anger like tangled circuit board wires. Two additional policemen stepped from the elevator with high powered rifles and rushed towards the office.

"Who told you I was here?" Jeanette screamed. She stood up and glared at the black female SWAT officer. "What the hell are you doing here? You've taken my life away from me! You are the damned problem! You!"

A third officer, a sharp shooter, took aim at Jeanette and held his position until she got the go ahead to shoot her.

"This belongs to me! This building is mine! You have no right here. I don't care what the Grants told you. This is mine, this company, my house. Mine!" Jeanette's face was bright red. Her eyes seemed to spit hate. "You don't understand who I am! You just watch what I can do."

"Mrs. Davidson, this is the last time we're asking." The sharpshooter placed her finger on the trigger. "Put the gun d…" Before the officer could finish, Jeanette shot herself in the head. It happened so quickly, no one believed they saw it. The blood and brain matter on the desk and rug told them otherwise. The smell of gunfire floated in the air like incense.

Hearing the gunshot, Tom fell against the nearest wall, and covered his eyes. Every thought in his head bounced up and down as if they were on a trampoline from hell. Nothing made sense.

Nothing made sense and all the activity going on around him didn't help. The muffled voices of the police asking him questions didn't register. His father's office furniture that was so pristine, polished, and orderly stood in stark contrast to the blood and brain matter scattered around Jeanette's body. The new memory of hearing gun shots mixed with the old memories of watching his father shoot animals, and the ominous appearance of two detectives, their faces empty of expressions had a unique cruelty that made Tom nauseous. All the lights were on now eliminating shadows.

There was no avoiding the horror that just took place or Jeanette's hair soaking in her blood, her face distorted, her eyes wide open like a terrified child. It made Tom gag. He thought he was now trapped in hell only he felt cold. What would he do with the images from this night?

Jeanette's gun had fallen to the floor, abandoned, like a toy cast aside by a fretful child. Her cell phone started to ring, and Tom jumped again. He saw the two detectives taking in every inch of his father's office. Tom watched them look at Jeanette's body and the surroundings for another minute. It was going to be a long night. The older detective told an officer to make sure the gun was bagged.

He walked over to Tom and asked, "Who are you?"

"Tom, Thomas Capwell."

The detective raised his eyebrows and asked, "You're related to her?"

"I'm her brother," Tom said.

"Where's her husband?" the second detective asked.

"They're no longer together. He's in Scarsdale. Her daughter's in New York and her son is in grad school, Yale. I'm the only next of kin here," Tom said.

"Okay, well, sorry for your loss Mr. Capwell. This is going to take some time to sort out. Where can we talk? There must be a conference room or something."

Tom led the detective and his partner a few doors down to his office. Ushering them in, he closed the door and sat behind his desk while the detectives pulled up two chairs. Tom noticed the younger detective was surveying his office.

"Okay, Mr. Capwell, I'm Detective Matthis." Pointing to the younger guy, Matthis said, "This is my partner, Detective Regan. Tell us in your own words what happened here tonight." Matthis' voice was drenched with weariness, his face the manifestation of earned gravitas.

Tom described what took place once he found his sister in their father's office. He went over the chain of events three times. Tom knew he was going to scream if he didn't get out of there soon. There were at least four policemen who saw Jeanette shoot herself, so what was the problem Tom wondered? But it was the motive that the detectives were trying to comprehend. At one point Tom thought the younger detective was bemused by all this.

Matthis loosened his tie and asked, "What's really going on here, Mr. Capwell? What was your sister's real motive? The Capwells are rich as cream, at least that's the way it appears. What's the financial reality of the Capwells? You guys going broke? Was that it?" If you judged by appearance, Matthis' best days were behind him. He was a little overweight and slightly balding but Tom sensed that was a distraction. The city would never send over the "B" team for a case of this magnitude and notoriety. Tom could already see the tabloid headlines.

It took him a half an hour to explain the finances of the company as diplomatically as possible. Regan never took his eyes off Tom. He searched every inch of Tom's face and hands, noted every innuendo of Tom's body language, looking for anything that didn't track. "This guy was no dummy," Tom thought.

"So, you're telling me, Mr. Capwell, that this Atlanta company now owns all of Capwell? Something's not adding up here. You're leaving something out. The sooner you tell us the whole story the sooner we can all go home," Matthis said.

Tom fell back in his chair, sighed heavily, and told them about the blackmail. For the first time the lead detective was speechless. He looked at his partner and mumbled, "Do you believe this? You've been blackmailing these folks in Atlanta for what? Two hundred years? Wow."

Regan who had a raspy voice said, "So you basically were forced into giving up your entire empire. More like shamed... They were going to go public if you didn't give in, and there's nothing you're going to do about it? This is too much. That's what your sister couldn't handle." Regan started tapping his upper lip with his fingers, looked at Tom and asked, "Did you ever think about just letting all this go? Hundreds of years..."

Matthis muttered, "Rich people's problems...okay Mr. Capwell."

When they finished with Tom, he went back to his father's office and asked one of the policemen what was the procedure? Where would they take Jeanette? Tom listened while watching the EMTs.

The coroner was there. He studied Jeanette and shook his head from side to side. The coroner and detectives had a brief whispered conversation. The coroner nodded his head in agreement to something that Matthis said and pronounced her dead. The EMTs attended to Jeanette's body.

One of the EMTs was holding a body bag. He unfolded and then unzipped it. With great care, they placed Jeanette in the body bag. The sound of the zipper closing gave Tom a sense of relief he had never known. He heard himself think, "Thank God she's gone." But deep down he wondered if her spirit would ever leave that building, if she would ever find peace.

Chapter Eighteen:
The New Reality

Carl pulled into the driveway of his Scarsdale home. He turned off the ignition and exhaled heavily. Denise and he had picked out this contemporary, two-story house set on two gracefully manicured acres. The house featured open spaces, built in bookcases, two wood burning fireplaces, hardwood floors and several impressive pieces of contemporary art that belonged to Denise. Every room had evidence of their two daughters. Dwell Magazine recently approached them about doing a feature on the house.

Carl stepped out of the car and was reminded of how cold it had become. He looked at the lawn and the house and smiled with gratitude. "Finally," he said softly and took from the trunk and back seat his garment bags, a suitcase and three bouquets of flowers in a shopping bag. Just as he was putting the key in the front door lock, the door opened revealing Denise. She was a compelling sight. It had something to do with the energy she generated that exceeded her height of five foot three. She had soothing dark brown eyes, curly black shoulder length hair, butterscotch skin, and a smile that would relieve any burden you carried, a good trait for a pediatric neurosurgeon. Denise was hard to ignore, one of those small but fierce characters Shakespeare wrote about in Midsummer's Night Dream.

Walking inside, Carl placed his garment bags, suitcases and shopping bag on the hall bench as Denise shut the door. She turned around, looked at Carl and he hugged her. They stood and held each other in silence for a few minutes. Whispering in her ear, he said, "Thank-God for you." Carl hugged her tightly and took a few steps back to look at her. He was beaming. He reached into the shopping bag and pulled up a bouquet of a dozen red roses.

Handing them to her, Carl said, "For you, because you're still here. I never thought this day would come. I think we're free. Kenneth's working on the divorce."

Denise smiled at the roses and looked into his eyes. "Carl, have you been listening to the news?"

Before he could answer, the sound of small feet racing down the stairs filled the air along with the voices of two little girls. "Daddy you're home! Are you going to stay? Will you have to go away again? You said you wouldn't," Frederica, the oldest one asked. The youngest one, Nicole, grabbed his leg, preventing him from going anywhere without her.

He bent down and hugged both of them. Nicole, wearing pink pajamas, held her stuffed bunny rabbit that had long floppy ears with one hand while climbing on his knee. "Dad's home. I won't be going away for long stretches anymore." He reached in the bag and produced two small bouquets of daisies. These are for the prettiest little girls in my life." Smiling, they took their flowers, their eyes glittered with joy.

The housekeeper, Mrs. Franklin, walked down the hall holding the phone. "Mr. Davidson, Tom Capwell is on the phone." She handed Carl the extension, looked at the girls and said, "C'mon you two. Let's fix some hot chocolate for all of you and we'll put these beautiful flowers in some water." Their faces lit up and they followed Mrs. Franklin while Carl took the phone.

Standing up he reached for Denise's hand and they walked into the living room. Both sank into their sectional sofa. They were embraced by its comfort and each other.

"Tom, what's going on? What?" Carl squeezed Denise's hand and then they interlocked their fingers. "No, I've been driving, listening to music. What did you say?" There was a long pause. "How many did she kill?"

Denise put her head on Carl's shoulder then looked into his eyes that were glistening with tears. "I guess that makes me a widower," Carl said. "Hold on a minute." Carl put the phone down and wiped his eyes. Denise found a tissue and gave it to him. Never letting go of her he mumbled, "Thank-you." He cleared his throat and asked Tom, "Where are you? How long did they talk to you?" Carl put his arm around Denise's shoulder as if she was some kind of flotation device that would prevent him from drowning. "Look, you don't have to do everything tonight, Tom. Give yourself a break. You're doing what? For God's sake, let Gillian do that. Okay! Okay! I got it. We'll talk in the morning." Carl hung up and looked at Denise. "It's over. She's dead. We can breathe."

"I had been listening to the news. Carl, I'm so very sorry," Denise said.

Carl kissed her. "Let's go get that hot chocolate." He didn't know whether to laugh or cry.

Tom was trying to recover from talking with the detectives. He had no idea what they were still doing in his father's office and didn't really care. There were calls to be made. He walked back to his office and phoned Kenneth. As soon as Tom finished that, he called his Administrative Assistant, Elaine. He wanted her to cancel tomorrow's meetings. She asked why and he told her to watch the news, and instead of going to the office tomorrow, to come to the estate and they would drive in together for the breakfast meeting already scheduled.

The Capwell Communications Director, Gillian Hunter, arrived with a pinched expression on her face, and tightened shoulder and neck muscles. In her early thirties, her facial features were overshadowed by this ominous frown. Carrying her black leather tote bag, she came close to stomping into Tom's office. She wore a navy blue pea coat, with navy slacks, navy cashmere turtleneck and a white silk scarf wrapped around her neck. Gillian's shiny, long brown hair, seemed to be always in motion even when she stood still. "Get a grip, Gillian," she told herself. "Get it together!"

Hearing her footsteps stop in his doorway, Tom looked up from his desk and asked, "What are you doing here?" He was a little stunned to see her. He was also relieved.

"What am I doing here? Tom, it's all over the news!" She told him there was a mob of reporters and television cameras outside. "What happened?! You should hear what people are saying. I need to know what's going on."

Tom motioned for her to sit and he told her exactly what took place. Gillian's mouth fell open. Now she understood the reason Charlotte Grant or Trixie tracked her down months ago and flew her to Atlanta for "lunch." Gillian knew better than to tell Tom about the meeting because he was holding on by a thread. The good news for Gillian was her certainty after lunch with Trixie, that she would have a place in the new order of things under the Grants. She was amazed she had kept her mouth shut all these months.

After a few minutes, Gillian put her hands up and said, "Enough. I really don't want to know anymore. I want to be able to say, I don't know, with some plausible deniability." They talked about next steps. She put on her tortoise rimmed reading glasses, pulled out a pad and started to take notes until she had all the information she thought she needed. Gillian walked to her office with a throbbing headache not quite believing Jeanette Capwell Davidson was gone. Gillian was also thinking about how she was going to position Tom, and the company to the press. Of course, the overriding monster was Jeanette Capwell. Gillian could hear the questions now. What she would say versus what she wanted to say were miles apart.

Gillian had always believed Jeanette was slightly mad if not psychotic. She took off her pea jacket, sat down, and opened her bottom desk drawer where she kept an excellent bottle of white Riesling. She pulled out the cork, found a wine glass, and filled it to the top. Taking a sip, she began to work on a statement. What would she say? Mrs. Davidson had been…no…Mrs. Davidson had a long history of emotional disorders. Yeah – that might work. Oh my God – what do I say about the role of race in all this? Somebody's going to ask why she targeted not just people of color but black women? Finishing her wine, Gillian muttered out loud, "Shoot me now!" The eleven o'clock news was a half hour away.

Tom went through every desk drawer until he found some aspirin. He opened a bottle of water on his desk, threw four aspirins in his mouth, gulped some water and swallowed. He leaned back in his chair, put his right fist up to his mouth and started biting on the forefinger lost in thought. After a minute or two that felt like hours, he reached for the phone and called Trixie. Her phone rang once.

"Tom, tell me something," Trixie said motioning for Peter to stay with her.

"She's gone," Tom said and slumped in his chair not sure where he would find the energy to open and close his eyes.

There was a pause on the other end before Trixie said anything. "What do you mean Tom? I don't want to assume anything. Gone where? Has she left the country?"

"No, she's dead. She shot herself in the head," he said struggling to sound like he was in control. He briefly described the shooting spree Jeanette went on including her suicide in their father's office.

"Tom. I am so sorry for you. I really am," Trixie said stunned but not surprised. "What are you going to do? Listen, I'm putting you on speaker. Peter is here."

"Okay, that's fine. The press has gathered outside the building. I've got, Gillian, our Communications Director, working on a statement. They will have questions. When I left the house, a bunch of them were already outside the gates..."

"You can bet they will have questions! What're you going to say Tom? This would be a good time for the left hand to know what the right hand is going to do."

"I think I'll try to tell the truth. That's the only way to purge ourselves of all this. I talked candidly with Gillian. She'll come up with just the right wording. She's good with nuanced statements regarding controversy or crisis events. I just think we've got to tell it like it is to the best of our ability."

"Yeah...the truth can be a powerful tool, Tom. Try to keep us informed. We've already got reporters calling here. Let's stay in touch and you take care. Try to eat something. Don't face 'em on an empty stomach!" Trixie hung up and looked at Wallace who had been seated next to her the whole time. "Is the gate closed?"

"Should be, but I'll go check again." He lifted his large body and walked out of the kitchen. Peter leaned back on the kitchen counter shaking his head.

Instantly, Trixie started giving orders. "Get our Communications' people out here, Madeline. Every last one of them. It's going to be a long night. Bell, let's fix some sandwiches or something for them to eat. Set it up in the den. Lots of coffee and tea. Make sure we've got some soda and bottled water too."

Touching her shoulder, Chloe said, "I'm going to check on Jacq."

"Good idea. Thank-you darlin'," Trixie said. She squeezed Chloe's hand and said quietly, "I don't know what I'd do without you. I love you." Chloe smiled and kissed her before leaving the kitchen.

Everybody moved into the den. Peter turned on the wide screen television. Cable networks were covering the incident. Slowly the staff arrived, some dressed in jeans, others still in business attire but every one of them ready to work like the Calvary preparing for battle. The Communication's Director for GFC, Katherine Cobb, an older British woman of indeterminate age with short silver hair, started to field calls from the morning news shows and newspapers.

After talking with Katherine, Trixie told everyone that she didn't want to issue a formal statement until the next morning. She wanted to talk with Katherine about various strategies.

Trixie looked from face to face and said, "Need I remind you the consequences of any unplanned leaks at this point?"

There was a collective mumble and head nodding indicating complete clarity. An unauthorized leak, from some anonymous staff member not explicitly approved by Trixie or Katherine, would result in the entire communication's department being fired, everyone, including secretaries and the cleaning staff. The policy had a chilling effect and worked very well.

Katherine sent one of her staff people down to the gate to let the reporters know there would be no statement, of any kind, until tomorrow. "Tell them they should all go home," Katherine said. "We want to give the Capwells the time and courtesy to address this first."

"The truth can also be a dangerous ally," said Trixie to no one in particular. "This might be a long night people. Make yourselves comfortable and wait for Katherine's instructions." Trixie motioned for Peter to follow her into the dining room. They sat down and Trixie said, "Well, I'll be damned. I told you that bitch would snap. My God!"

Peter looked at his sister and said, "You called it. You said she'd crack in some way. Did you think she'd kill all those people?"

"I didn't want her to kill anybody, but I knew she had so much hate and anger in her she would take it out on somebody. It might've been Carl – but he hightailed it out of there - or Tom. But I saw the look in her eyes. She needed Tom too much to ever admit it. She wouldn't kill her baby brother. He was the only decent thing in her life. What she really wanted to do was kill Kate. Short of that, she went after every black woman she could find. But, see Peter, this is what happens when we don't find a way to atone for our sins."

"How do we do that? Reparations? Apologize? It's hard…"

"I don't know, but we could start by owning up to what slavery did and its ongoing impact. People need to open their eyes and their hearts. All these so called religious people talking outta both sides if their mouths. Stop being gripped by fear. Toughen up, people! Toughen up. Stop acting like they're so damned delicate. If you say boo, they'll die! It's the fear of hearing the truth 'cause then they'd have no choice but addressing it otherwise that image they have of themselves as 'good' people is shot to hell."

They sat in silence for a few minutes with Peter studying his sister's face. He liked to think that he understood his big sister like no one else. But sometimes he found himself wondering what really made her tick and who she really was. There are still so many layers of her. He clenched his jaw so he wouldn't smile remembering a fight she got in when they were in grade school. A little boy who sat in front of her used the "N" word referring to a classmate. Trixie reached forward, put her hands around his throat, threw him to floor, and was ready to beat the livin' be Jesus out of him had the teacher not pried her loose from this poor kid. She was sitting on top of him and managed to get one or two good punches in, shocking her teacher and terrifying this little boy. To this day if he saw her on the street in downtown Atlanta, he crossed over, or at a social event, he would leave! The story spread like a deadly virus. Trixie stomped out of school that day, her face scrunched up, looking mean as spit, that long French braid she had still perfectly centered, daring anybody to confront her. Christian evangelicals talk about being reborn. On that day, Trixie, aka Charlotte Alison

Grant, was reborn as a social justice fighter with one hell of a legacy shoring her up.

Leaving those memories behind, Peter came back to the present and said, "I have to change the subject, Trix. Let me ask you, have you thought about the Capwell office building?"

"Well, I have now! We're gonna sell that sucker. Let her spirit wander around and haunt a bunch of other people! We'll take the money and give it... No! You know what we can do? We can set up a bunch of trusts for the families of those people that lunatic shot. I've already got Madeline finding out about them. Maybe we ought to fly up there and meet with them... I don't know. We'll figure it out."

Peter looked at his sister, raised his eyebrows and smiled. He lowered his head for a moment then looked up at her and asked, "You know what pisses me off?"

"What?"

Peter stood up and bent his neck from side to side before speaking.

"There're gonna be a whole bunch of people who just won't get it. They can't wrap their heads around us at all."

"Hmph. Sad isn't it? Baby brother, why do you think so few white people are as outraged and genuinely disgusted by slavery and its legacy as we are? Even fewer want to face what's been done to Native people. Something's really wrong with us, baby brother. It's gonna bring us down. You wait and see. Did Madeline tell you what she found in Alistair's diaries about the Cherokees?"

"No!"

"Let's just say Alistair was one complex man. Try to talk to people today about Native Americans. They look at you like you're crazy. For some reason people think they've vanished! I wish somebody would try to say that to Wallace or Frank! Whoa! This is what puzzles me; why is it more people who look like us don't pick up the sword and fight the hate... Shoot, pretty soon we're going to be outnumbered anyway."

"You remember what Mama said about hate?"

"Do I?! Sustained hate kills, that's what she said. How could we forget? It was like some kinda prayer or mantra. First heard it when I was five or six and got in a fight at school with that evil little girl, Mary Esther!"

This time Peter couldn't hide his smile. "Trix, you got in a lot of fights at school."

"Well, hell, somebody's gotta fight. Mary Esther was just plain mean! But what Mama said really sunk in when I started to be fascinated by American history and our family's part in slavery... And then, I was sixteen, seventeen and we were at the plantation for the Grant annual reunion... I walked over to the family cemetery and saw Kate's grave. That's when I got the full story about Kate, Alistair, Sinclair, Bridget and Patrick and Alistair's second wife... I remember now, it was the summer before I started college. You know who kept that story, passed it on down from the late 1700s until now? Alistair's slaves and their descendants, some of whom were Bell's people. That's the only way we knew the whole story until Madeline found the diaries. Anyway, I was standing there looking at the headstones when Mama walked up to me. She put her hands on my shoulders, looked me straight in the eye and said..."

Peter jumped in and said, "Sustained hate kills. I remember, Trix." He paused and studied his sister. "Nobody expected you to be such a fighter, at least not at first."

"You've got to fight to defend yourself, for what's right, and most of all for what you believe in. Ask ten average people what they believe in. Try it. They couldn't tell you."

Peter nodded his head and said, "I know. You're right. I've tried it."

"The Capwells are despicable, Peter, and you know it. They rode off into the sunset of hypocrisy like they were the good guys. Not on my watch. We've all got blood on our hands from slavery. Every last one of us. Nobody's got clean hands. Don't ever forget that."

"We're all under your spell, you know that, don't you?" He grabbed her hand and smiled.

"Oh, stop it! You make me sound like some magical being! Please," exclaimed Trixie! She pulled her hand out of his and tried to suppress a small smile.

"Yeah - magic? You walk your talk. That's magic today, and I love you for it...even though it gets a little sketchy from time to time," and he laughed. "You're hard core, big sister."

"You know and I know, it's easy to walk your talk when you're rich. What am I risking? Nothing. We'll be fine. Now, c'mon, we need to get on the same page about tomorrow." They walked back to the den where everyone was still glued to the television. About half an hour later, Tom called.

"Talk to me Tom, tell me what's going on if you can," Trixie said.

"Yeah – the detectives talked to me for an hour at least. Jeanette was the shooter. There's surveillance footage from Sak's and the streets. But the police want to search the house, see where my father's gun collection is located. The lead detective is having a really hard time understanding, no, accepting the motive."

"I'm sure of that," Trixie said and rolled her eyes.

"Kenneth arrived a few minutes ago. I'm letting him deal with the police now. Reporters are still at the house and outside the building. Somebody said the Mayor is trying to reach me. I've decided to let our Communication's Director, Gillian, give the press a brief statement. I guess…I don't know."

"What're you going to tell them?" Trixie asked and reached for a pad and pencil to take notes with one hand and gestured to Katherine with the other while securing the phone to her shoulder with her ear.

"Oh yeah – the sale of the company to G.F.C was too much for Jeanette. But the lies stop tonight. The truth is the only good that can come out of this."

They talked for a few more minutes then Trixie and everyone else continued to watch the news. Katherine took notes as she watched and listened to various reporters covering the story. Chloe walked in, sat down and continued to watch the news while thinking about Jacq's drawing including what no one talked about but saw.

Trixie's cell phone rang. She looked at it and recognized Tom's number.

"Tom?"

"I'm going down now to give a statement. I've got to try and keep it together."

"I thought you were going to let Gillian do that."

"No…that's the coward's way out. I changed my mind. I have to do this. Gillian's here. It'll be okay. Good-bye."

Tom met the press in the lobby of the Capwell office building and gave a very composed, somber statement, alluding to the stress Jeanette was under due to the takeover of their empire by G.F.C. He then turned and left, answering no questions from the press, leaving Gillian to handle everything and fill in the blanks.

"Well," Trixie muttered, "so much for facing and telling the truth. E for effort Tom. And so it goes…" Trixie walked back to the kitchen. She developed a craving for something sweet, anything, cake, pie, ice cream, cookies. Opening the refrigerator, she found a left-over piece of sweet potato pie. She took it out and closed the door only to find Jacq standing there with Mr. Bunny.

"Hi, Mama."

"Baby what are you doing up? It is way too late for you. Are you okay?" Trixie put the pie on a nearby counter and picked up her daughter. "What's going on?"

"The lady with the sad colors is dead, isn't she? Like in my drawing."

"Yes. She is. Tell me what's bothering you, baby?"

Jacq clutched Mr. Bunny and asked, "She did bad things so will God still love her?"

Trixie let out a big sigh and sat her daughter on the counter. Holding Jacq's face in her hands, Trixie said, "Baby, God loves everybody even if you do bad things. He doesn't like it if you do bad things, but He still loves you. God will forgive you."

"But what about the bad things you do or I do? That sad lady hurt people."

Trixie lifted herself and sat next to Jacq on the kitchen counter before she said anything more. "I think God has a way of making you face the bad things you've done on earth and it's not burning in hell either! Some people will say that. I don't believe that, and I don't want you to believe that either. Listen, baby...Mrs. Davidson, the lady with the sad colors, is probably having a long conversation with God about all that she did, and God stands there while she lives and feels all the bad things she did to people while she was here. And that's probably a lot worse than burning in hell. She's got to come to terms with all that."

Jacq's eyebrows almost met in the middle as she frowned. "So, will God help her learn what was bad and why?"

"I think so. I certainly hope so," Trixie said and smoothed her daughter's hair.

"So, God teaches her about the bad things she did and forgives her because He loves her?"

Trixie nodded her head before saying anything. "God does."

"So, can we forgive each other if we do bad things to each other?"

"If we were perfect we should be able to do that. Most people aren't perfect, Jacq. I know I'm not. C'mon, I want you to go back to bed. You stop worrying about Mrs. Davidson." Trixie got down from the counter, picked up Jacq (and Mr. Bunny) and took her upstairs to bed fighting back tears over the implications of her talk with Jacq.

Work at the Grant estate continued until the early morning hours before everyone left. Drained, Trixie walked up to her bedroom. Wrapped in an orange cashmere robe, Chloe was reading a biography of Claude Monet.

"You didn't have to wait up for me," Trixie said as she sat down on the edge of the bed. She took a deep breath, exhaled slowly and looked at Chloe.

"I didn't have to, but I wanted to. Are you okay?"

"Let me get ready for bed. I'll be just a minute." She took a few steps and turned around to look at Chloe. "You know, Tom has to plan Jeanette's funeral. Damn. He drew the short straw in all this." She continued to the bathroom.

Chloe could hear the water running while Trixie washed her face and brushed her teeth. Chloe fluffed up the pillows and opened a window an inch or two before getting back in bed. Lying on the night stand was their daughter's drawing.

Dressed for bed, Trixie got in and rested her head on Chloe's shoulder.

"How do you feel?" Chloe asked and put her arm around Trixie. "Really, this whole ordeal... Trix, where are you putting all this?"

"It occupies my very flawed soul. Funny feeling being right about all this," Trixie said. "Sometimes it's a burden. I wish the world was different, but it's not. And what about you? How are you holding up? What does it feel like watching all this?"

"Don't worry about me. I'm fine. Is it true? Is she really dead?"

"Yes, she's dead. She blew her brains out," Trixie said.

"So, Jacq's drawing was correct? The gun she drew pointed at the woman's head and the pool of blood?"

"Yes, the drawing was right and damned accurate." Trixie then told Chloe about the conversation she had with Jacq in the kitchen.

"Oh, my Lord... Our little girl's an old soul..." Lying in each other's arms, Chloe said, "Jeanette really killed herself. I find it so hard to believe. I never thought she would do that even though you were convinced of it after you met her."

"Umm-hmm…no winners here, love. I never understood why so many people think this poison will all just go away and nobody will have to pay for this evil. It won't. Mention racism, genocide and slavery… White people go running and screaming from the room. My God," Trixie said and sighed. "You see what happened to the Capwells, specifically Jeanette. Something went wrong, real wrong with her. Talk about wrestling with demons… My God…"

"What do you think black people do?" Chloe asked.

"Pray and fight in ways we couldn't begin to imagine or understand. They know how to survive."

Chloe smoothed Trixie's hair and said, "Don't you ever worry about someone coming for the Grants?"

Sitting up in bed, Trixie looked at Chloe and said, "Oh yes. They're coming. Maybe not in our life time, maybe Jacq will have to address our part in this mess. Buying and selling black people into slavery, slaughtering red people for their land… Who the hell thought that was ever a good idea? And then thought there'd be no payback! Is it me?" Trixie asked and leaned back against Chloe.

"No, my love. It's not you," Chloe said. "What is it that Bell always says when something like this happens?"

"God don't love ugly, and don't care much about pretty," Trixie said.

Chloe kissed her and turned out the light.

Chapter Nineteen:
Secret Reflections

Senior staff at the Atlanta headquarters for Grant Family Companies had been working sixteen-hour days since the Capwell take-over. Staff used the company jet to fly back and forth to Boston the way average people used cabs and public transportation. Peter often forgot what day it was, and Trixie had been unusually quiet. She watched every move, knew exactly what was going on with the senior staff and attended every meeting that addressed the take-over. Consistent with her style, she missed nothing. She kept in touch with Tom. Trixie knew that within six months, the Capwell empire would be a fading memory to the public. GFC will completely swallow it up. Meanwhile Christmas was approaching.

Chloe walked in the living room after dinner holding a yellow legal pad and pencil. "Trix, Christmas is in two weeks and everyone's coming here this year."

Trixie was tending the fireplace and looked at Chloe after arranging another log. "Why do we do this? Subject ourselves to this madness? We've got a dozen people coming for dinner, four of them under the age of eight and another five or six coming for desert. We need to have our heads examined!"

Chloe laughed and sat down on the couch. "Trixie, what's going on with you? You've been...I don't know...different ever since the Capwell take-over."

A small smile emerged from Trixie's mouth. "How have I been different?"

"Quiet. Earlier this week, I woke up around 2 AM and you weren't in bed. I went looking for you. You were sitting down here reading and just staring into space. I didn't want to intrude but I know there's something on your mind."

"You don't miss much, do you love?"

"I've been taking lessons from you!"

"I was re-reading that poem I told you about, A Good Anger, by Marge Piercy.

"A good anger? With you, that scares me!"

Trixie sighed and looked at Chloe before speaking. "Peter's not the only one in this family who reads and recites poetry. Listen, it's not long. 'Anger shines through me. Anger shines through me./ I am a burning bush./ My rage is a cloud of flame./ My rage is a cloud of flame in which I walk/seeking justice / like a precipice./How the streets / of the iron city / flicker. Flicker, / and the dirty air / fumes. / Anger storms / between me and things, / transfiguring, / transfiguring. / A good anger acted upon / is beautiful as lightning / and swift with power. / A good anger swallowed, / a good anger swallowed / clots of blood / to slime.'
***

Chloe was transfixed. She and Trixie had been married for ten years and together for almost sixteen, but Chloe had never seen this side of Trixie whose energy and spirit at that moment made everything still with an omniscient silence.

Trixie looked at Chloe as if returning from some faraway place. She sat down next to Chloe on the couch. "Sometimes anger is necessary. Okay darlin', let's see what you've got on this list."

Chloe knew she wasn't going to get Trixie to say anything else about what she was thinking at this moment until she was ready, and Trixie wasn't ready. Chloe had a feeling Trixie wasn't ever going to talk about what was going on inside her right now. The last time Trixie was this quiet was fifteen years ago when her father died. She shut down, flew off to their place in Colorado, and didn't talk to anybody for almost two weeks. Everybody was worried but Trixie returned and never said a word about the trip or what she did.

Chloe and Trixie spent the next hour going over the list of things that had to be done to prepare for Christmas before turning in for the evening.

Trixie, showered, got in bed and inched over to Chloe's waiting arms. "Thank-you for being here, Chlo..."

"You don't have to thank me! I want to be here. You're the love of my life. Where else would I be if not here with you and Jacq?"

Trixie kissed Chloe and turned out the light. Chloe fell asleep within minutes. Trixie managed to nod off but got no more than two to three hours of sleep.

Chapter Twenty:
A Quick Trip

Peter looked over the rim of his coffee mug as Trixie walked in and sat down across from him at the kitchen table. He smiled and said, "Don't we look like the epitome of dignity this morning. What happened? Johnny Cash, The Man In Black, your stylist?" He grinned at his sister.

Trixie smiled, poured herself a cup of coffee and proceeded to put in three teaspoons of sugar and enough cream to turn the coffee from dark brown to light tan. She was wearing an elegant, black pants suit. She threw the matching overcoat onto the chair next to her. The black overcoat looked fairly ordinary, even modest, until you opened it. Her coat was lined with mink. Trixie sat down and drank her own version of café au lait. "I've got a quick trip to make today."

"Trip where?"

"D.C. I'll tell you about it when I get back."

"I have to go up to Boston today. You should've said something."

"Peter, I'm taking the family jet. The company plane is all yours." She finished drinking her coffee and quickly ate a freshly baked corn muffin Bell had made.

"Are you okay?" Peter asked as he looked at her the way a doctor looks at a patient with a mysterious ailment.

Giving her brother a look highlighted by a frown, Trixie said, "Look, what is it with everybody? I am fine, okay? First Chloe, now you. You two been comparing notes?" Trixie stood, put on her coat and gave her brother a snarky look.

Peter put both hands up and said, "We're just concerned."

"Concern yourself with Capwell. The new year is coming, and I want Capwell fully integrated in GFC. No one's going to remember Capwell by spring. By the time marketing and our public relations' departments finish Capwell will never have existed in the minds of the general public. I gotta go. Safe travels to you! When are you leaving?"

"Around 11AM. I've got some things to do at the office first," Peter said. "Hey, you're not fooling me. You're no more going to D.C. than I'm going to the moon this afternoon. You hate D.C. When we do go, I have to drag you! So, where are you really going?"

"Okay. I'm going up to Manhattan to do some Christmas shopping. You need to be quiet. Don't tell anybody."

He got up, walked over to her, and put his hands on her shoulders. As his fingers felt the outline of her shoulders, for a second, Trixie seemed delicate. "Just remember, we love you. We've always got your back."

Trixie smiled. "I know." She took her hand bag, put on her sunglasses and walked out.

As she left, Peter wondered what she was really up to. Watching her walk away, his gut told him she wasn't going to New

York either. He stretched to his full height of six foot three, folded his arms across his chest with his feet firmly planted on the ground and noticed his heart was beating a little faster than it should've been. He knew something important was going on with his sister and he really didn't have a clue as to what it was. That scared him.

Trixie was driven to the airport's terminal for private planes. She got out of the limo, thanked the chauffeur, and told him she would call when she was on her way back to Atlanta. Once on the plane, she opened the cockpit door and spoke to the pilot. "Steven, what's the weather look like up there?"

"Boston's clear as a bell, Ms. Grant. We should have no trouble."

"Great. How long before we take off?"

"Ten, fifteen minutes at the most."

"Good enough. Thank-you." She took off her coat, hung it up and sat down. She buckled her seat belt and started to think. Silence watched her and protected her. All anyone would hear would be the soft hum of a finely tuned machine eventually gliding through the air, pushing the clouds away revealing sunlight that exposed everything.

Mt. Auburn Cemetery had to be one of the most beautiful cemeteries in America. It was so tranquil. The beauty of the landscaping created the kind of atmosphere that nurtures a sense of peace. Mt. Auburn was not a scary cemetery. It would never be featured in a horror movie! People got married at Mt. Auburn because it's so exquisite, and in the spring around sunset with trees blooming and flowers appearing like debutantes being introduced to society, it took on another world quality.

As they drove slowly down the narrow paths, Trixie heard herself thinking, "This is a fancy cemetery for fancy people." She had read online that King Edward VII had visited Mt. Auburn, and so did Emily Dickinson, and Herman Melville. Being carefully driven by the Bigelow Chapel, Trixie could almost hear its architecture whispering Anglican hymns from England. It made sense that this cemetery was a historical landmark.

The limousine continued to snake its way through the narrow pathways until arriving at the Capwell plot. Jeanette's parents were buried there. The big brother who could do no wrong was also there. Trixie wondered why he hadn't been buried at Arlington National Cemetery. But she didn't dwell on it. Next to the perfect brother was Jeanette. There was a dark grey granite plaque in the ground with her name, date of birth and death. Nothing else.

Trixie bent down, balancing herself on her left knee and took off her sunglasses. "Well Jeanette, here we are again, two women who were loved by their daddies. I needed to come here and … well, I just needed to come here and have one last talk with you. You know what Chloe asked me? She wanted to know why we just couldn't forgive each other. I'm not that good, Jeanette, and can't let it go; can't let go what you embodied. I don't know all of what you endured, what you witnessed during your life. But I do know what evil you helped perpetuate. You and I know that forgiveness is a complex activity. Imagine what it takes to let go of this in the spirit of forgiveness? I can't let go of what my family did. The truth is I don't want to let it go. Evil in each generation must be remembered with religious regularity least we forget, and have lapses of judgment and decency.

But what I can do is express lament for both of us. I bet you don't know what lament is. A straight forward expression of grief or regret. The Irish know how to grieve. I used to hear my grandmother, who was Irish, talk about the old ways. In ancient Ireland, way back in the day, women would come, and just wail these high-pitched cries that could go right through you when someone they knew died. They called it the caoineadh.* Grandmother told me within the sound of those cries you'll find the history of a person's life as these women knew you. Maybe those women you killed... maybe they cried for you knowing you were racing towards death, knowing and understanding you better than you knew yourself."

Trixie stood up, and looked at Jeanette's grave with no expression on her face before speaking. " 'From the cowardice that shrinks from new truth; from the laziness that is content with half-truths; from the arrogance that thinks it knows all truth, O God of truth deliver us.' That's it Jeanette. That's all I have to say. May God's peace finally be with you." Trixie pulled her coat collar up around her ears, put on her sunglasses, and walked back to the limo. The chauffeur opened the door, and waited for her to get in. As the limo pulled away, Trixie whispered to herself, "Be merciful to me, O God. Be merciful...to all of us."

*The Anam Cara, A Book of Celtic Wisdom, by John O'Donohue, page 208

**A Grateful Heart, J.M. Ryan, editor, page 206

***To Be Of Use, Poems, by Marge Piercy, page 22

Acknowledgments

Dinner with Trixie... would never have been born without the "midwives" of the Jackson Women's Writers Group of Jackson, New Hampshire. Trixie was born from a prompt, and grew into a contemporary statement about what author, activist and evangelical minister, Jim Wallis, calls America's original sin. This is a subject very close to my heart and to who I am as a woman of color in this country.

I thank my agents, Eric and Karen Canton, for believing in me and this work. Dinner With Trixie... is radically different in tone and subject from my memoir previously released. I'm grateful for their ability to absorb the literary whiplash of Trixie and recognize its value. I'm also grateful for the ongoing commitment, investment, and partnership of Black Pawn Press.

I thank my New Hampshire "posse," Joanne Clary and Donna Rae Menard, for their feedback, inquiries, and support while writing this book. To the members of Trinity Church Boston's Antiracism Team, I thank them for helping deepen my understanding of the pervasive and ingrained reality of racism in the United States, and how we're all poisoned from it.

I thank the trainers of the Crossroads Antiracism Organization for helping equip me with intellectual and emotional intelligence to dissect racism from its most blatant demonstrations to the subtle micro aggressions that so many of us who are not white have to endure on a daily basis, and hope and pray we're not destroyed in ways we can't even imagine or recognize until it's too late.

A special thank-you to Cindy Uhl who reminded me of how important a commitment to understanding racism is along with the need for courage.

There have been a wide array of people I've worked with and known who, unbeknownst to them, provided extraordinary opportunities to observe and experience the paradox of America when it comes to race and class. A special acknowledgement goes to the late Senator Edward Kennedy, Reverend Jesse Jackson, former State Representatives Mel King and Doris Bunte, of the Commonwealth of Massachusetts, Rose von Thater Braan-Imai, friend, role model, Tuscarora Elder, sister from another mother, founding Co-Director of Silver Buffalo Consulting, and James Sakej Youngblood Henderson, international human rights lawyer, educator, and member of the Bear Clan of the Chickasaw Nation, whose wisdom is inescapable and unforgettable once you're in his presence. I thank the readers for allowing Trixie and Jeanette to illustrate one aspect of the truth, destruction, and growing complexity of racism's ongoing legacy in America.

Janis A. Pryor

September 2018

About the Author

Janis has spent most of her adult life trying to help save the world as a political operative and a media professional. Some of her bosses have included the late Senator Edward Brooke, the late Senator Ted Kennedy, John Kerry, Secretary of State for the Obama administration, Reverend Jesse Jackson and Boston's Ten Point Coalition. Specifically, as a media professional, Janis has been a television producer, broadcast editorial journalist, radio talk-show host of a syndicated program, broadcast to thirty plus stations across the Commonwealth of Massachusetts, co-author of a local bi-weekly political column for the Cambridge Chronicle, occasional freelance writer with pieces published in the Middlesex News, the Boston Herald and Boston Magazine.

She won the International Television and Film Award for cultural programming, the Iris Award for talk-show programming (television) and been an Emmy nominee for broadcast editorial journalism. Janis was hired by Northeastern University to help create its first professional public relations department.

Janis is a native New Yorker, a southerner by upbringing and a New Englander by choice. She went to some of the most progressive schools on the east coast including the High School of Music & Art as an art major. Janis graduated from Bennington College with a major in studio art (painting and architecture), and secondary studies in cultural anthropology. Her primary residence is Jackson, New Hampshire.

CPSIA information can be obtained
at www.ICGtesting.com
Printed in the USA
BVHW042144050319
541896BV00016B/151/P